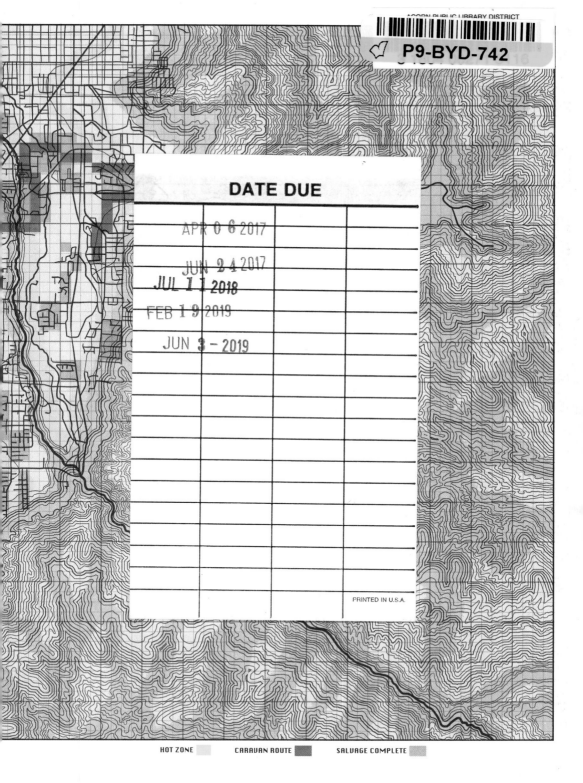

DATE DUE

HOT ZONE   CARAVAN ROUTE   SALVAGE COMPLETE

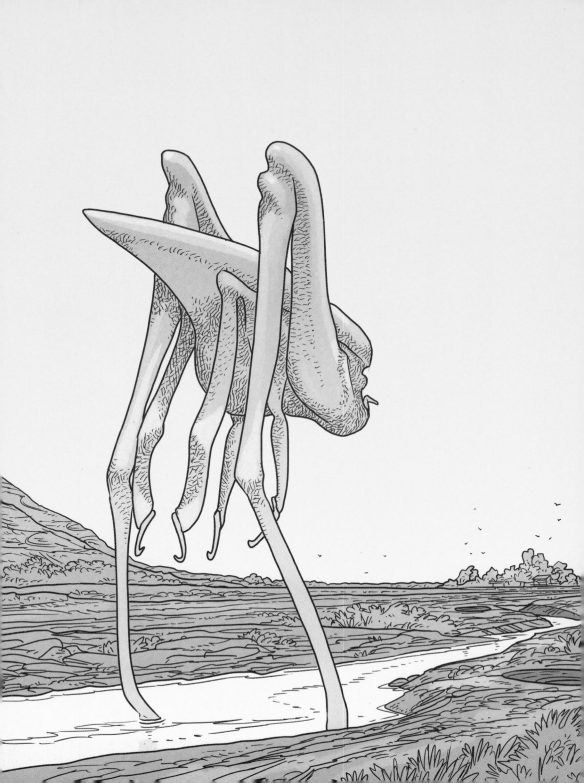

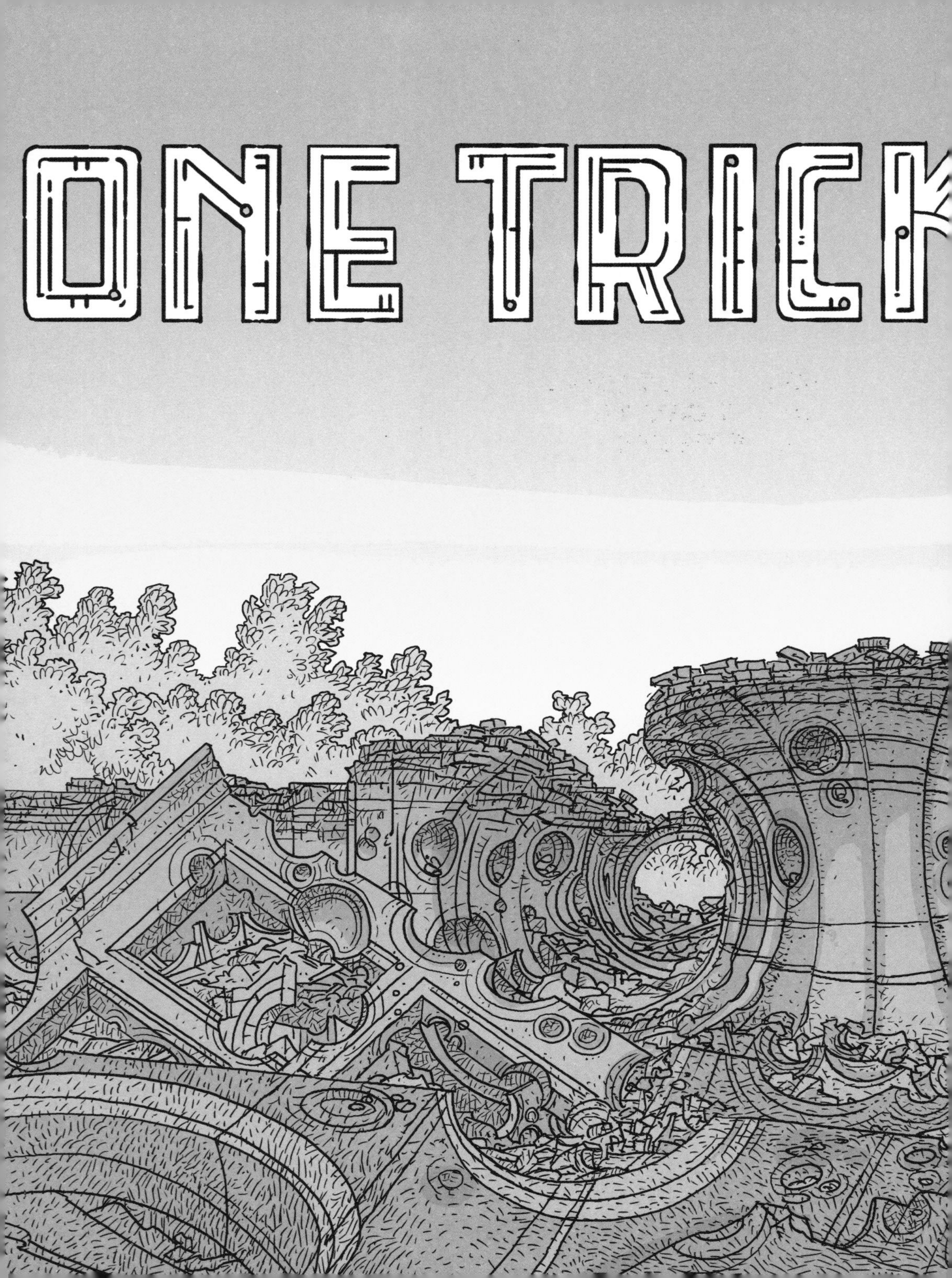
ONE TRICK

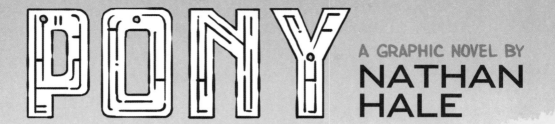

PONY

A GRAPHIC NOVEL BY
NATHAN HALE

AMULET BOOKS
NEW YORK

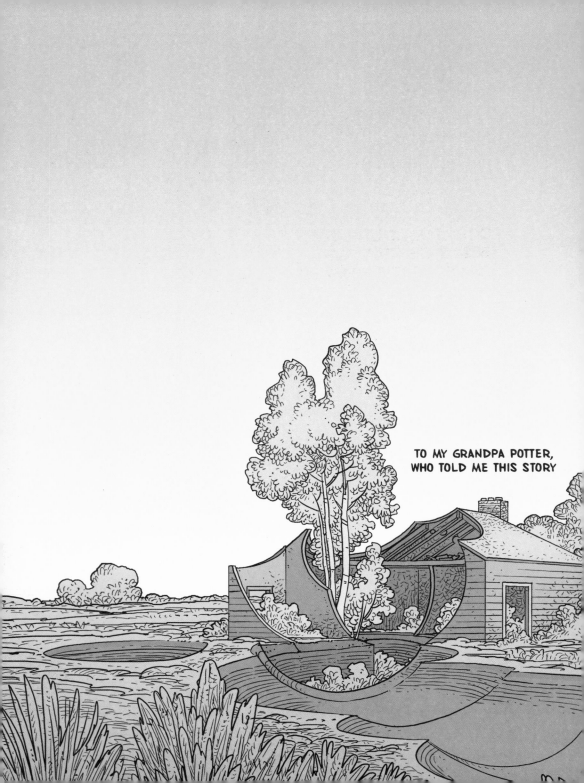

TO MY GRANDPA POTTER,
WHO TOLD ME THIS STORY

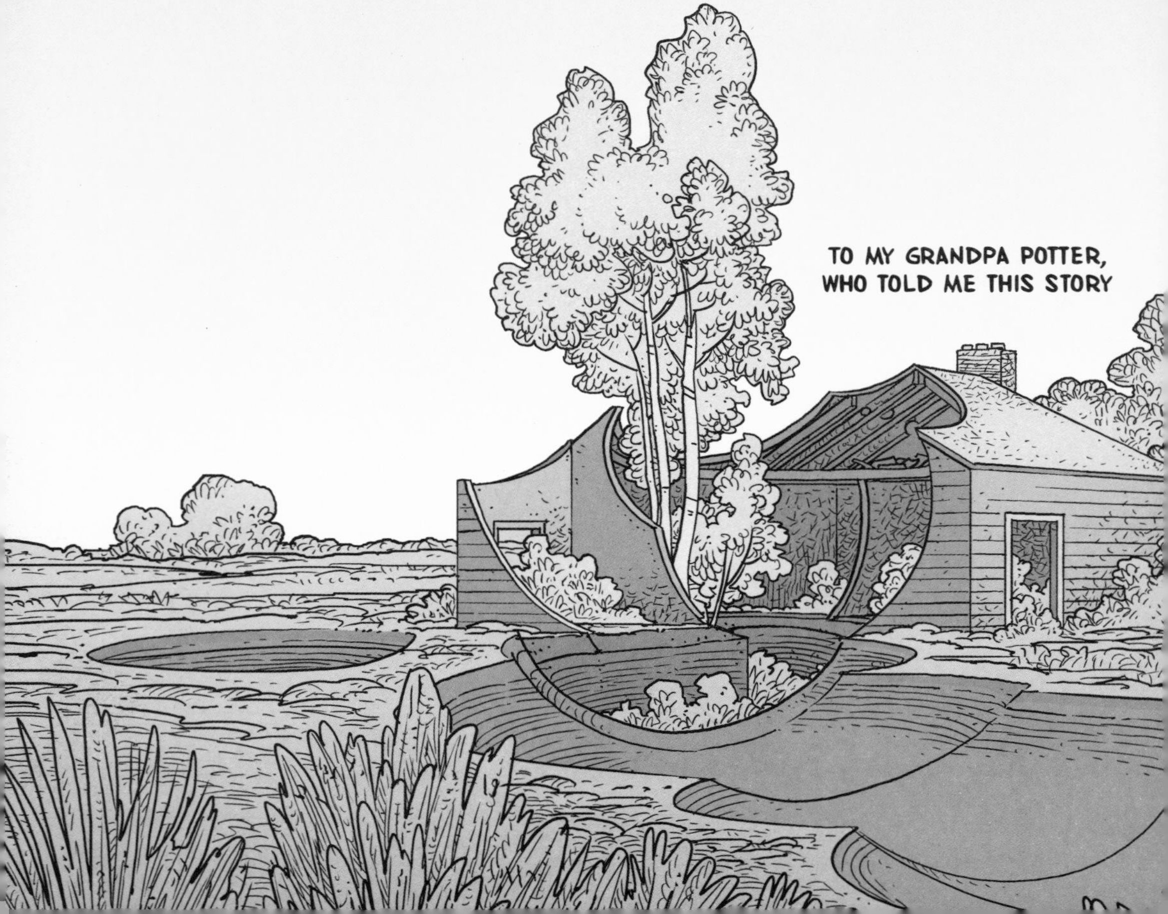

CATALOGING—IN—PUBLICATION DATA HAS BEEN APPLIED FOR
AND MAY BE OBTAINED FROM THE LIBRARY OF CONGRESS.

ISBN: 978-1-4197-2128-1

TEXT AND ILLUSTRATIONS COPYRIGHT © 2017 NATHAN HALE
BOOK DESIGN BY NATHAN HALE AND CHAD W. BECKERMAN

PRINTED AND BOUND IN CHINA
10 9 8 7 6 5 4 3 2 1

AMULET BOOKS ARE AVAILABLE AT SPECIAL DISCOUNTS WHEN
PURCHASED IN QUANTITY FOR PREMIUMS AND PROMOTIONS
AS WELL AS FUNDRAISING OR EDUCATIONAL USE. SPECIAL
EDITIONS CAN ALSO BE CREATED TO SPECIFICATION. FOR
DETAILS, CONTACT SPECIALSALES@ABRAMSBOOKS.COM OR
THE ADDRESS BELOW.

ABRAMS The Art of Books
115 West 18th Street, New York, NY 10011
abramsbooks.com

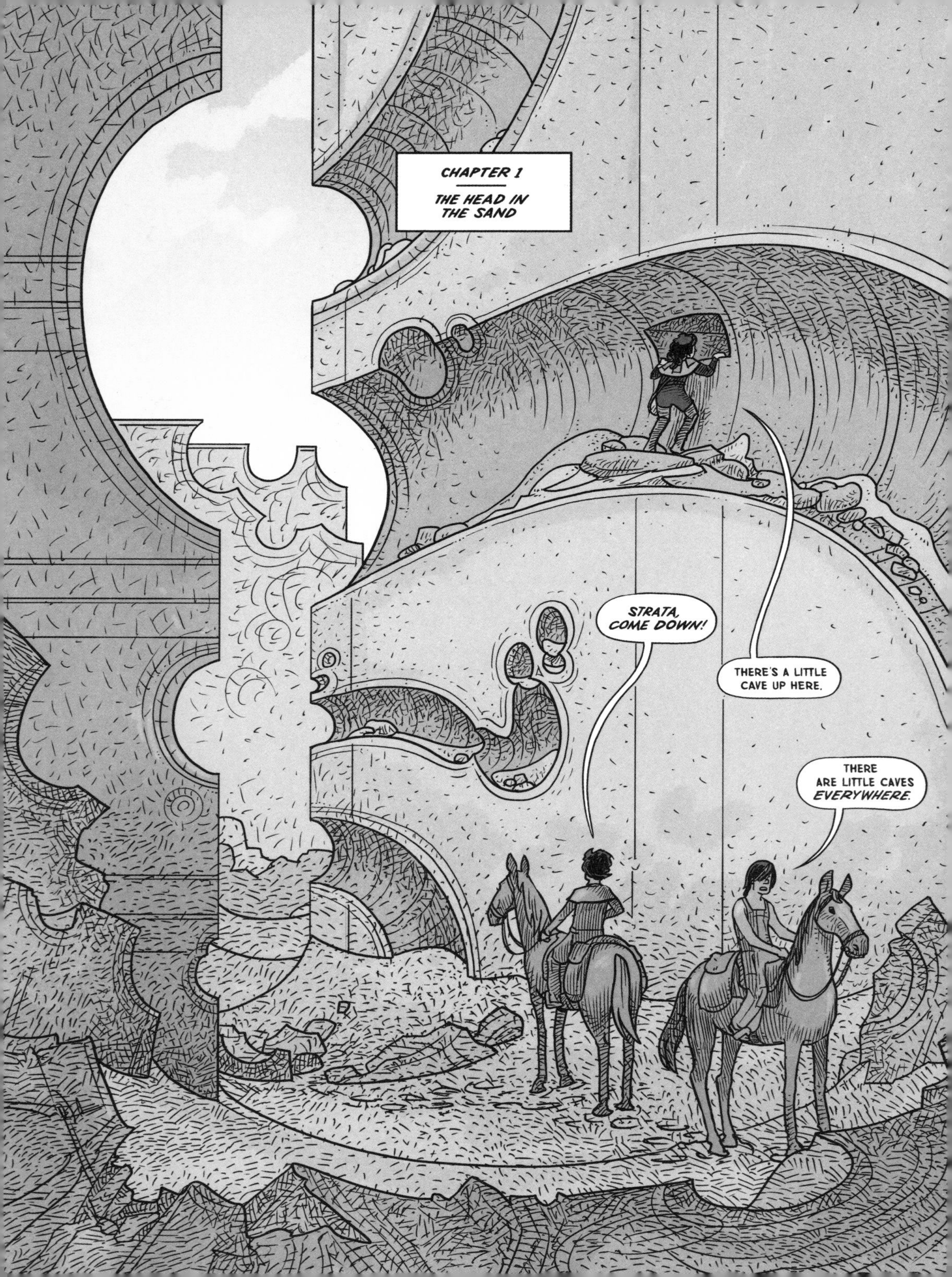
CHAPTER 1
THE HEAD IN THE SAND
STRATA, COME DOWN!
THERE'S A LITTLE CAVE UP HERE.
THERE ARE LITTLE CAVES *EVERYWHERE*.

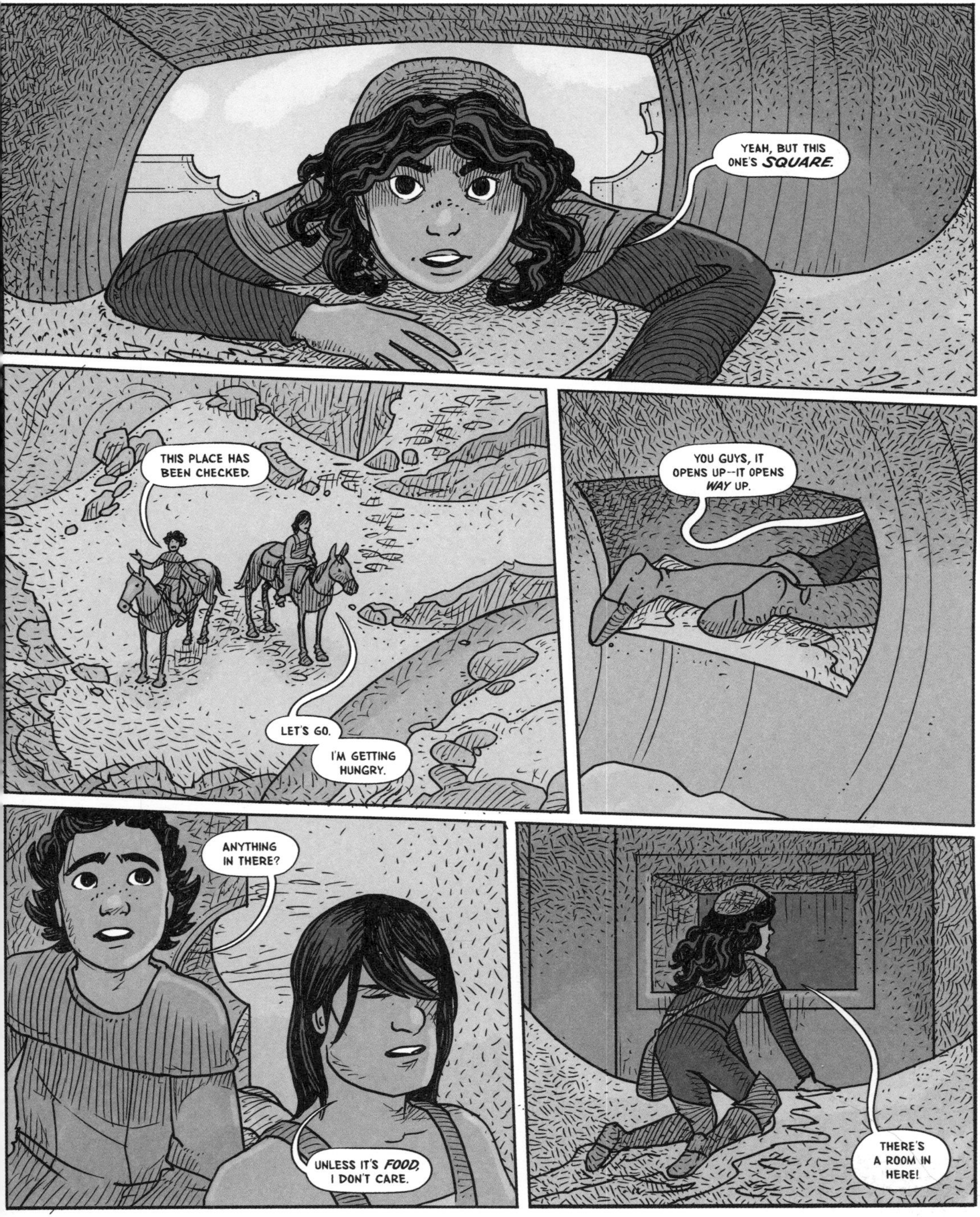
YEAH, BUT THIS ONE'S *SQUARE.*
THIS PLACE HAS BEEN CHECKED.
LET'S GO.
I'M GETTING HUNGRY.
YOU GUYS, IT OPENS UP--IT OPENS *WAY* UP.
ANYTHING IN THERE?
UNLESS IT'S *FOOD,* I DON'T CARE.
THERE'S A ROOM IN HERE!

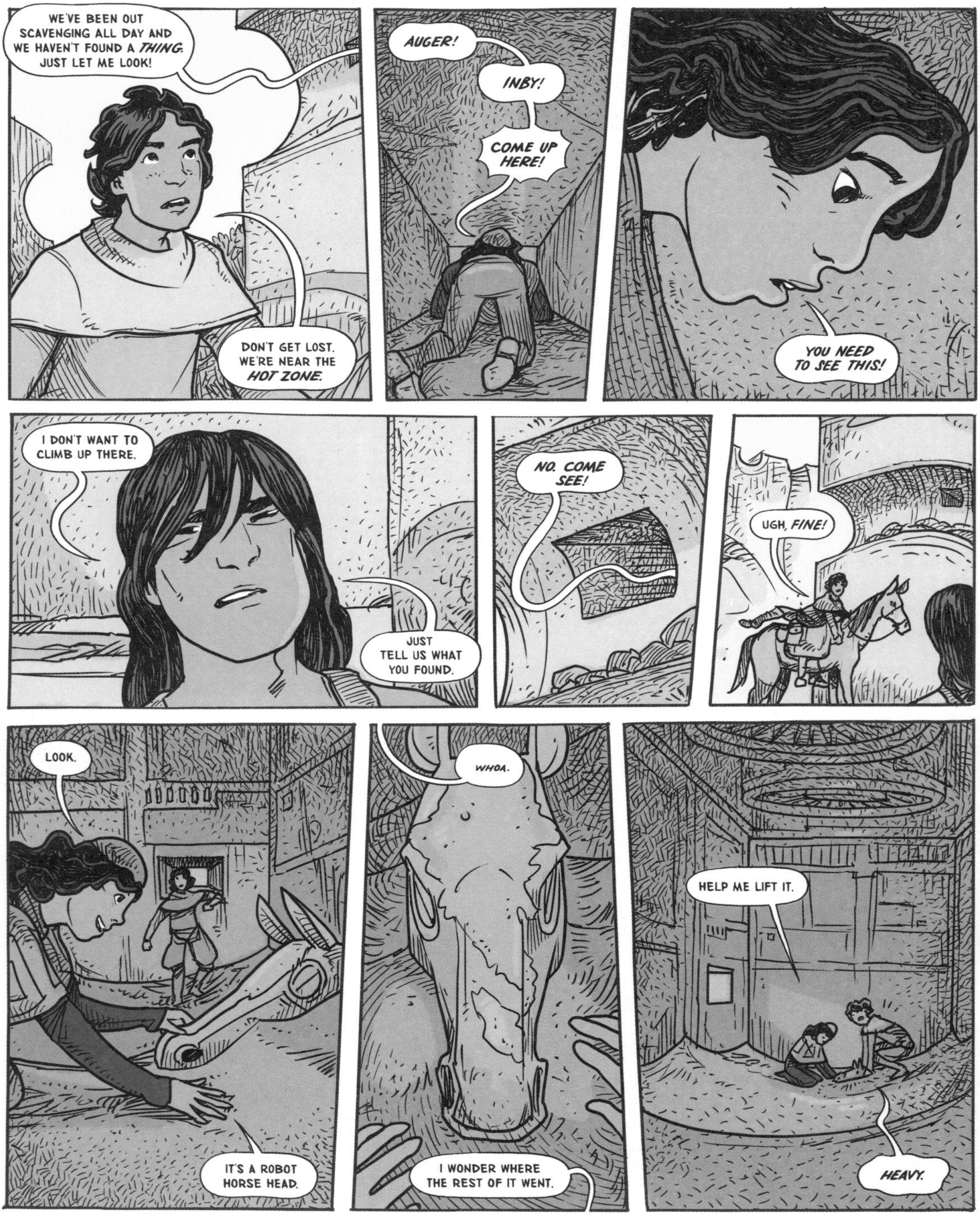
WE'VE BEEN OUT SCAVENGING ALL DAY AND WE HAVEN'T FOUND A *THING*. JUST LET ME LOOK!
DON'T GET LOST. WE'RE NEAR THE *HOT ZONE*.
AUGER!
INBY!
COME UP HERE!
YOU NEED TO SEE THIS!
I DON'T WANT TO CLIMB UP THERE.
JUST TELL US WHAT YOU FOUND.
NO. COME SEE!
UGH, *FINE!*
LOOK.
IT'S A ROBOT HORSE HEAD.
WHOA.
I WONDER WHERE THE REST OF IT WENT.
HELP ME LIFT IT.
HEAVY.

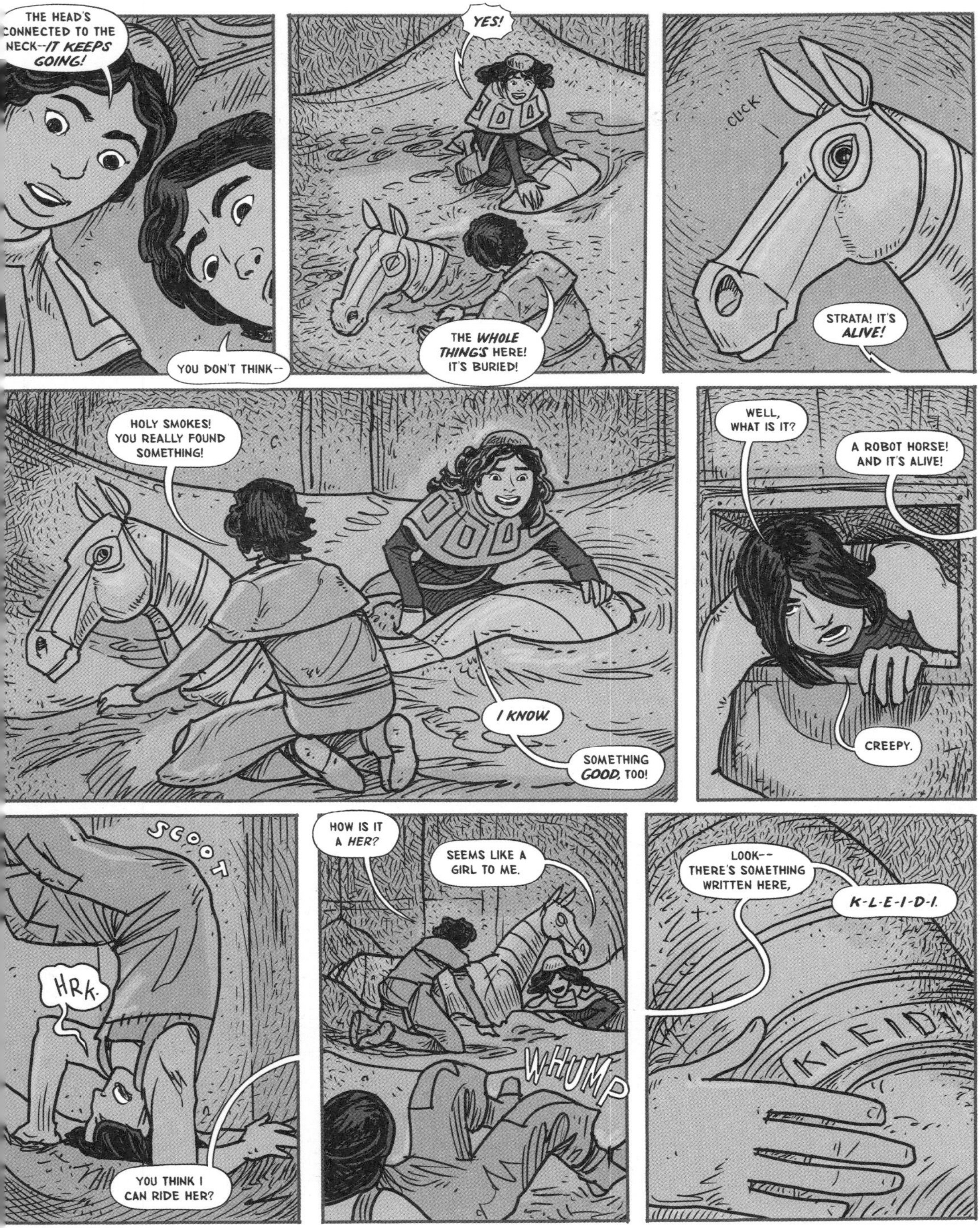
THE HEAD'S CONNECTED TO THE NECK--*IT KEEPS GOING!*
YOU DON'T THINK--
YES!
THE *WHOLE THING'S* HERE! IT'S BURIED!
CLICK
STRATA! IT'S *ALIVE!*
HOLY SMOKES! YOU REALLY FOUND SOMETHING!
I KNOW.
SOMETHING *GOOD,* TOO!
WELL, WHAT IS IT?
A ROBOT HORSE! AND IT'S ALIVE!
CREEPY.
SCOOT
HRK.
YOU THINK I CAN RIDE HER?
HOW IS IT A *HER?*
SEEMS LIKE A GIRL TO ME.
WHUMP
LOOK-- THERE'S SOMETHING WRITTEN HERE,
K-L-E-I-D-I.
KLEIDI

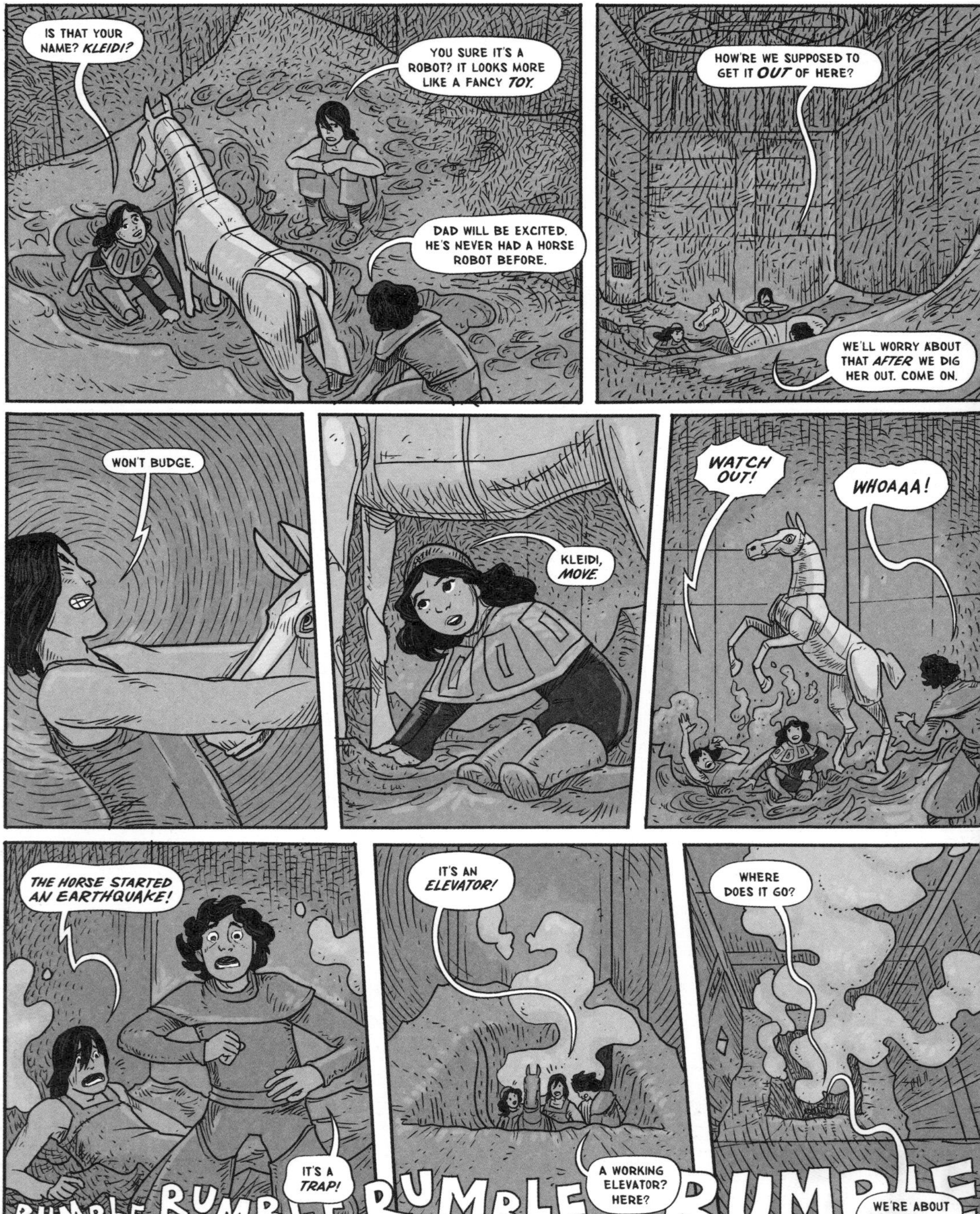
IS THAT YOUR NAME? *KLEIDI?*
YOU SURE IT'S A ROBOT? IT LOOKS MORE LIKE A FANCY *TOY.*
DAD WILL BE EXCITED. HE'S NEVER HAD A HORSE ROBOT BEFORE.
HOW'RE WE SUPPOSED TO GET IT *OUT* OF HERE?
WE'LL WORRY ABOUT THAT *AFTER* WE DIG HER OUT. COME ON.
WON'T BUDGE.
KLEIDI, *MOVE.*
WATCH OUT!
WHOAAA!
THE HORSE STARTED AN EARTHQUAKE!
IT'S A *TRAP!*
IT'S AN *ELEVATOR!*
A WORKING ELEVATOR? HERE?
WHERE DOES IT GO?
WE'RE ABOUT TO FIND OUT.
RUMBLE RUMBLE RUMBLE RUMBLE

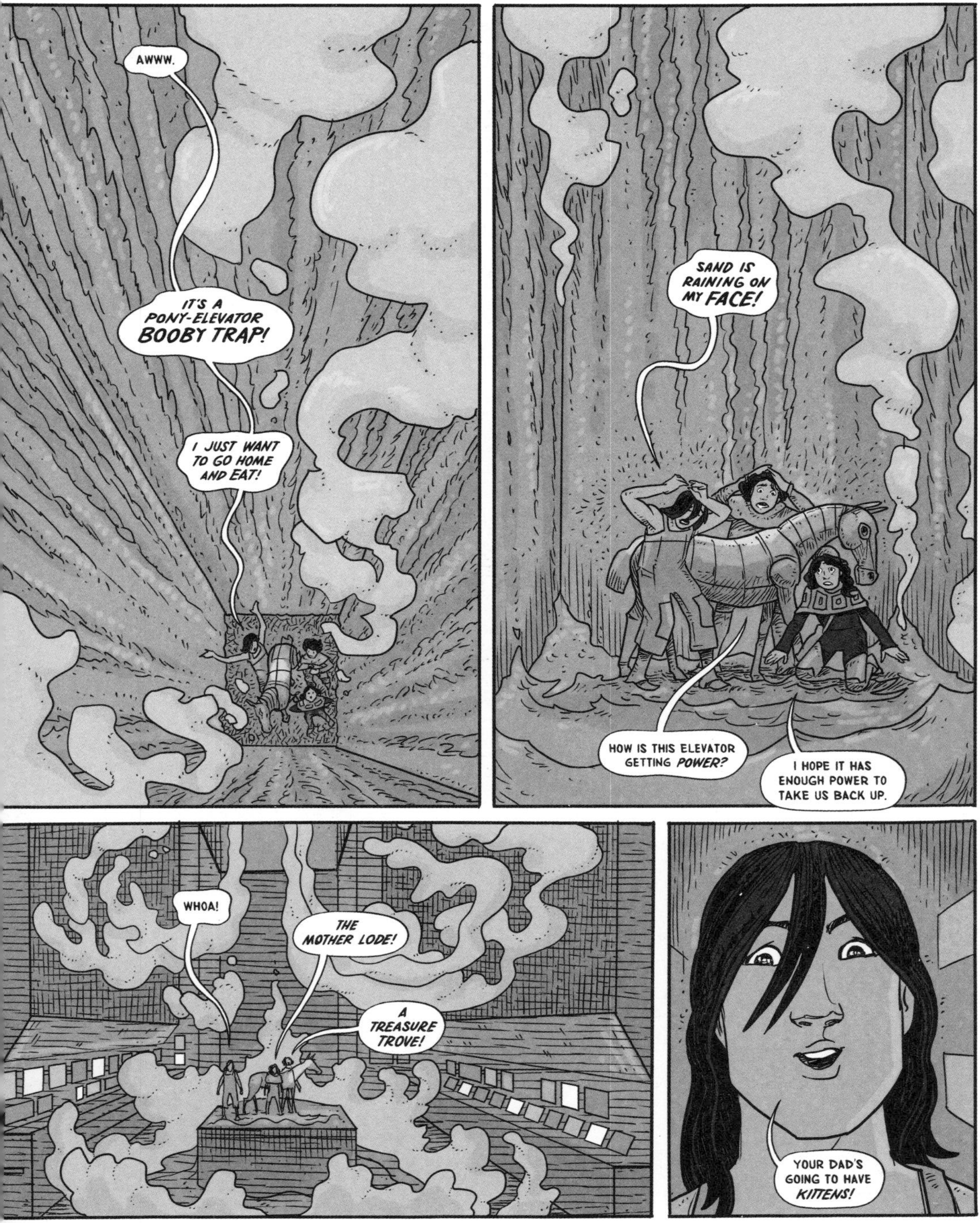
AWWW.
IT'S A PONY-ELEVATOR BOOBY TRAP!
I JUST WANT TO GO HOME AND EAT!
SAND IS RAINING ON MY FACE!
HOW IS THIS ELEVATOR GETTING POWER?
I HOPE IT HAS ENOUGH POWER TO TAKE US BACK UP.
WHOA!
THE MOTHER LODE!
A TREASURE TROVE!
YOUR DAD'S GOING TO HAVE KITTENS!

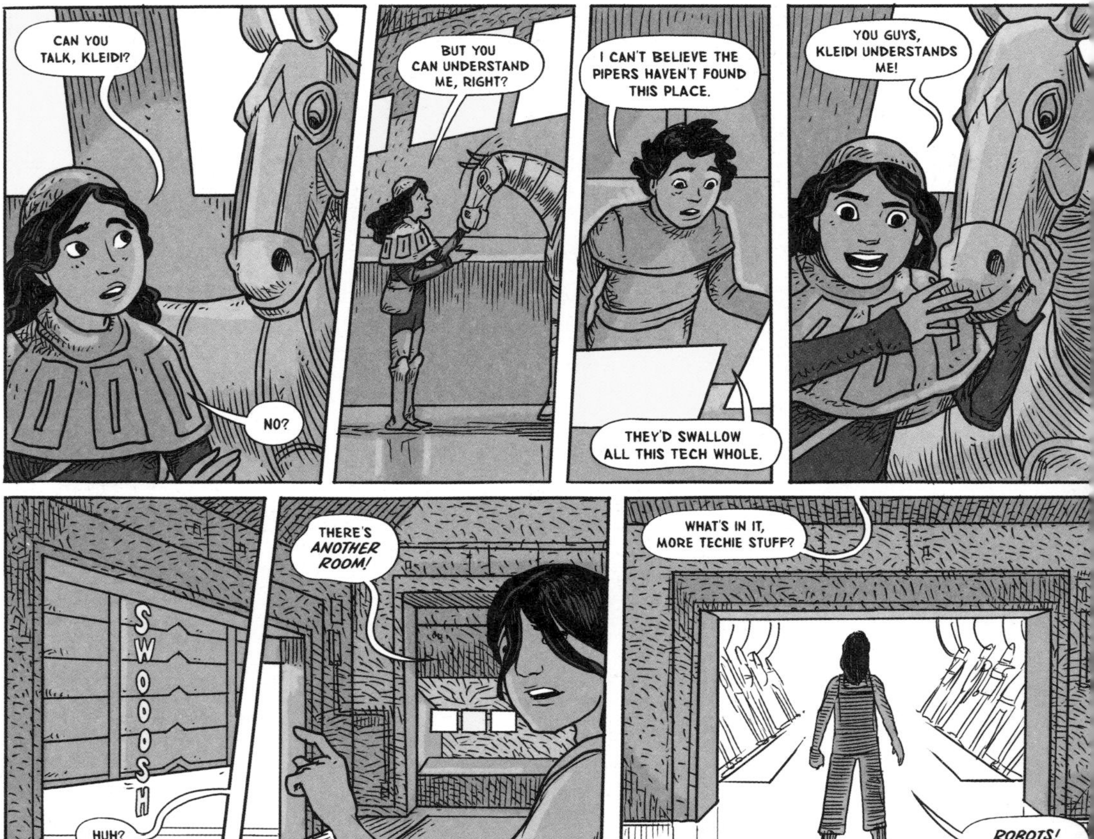
CAN YOU TALK, KLEIDI?
NO?
BUT YOU CAN UNDERSTAND ME, RIGHT?
I CAN'T BELIEVE THE PIPERS HAVEN'T FOUND THIS PLACE.
THEY'D SWALLOW ALL THIS TECH WHOLE.
YOU GUYS, KLEIDI UNDERSTANDS ME!
SWOOOSH
HUH?
THERE'S *ANOTHER ROOM!*
WHAT'S IN IT, MORE TECHIE STUFF?
ROBOTS! LOTS OF THEM!
THIS IS MORE THAN WE HAVE IN THE *ENTIRE* CARAVAN!
AND THEY'RE NEW! *SHINY AND NEW!*
THIS ONE'S MINE. THIS WILL BE MY PERSONAL ROBOT.

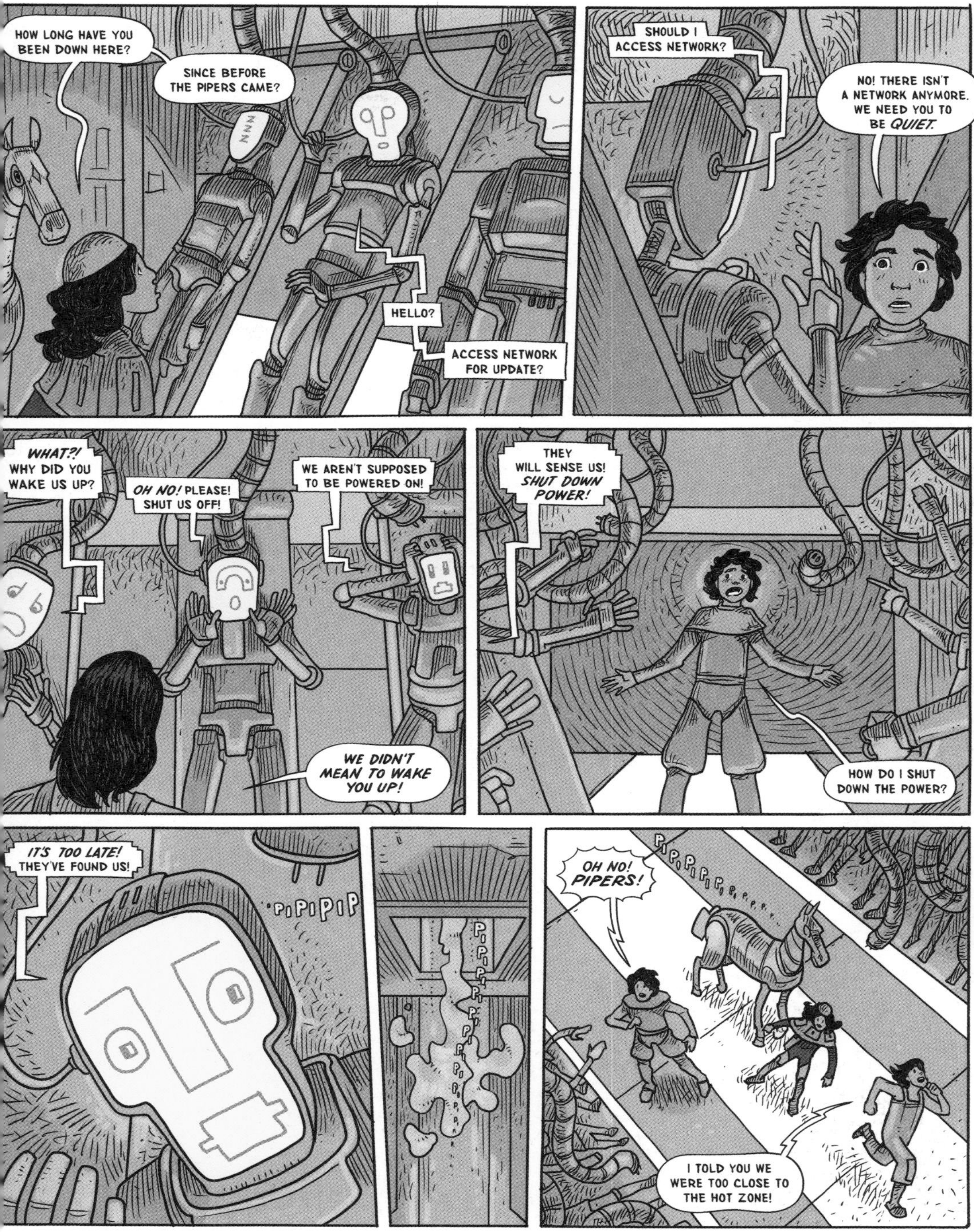

HOW LONG HAVE YOU BEEN DOWN HERE?
SINCE BEFORE THE PIPERS CAME?
ZZZ
HELLO?
ACCESS NETWORK FOR UPDATE?
SHOULD I ACCESS NETWORK?
NO! THERE ISN'T A NETWORK ANYMORE. WE NEED YOU TO BE *QUIET.*
WHAT?! WHY DID YOU WAKE US UP?
OH NO! PLEASE! SHUT US OFF!
WE AREN'T SUPPOSED TO BE POWERED ON!
WE DIDN'T MEAN TO WAKE YOU UP!
THEY WILL SENSE US! *SHUT DOWN POWER!*
HOW DO I SHUT DOWN THE POWER?
IT'S TOO LATE! THEY'VE FOUND US!
PIPIPIPIP
PIPIPIPIPIPIPI
OH NO! PIPERS!
PIPIPIPIPIPIPIPIP
I TOLD YOU WE WERE TOO CLOSE TO THE HOT ZONE!

WE'RE DOOMED!
BUBBLES! THEY'RE HERE!
PPPPPPPPPP
PIPERS!
PPPPPPP

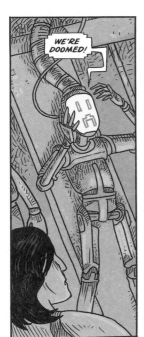

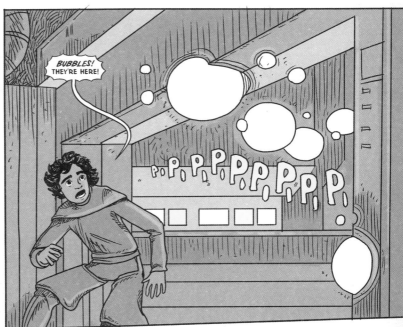

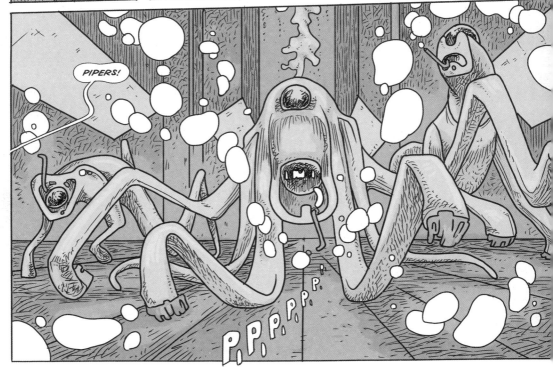

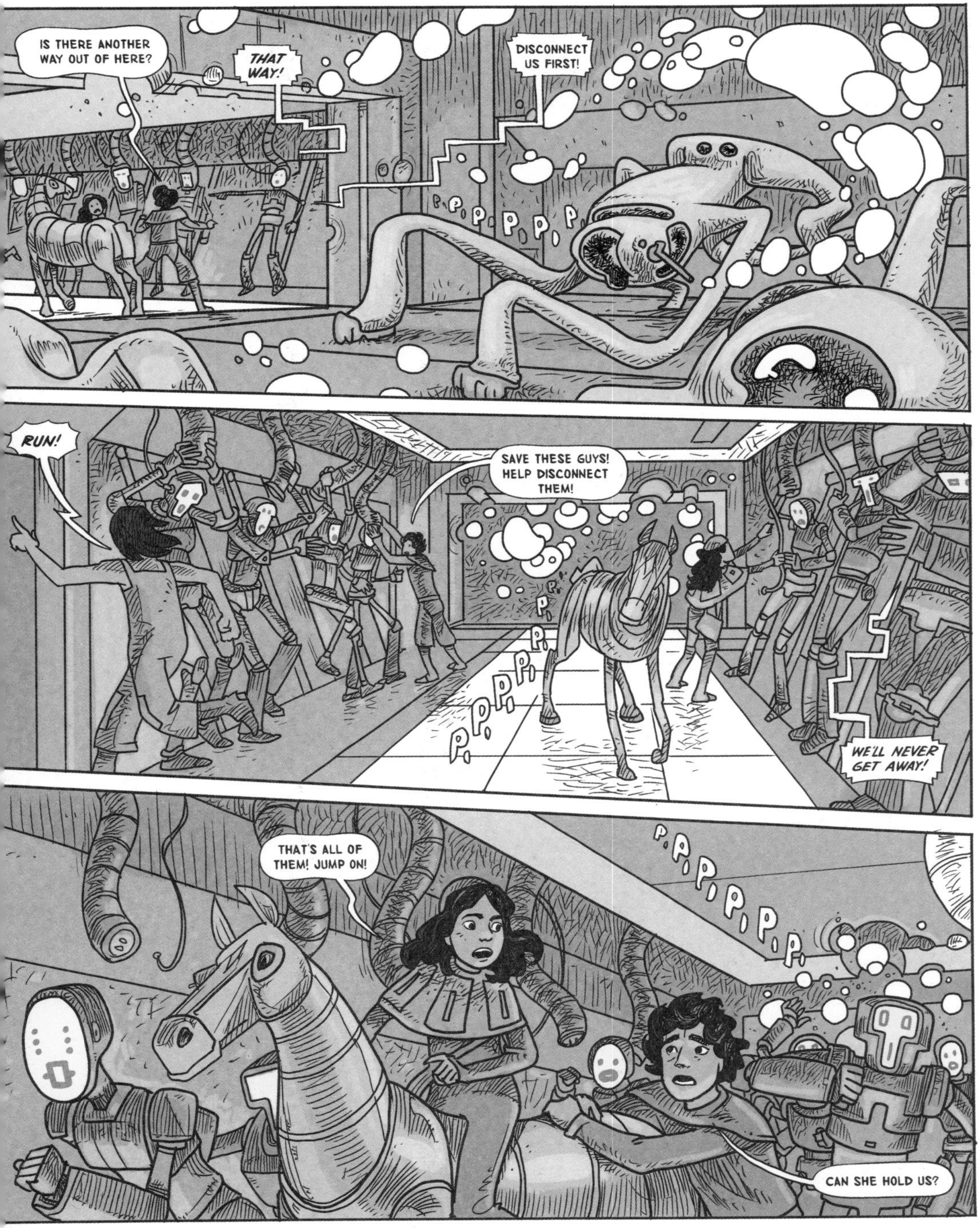
IS THERE ANOTHER WAY OUT OF HERE?
THAT WAY!
DISCONNECT US FIRST!
P P P P P P
RUN!
SAVE THESE GUYS! HELP DISCONNECT THEM!
P P P P P P P
WE'LL NEVER GET AWAY!
THAT'S ALL OF THEM! JUMP ON!
P P P P P P P P
CAN SHE HOLD US?

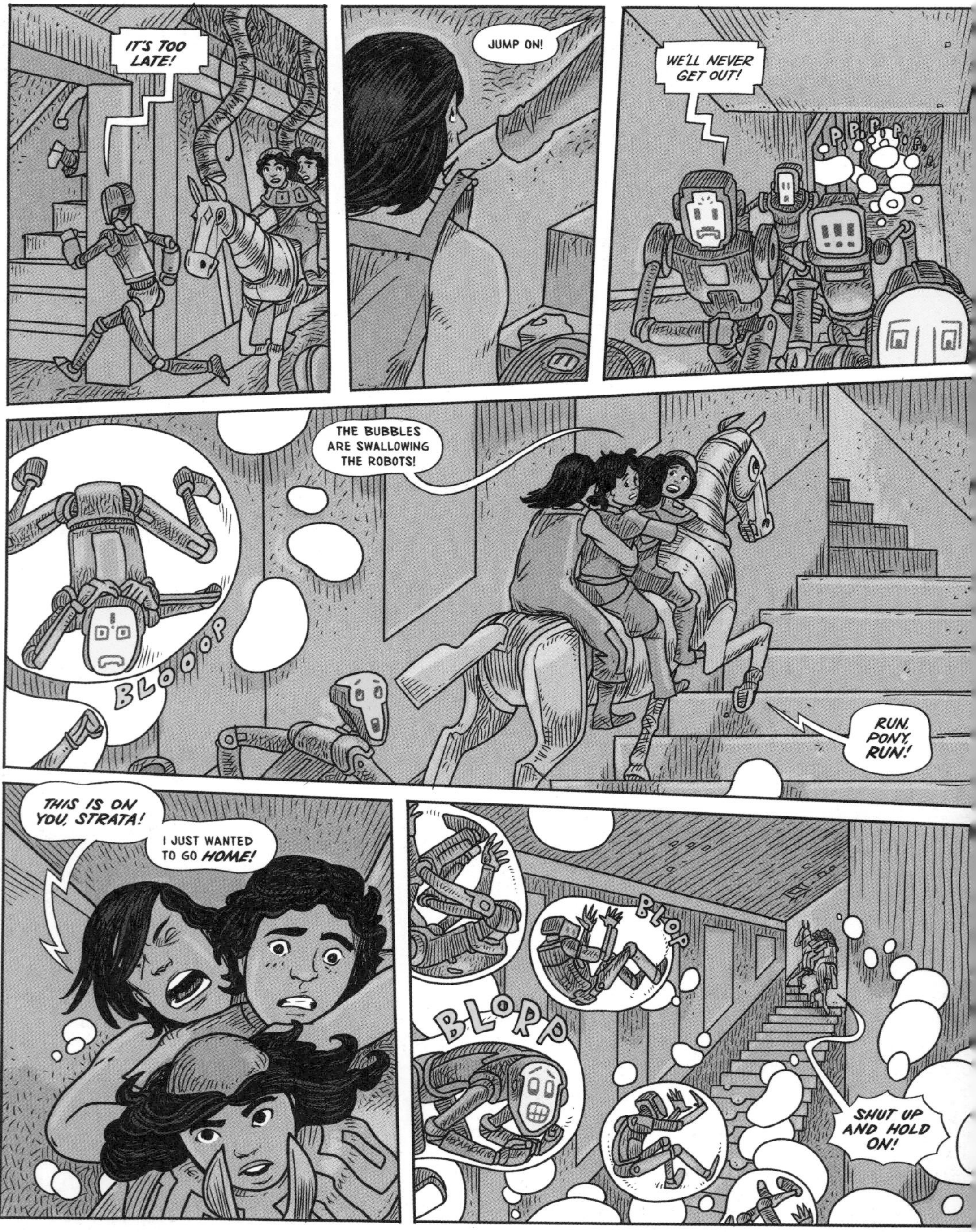
IT'S TOO LATE!
JUMP ON!
WE'LL NEVER GET OUT!
PPPPOPP
!!!
THE BUBBLES ARE SWALLOWING THE ROBOTS!
BLOOOP
RUN, PONY, RUN!
THIS IS ON YOU, STRATA!
I JUST WANTED TO GO HOME!
BLOP
BLORP
SHUT UP AND HOLD ON!

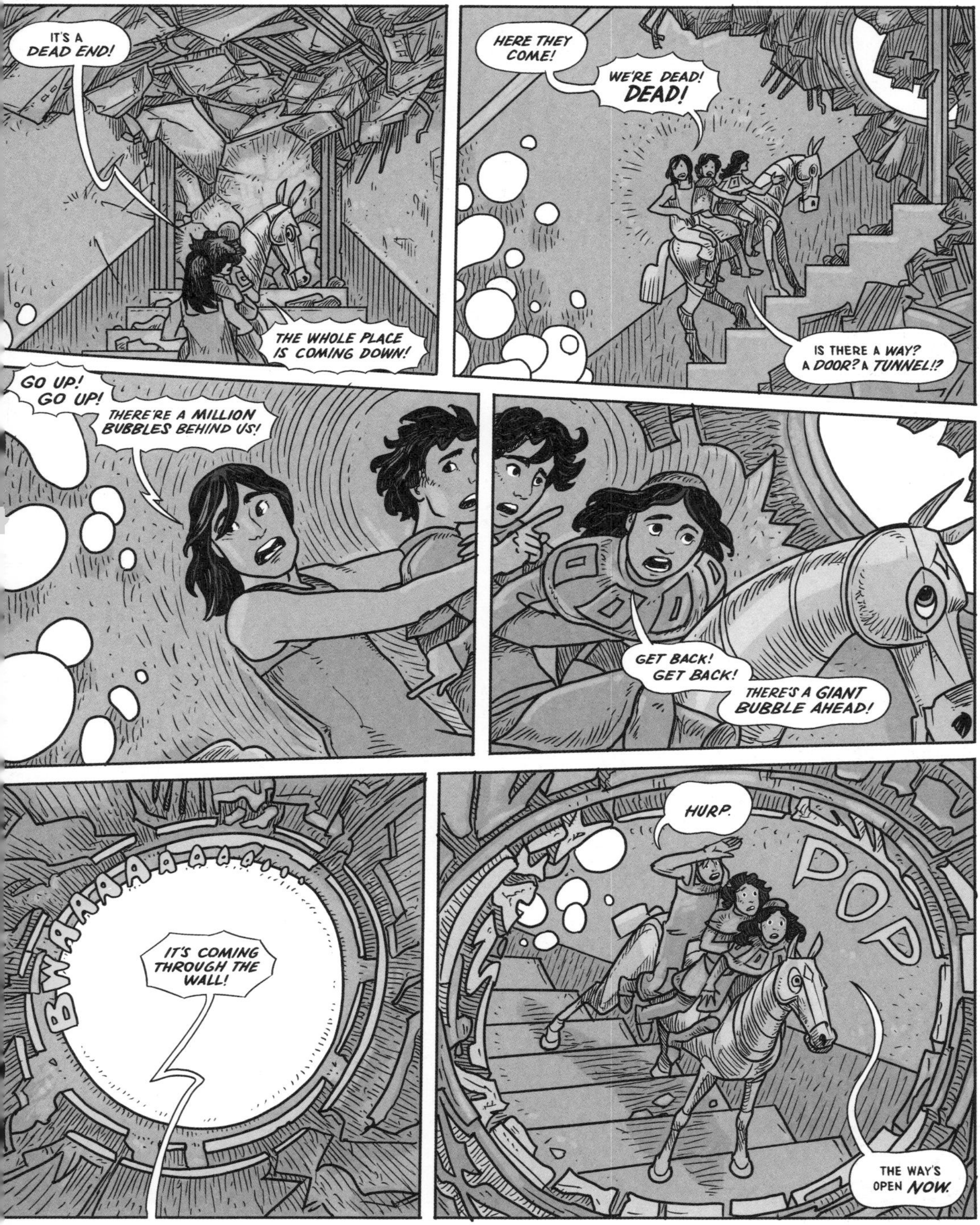
IT'S A DEAD END!
THE WHOLE PLACE IS COMING DOWN!
HERE THEY COME!
WE'RE DEAD! DEAD!
IS THERE A WAY? A DOOR? A TUNNEL!?
GO UP! GO UP!
THERE'RE A MILLION BUBBLES BEHIND US!
GET BACK! GET BACK!
THERE'S A GIANT BUBBLE AHEAD!
BWAAAAAAAAA...
IT'S COMING THROUGH THE WALL!
HURP.
POP
THE WAY'S OPEN NOW.

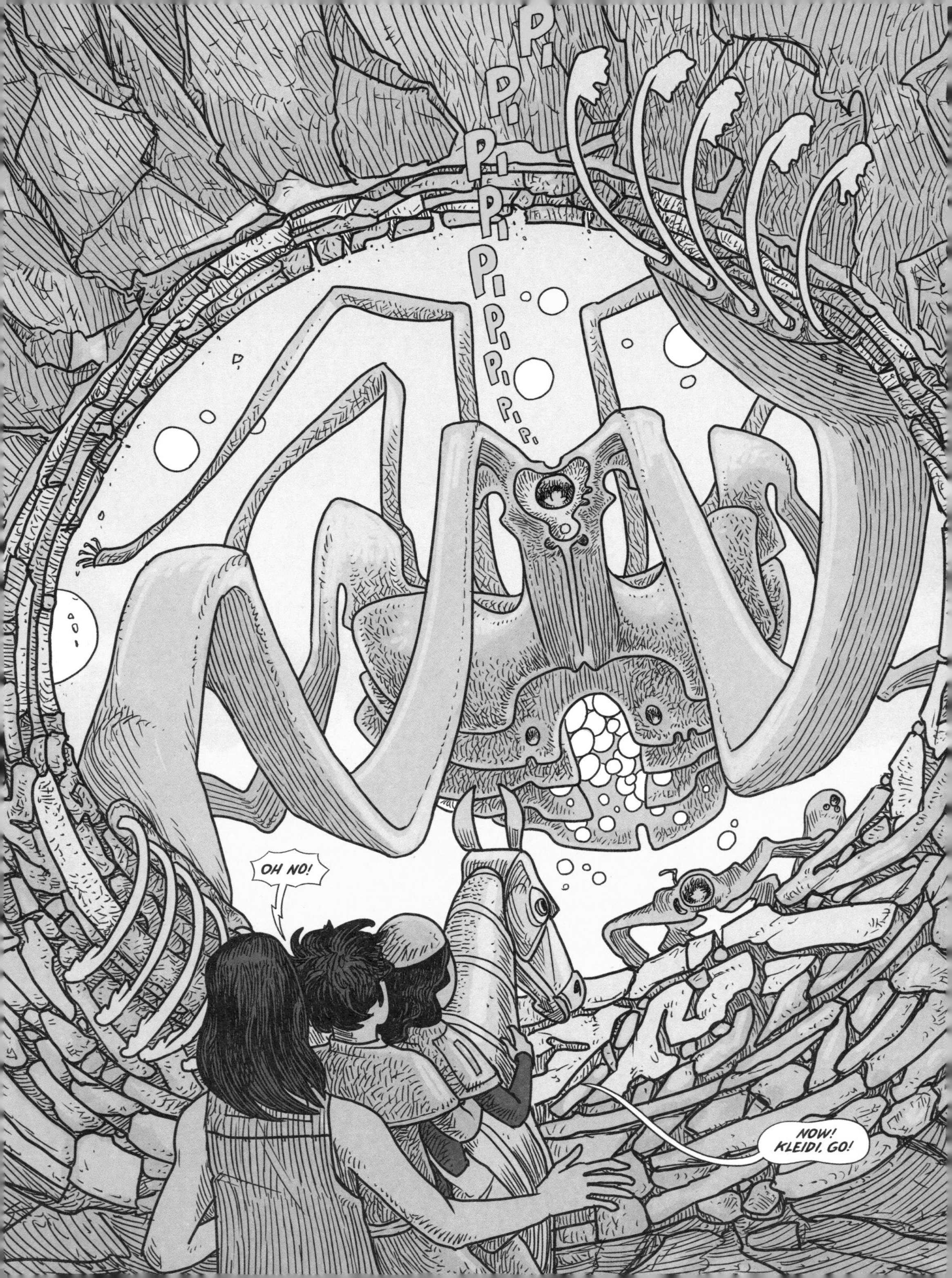
PI PI PI PI PI PI PI PI PI PI
OH NO!
NOW! KLEIDI, GO!

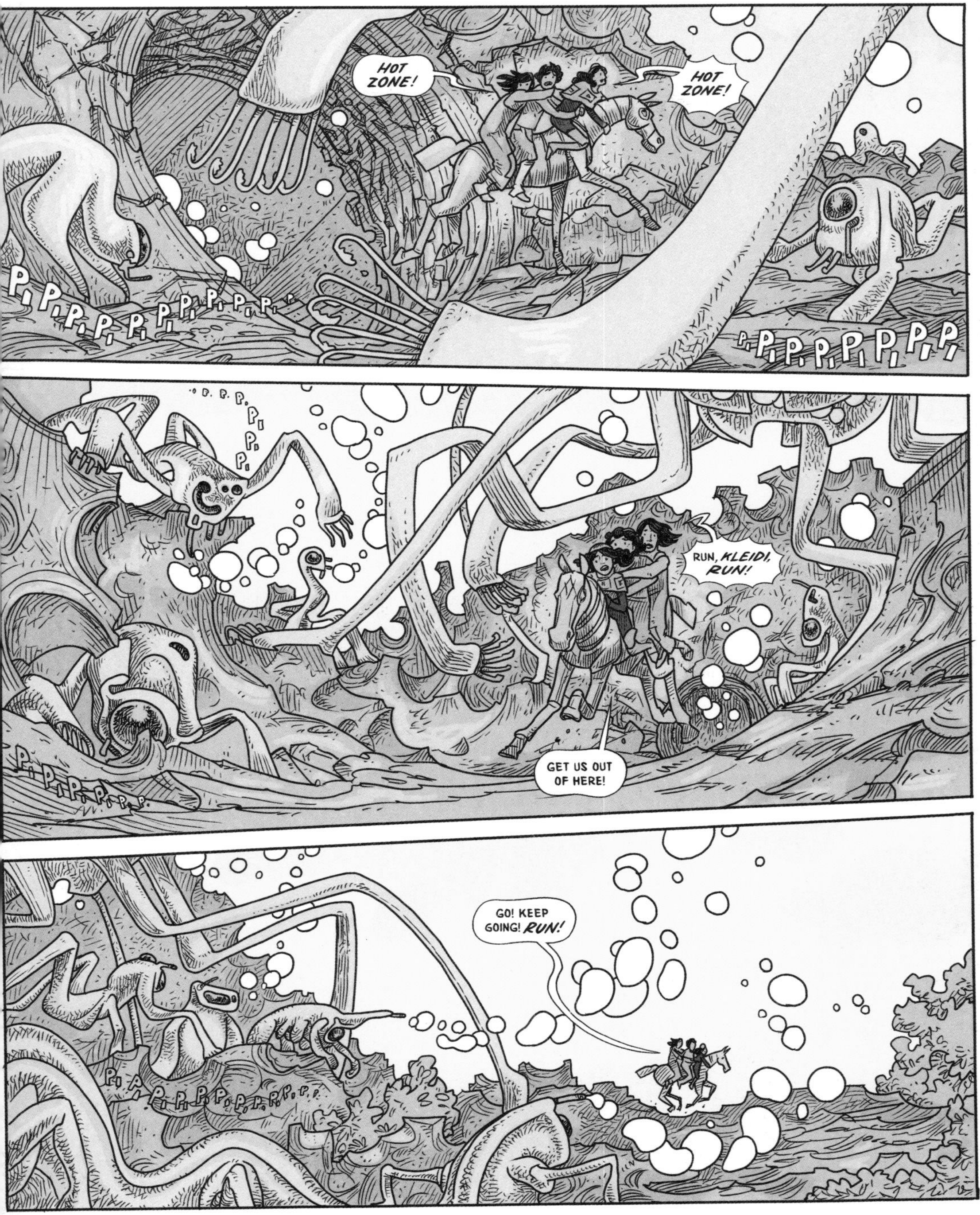
HOT ZONE!
HOT ZONE!
RUN, KLEIDI, RUN!
GET US OUT OF HERE!
GO! KEEP GOING! RUN!

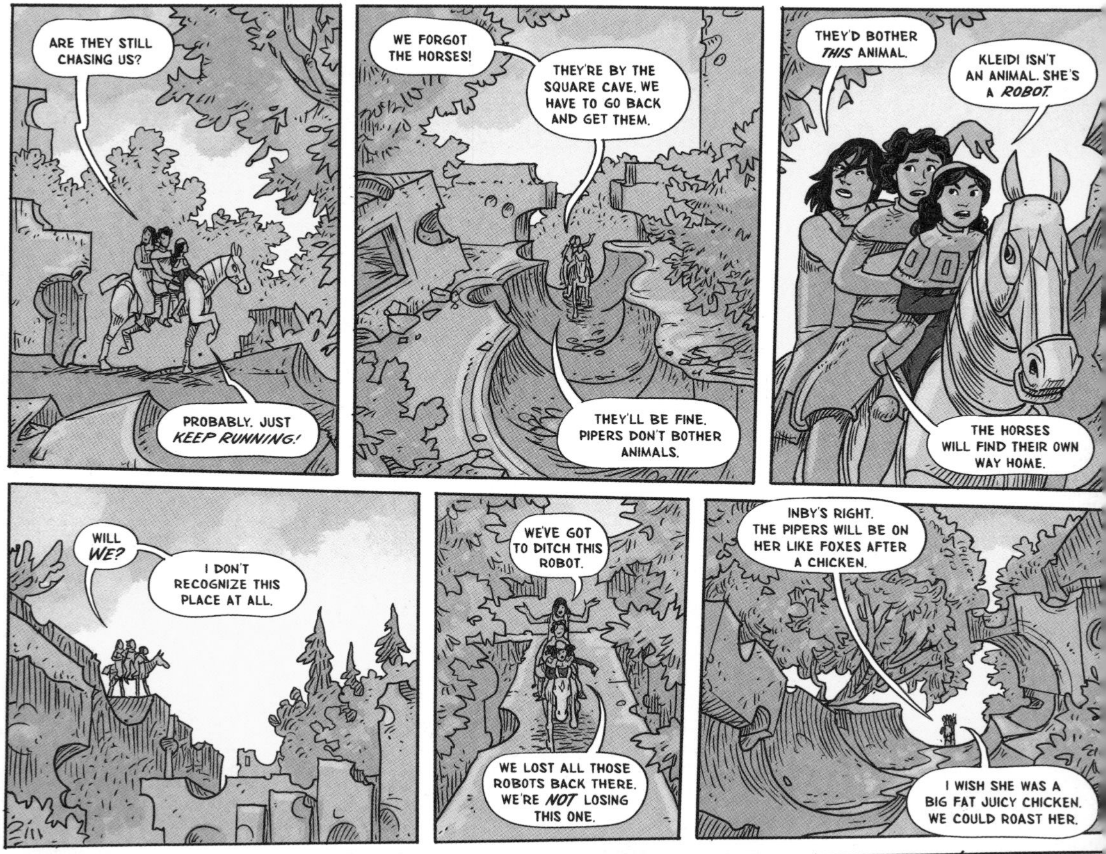

ARE THEY STILL CHASING US?
PROBABLY. JUST *KEEP RUNNING!*
WE FORGOT THE HORSES!
THEY'RE BY THE SQUARE CAVE. WE HAVE TO GO BACK AND GET THEM.
THEY'LL BE FINE. PIPERS DON'T BOTHER ANIMALS.
THEY'D BOTHER *THIS* ANIMAL.
KLEIDI ISN'T AN ANIMAL. SHE'S A *ROBOT.*
THE HORSES WILL FIND THEIR OWN WAY HOME.
WILL *WE?*
I DON'T RECOGNIZE THIS PLACE AT ALL.
WE'VE GOT TO DITCH THIS ROBOT.
WE LOST ALL THOSE ROBOTS BACK THERE. WE'RE *NOT* LOSING THIS ONE.
INBY'S RIGHT. THE PIPERS WILL BE ON HER LIKE FOXES AFTER A CHICKEN.
I WISH SHE WAS A BIG FAT JUICY CHICKEN. WE COULD ROAST HER.
WE *BARELY* MADE IT OUT OF THERE!
WE'RE *LUCKY* TO BE *ALIVE!*
SITTING ON A ROBOT WITH THIS MANY PIPERS AROUND IS *INSANE!*
FINE. THEN YOU CAN *WALK* HOME.
I'LL RIDE KLEIDI BACK. *ALONE.*
WELL? GET *OFF.*
THEN IT'S SETTLED. TAKE US HOME, KLEIDI.

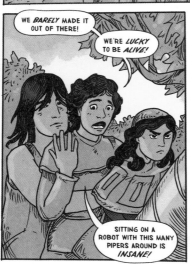

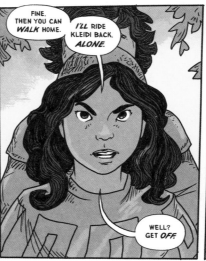

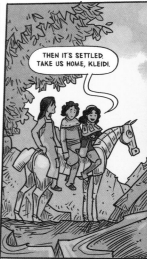

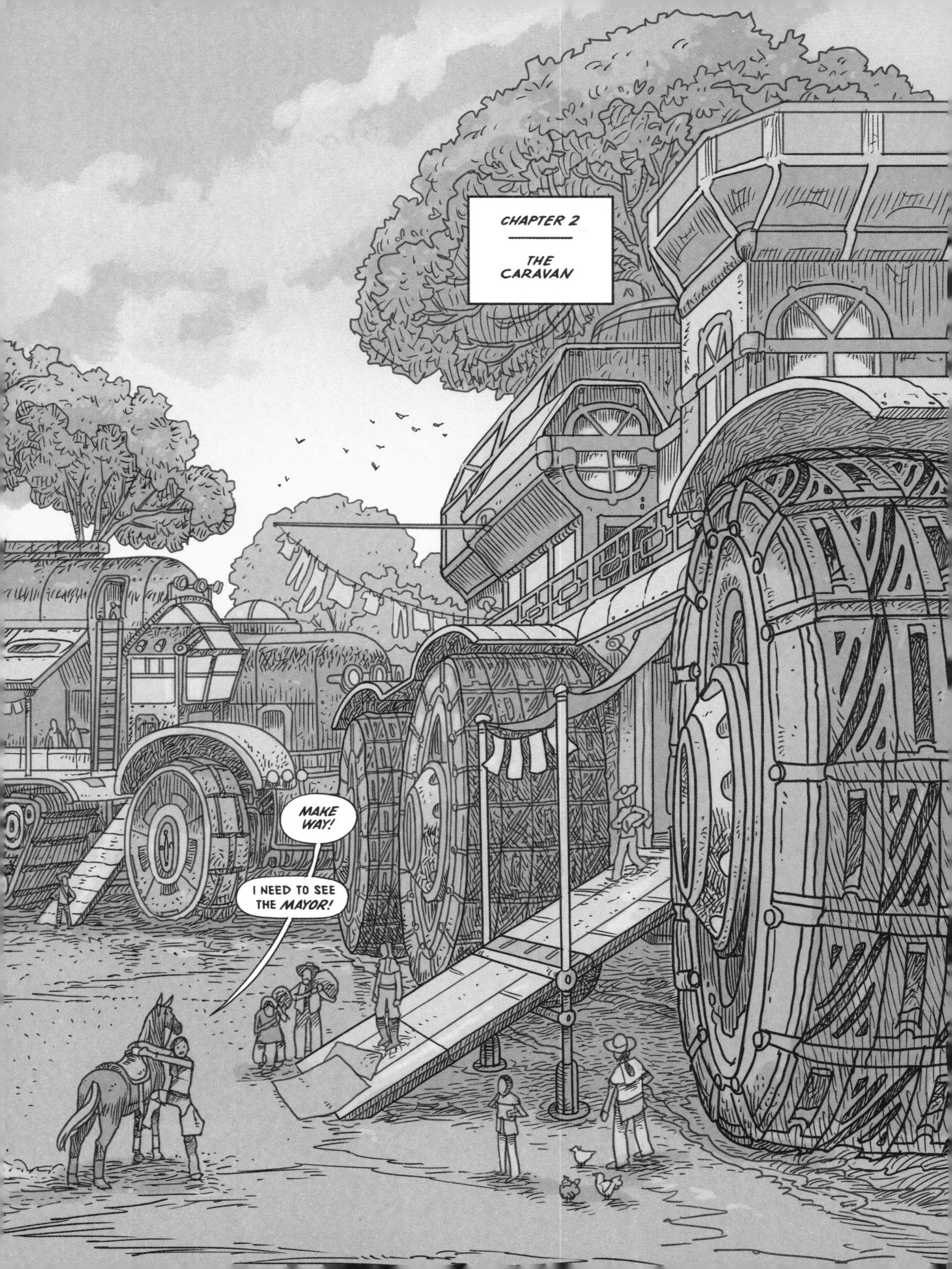
CHAPTER 2
THE CARAVAN
MAKE WAY!
I NEED TO SEE THE MAYOR!

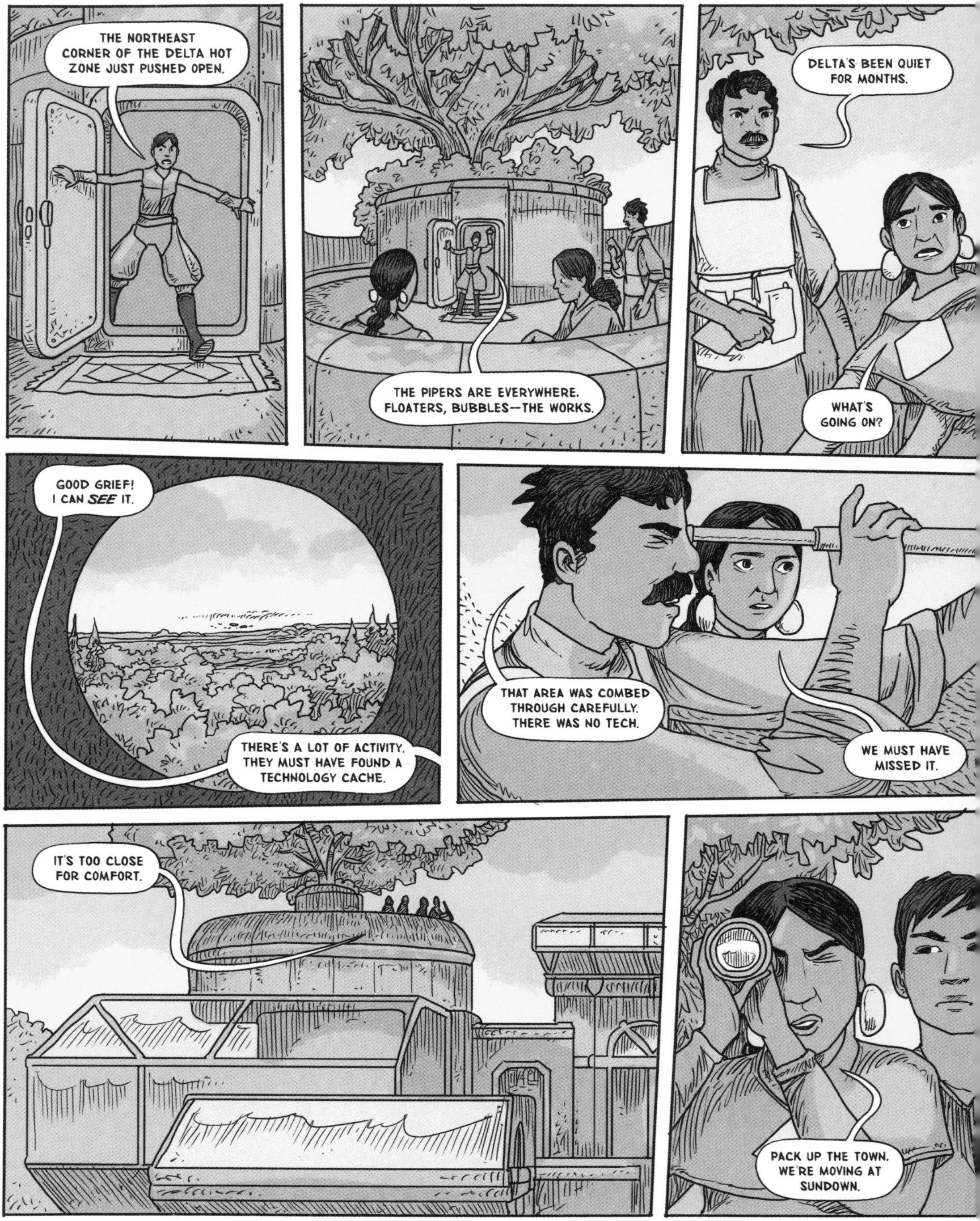
THE NORTHEAST CORNER OF THE DELTA HOT ZONE JUST PUSHED OPEN.
THE PIPERS ARE EVERYWHERE. FLOATERS, BUBBLES--THE WORKS.
DELTA'S BEEN QUIET FOR MONTHS.
WHAT'S GOING ON?
GOOD GRIEF! I CAN *SEE* IT.
THERE'S A LOT OF ACTIVITY. THEY MUST HAVE FOUND A TECHNOLOGY CACHE.
THAT AREA WAS COMBED THROUGH CAREFULLY. THERE WAS NO TECH.
WE MUST HAVE MISSED IT.
IT'S TOO CLOSE FOR COMFORT.
PACK UP THE TOWN. WE'RE MOVING AT SUNDOWN.

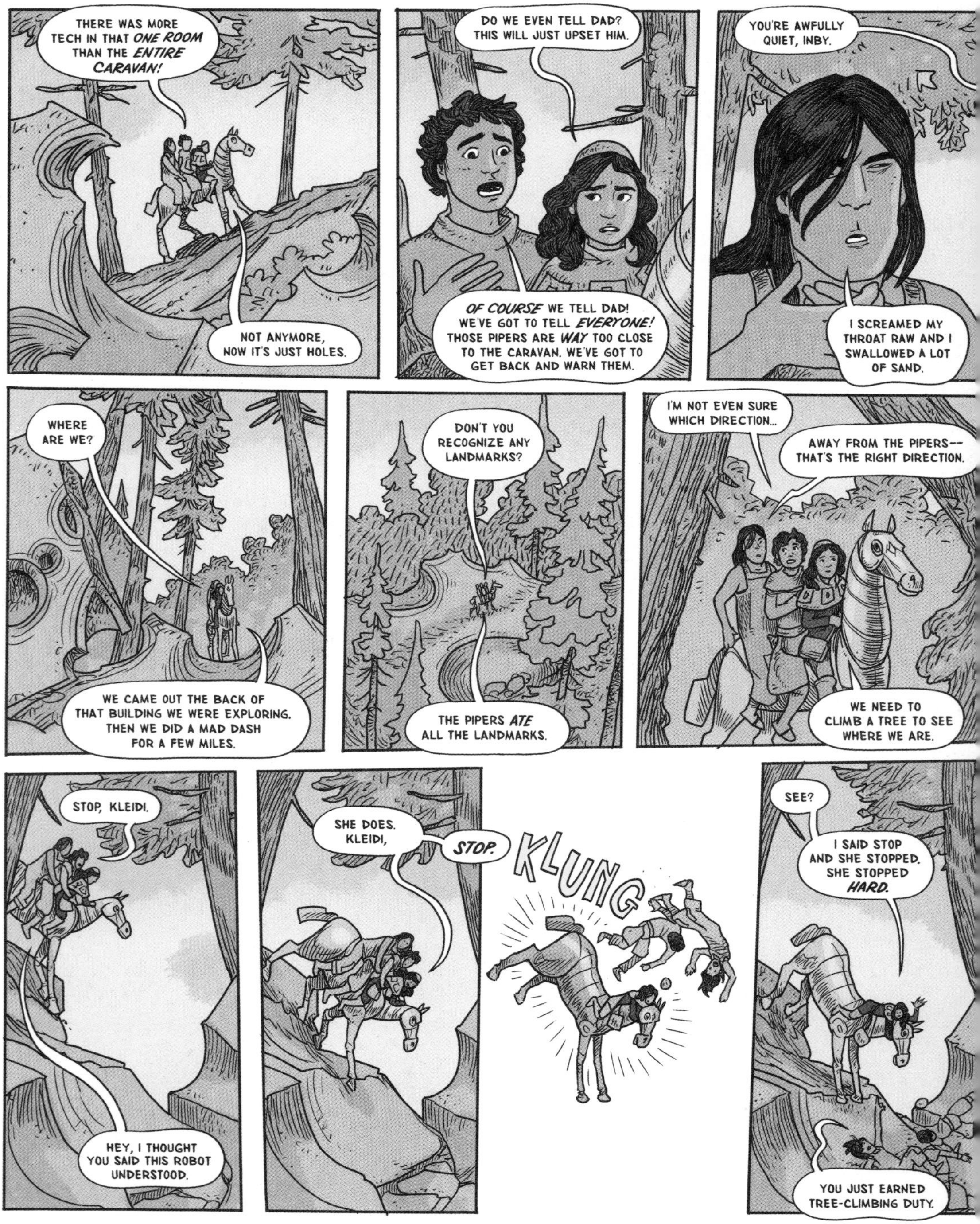
THERE WAS MORE TECH IN THAT *ONE ROOM* THAN THE *ENTIRE CARAVAN!*
NOT ANYMORE, NOW IT'S JUST HOLES.
DO WE EVEN TELL DAD? THIS WILL JUST UPSET HIM.
OF COURSE WE TELL DAD! WE'VE GOT TO TELL *EVERYONE!* THOSE PIPERS ARE *WAY* TOO CLOSE TO THE CARAVAN. WE'VE GOT TO GET BACK AND WARN THEM.
YOU'RE AWFULLY QUIET, INBY.
I SCREAMED MY THROAT RAW AND I SWALLOWED A LOT OF SAND.
WHERE ARE WE?
WE CAME OUT THE BACK OF THAT BUILDING WE WERE EXPLORING. THEN WE DID A MAD DASH FOR A FEW MILES.
DON'T YOU RECOGNIZE ANY LANDMARKS?
THE PIPERS *ATE* ALL THE LANDMARKS.
I'M NOT EVEN SURE WHICH DIRECTION...
AWAY FROM THE PIPERS-- THAT'S THE RIGHT DIRECTION.
WE NEED TO CLIMB A TREE TO SEE WHERE WE ARE.
STOP, KLEIDI.
HEY, I THOUGHT YOU SAID THIS ROBOT UNDERSTOOD.
SHE DOES. KLEIDI,
STOP.
KLUNG
SEE?
I SAID STOP AND SHE STOPPED. SHE STOPPED *HARD.*
YOU JUST EARNED TREE-CLIMBING DUTY.

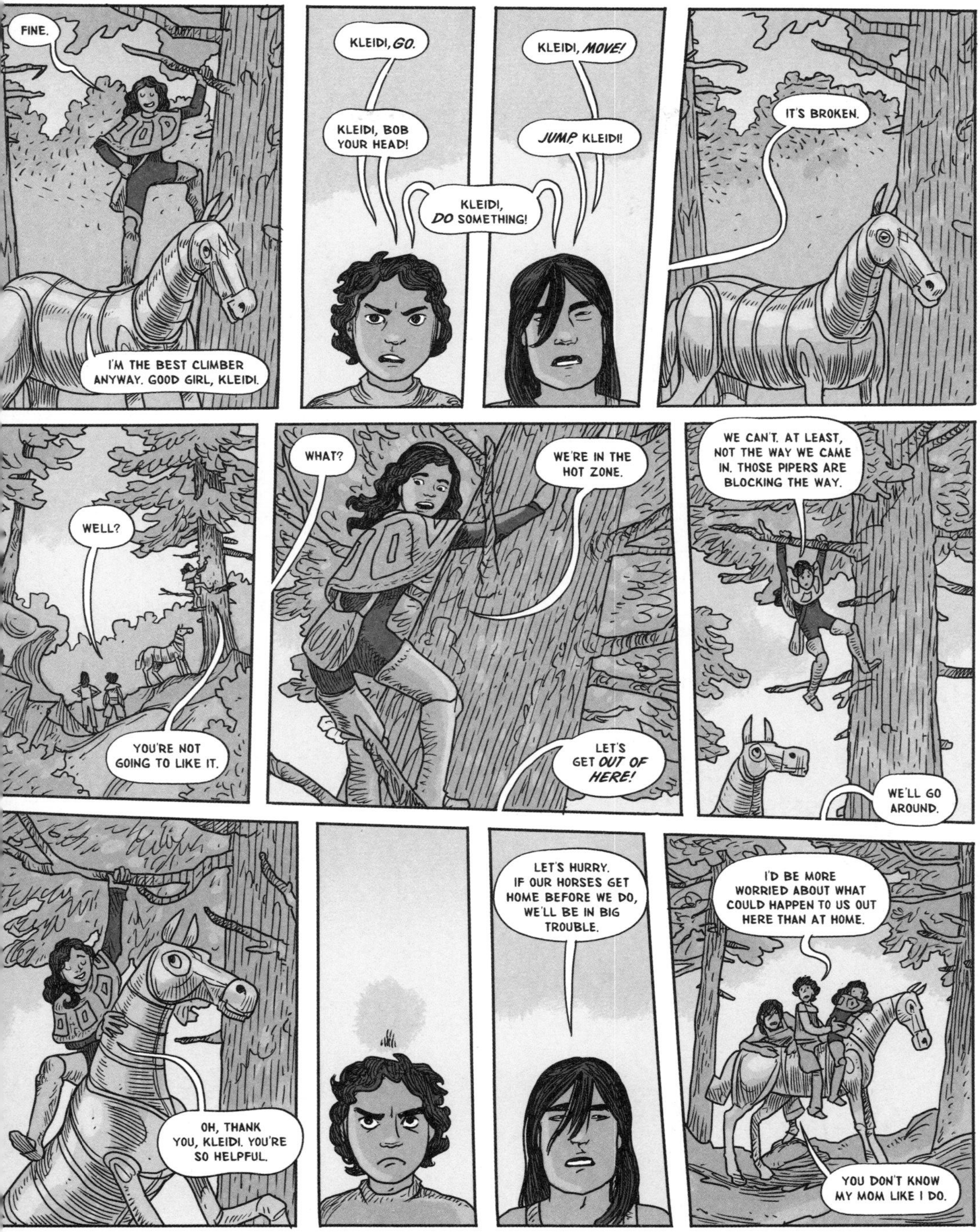
FINE.
I'M THE BEST CLIMBER ANYWAY. GOOD GIRL, KLEIDI.
KLEIDI, GO.
KLEIDI, BOB YOUR HEAD!
KLEIDI, MOVE!
JUMP, KLEIDI!
KLEIDI, DO SOMETHING!
IT'S BROKEN.
WELL?
YOU'RE NOT GOING TO LIKE IT.
WHAT?
WE'RE IN THE HOT ZONE.
LET'S GET OUT OF HERE!
WE CAN'T. AT LEAST, NOT THE WAY WE CAME IN. THOSE PIPERS ARE BLOCKING THE WAY.
WE'LL GO AROUND.
OH, THANK YOU, KLEIDI. YOU'RE SO HELPFUL.
LET'S HURRY. IF OUR HORSES GET HOME BEFORE WE DO, WE'LL BE IN BIG TROUBLE.
I'D BE MORE WORRIED ABOUT WHAT COULD HAPPEN TO US OUT HERE THAN AT HOME.
YOU DON'T KNOW MY MOM LIKE I DO.

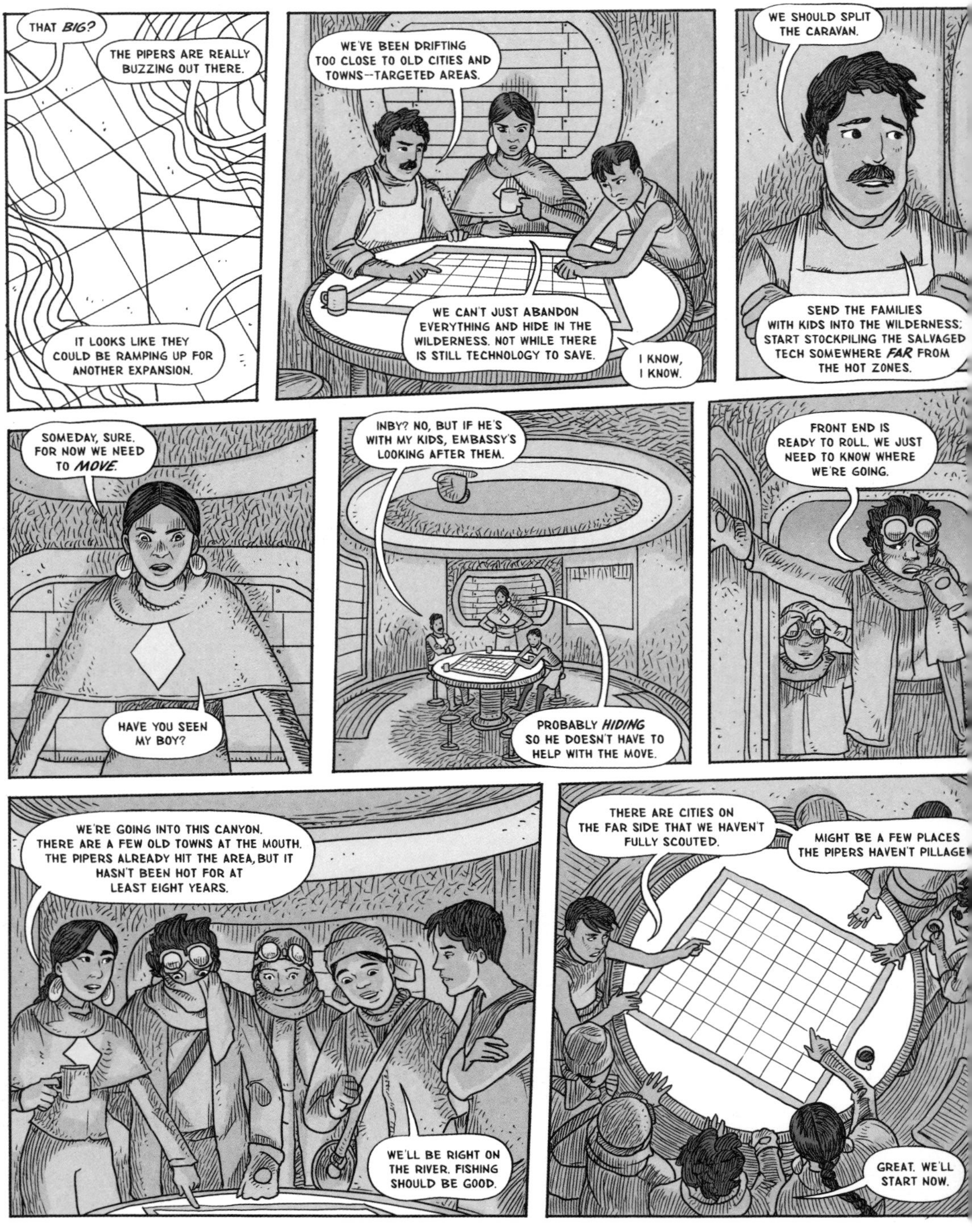
THAT BIG?
THE PIPERS ARE REALLY BUZZING OUT THERE.
IT LOOKS LIKE THEY COULD BE RAMPING UP FOR ANOTHER EXPANSION.
WE'VE BEEN DRIFTING TOO CLOSE TO OLD CITIES AND TOWNS--TARGETED AREAS.
WE CAN'T JUST ABANDON EVERYTHING AND HIDE IN THE WILDERNESS. NOT WHILE THERE IS STILL TECHNOLOGY TO SAVE.
I KNOW, I KNOW.
WE SHOULD SPLIT THE CARAVAN.
SEND THE FAMILIES WITH KIDS INTO THE WILDERNESS; START STOCKPILING THE SALVAGED TECH SOMEWHERE FAR FROM THE HOT ZONES.
SOMEDAY, SURE. FOR NOW WE NEED TO MOVE.
HAVE YOU SEEN MY BOY?
INBY? NO, BUT IF HE'S WITH MY KIDS, EMBASSY'S LOOKING AFTER THEM.
PROBABLY HIDING SO HE DOESN'T HAVE TO HELP WITH THE MOVE.
FRONT END IS READY TO ROLL. WE JUST NEED TO KNOW WHERE WE'RE GOING.
WE'RE GOING INTO THIS CANYON. THERE ARE A FEW OLD TOWNS AT THE MOUTH. THE PIPERS ALREADY HIT THE AREA, BUT IT HASN'T BEEN HOT FOR AT LEAST EIGHT YEARS.
WE'LL BE RIGHT ON THE RIVER. FISHING SHOULD BE GOOD.
THERE ARE CITIES ON THE FAR SIDE THAT WE HAVEN'T FULLY SCOUTED.
MIGHT BE A FEW PLACES THE PIPERS HAVEN'T PILLAGE
GREAT. WE'LL START NOW.

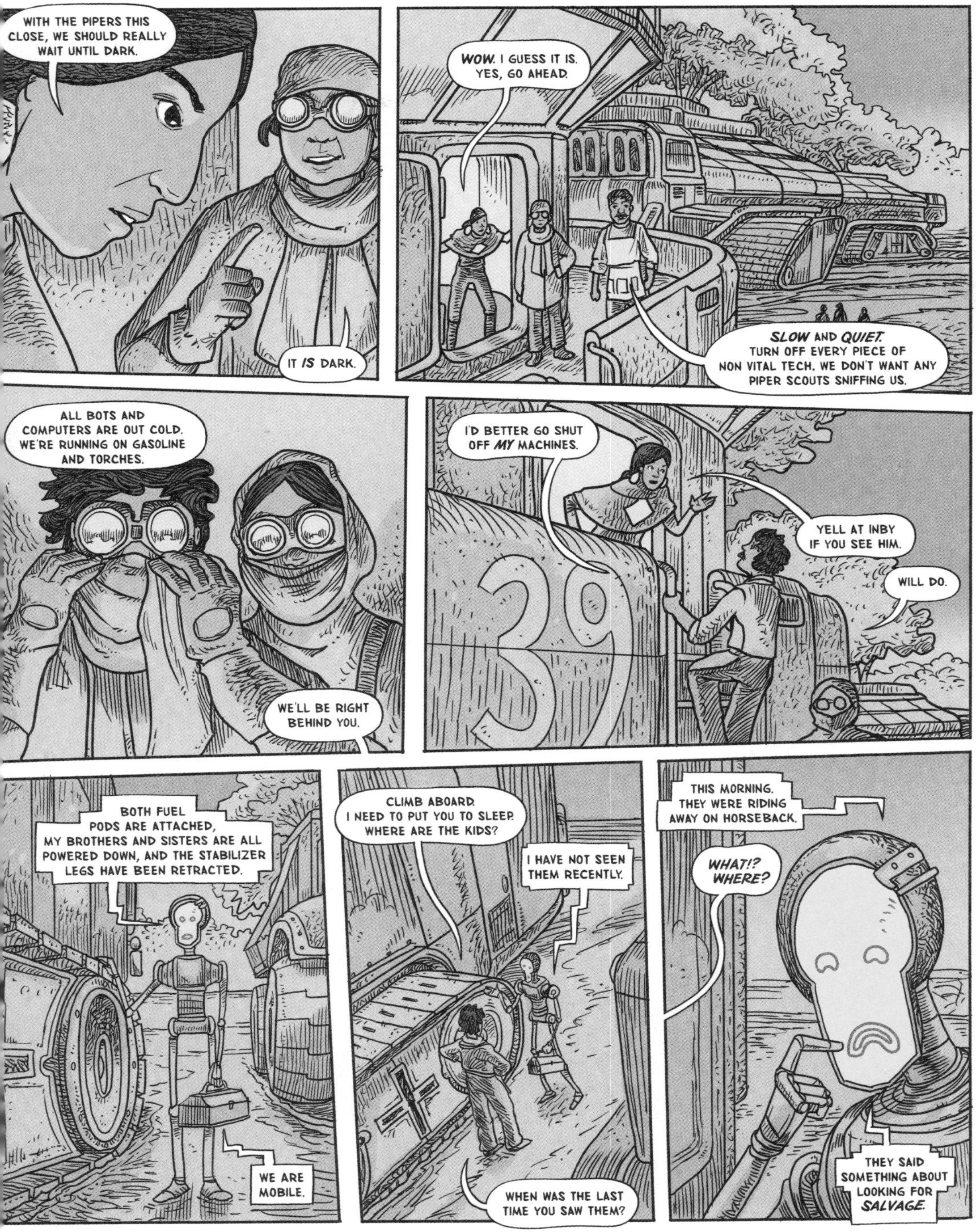
WITH THE PIPERS THIS CLOSE, WE SHOULD REALLY WAIT UNTIL DARK.
IT IS DARK.
WOW. I GUESS IT IS. YES, GO AHEAD.
SLOW AND QUIET. TURN OFF EVERY PIECE OF NON VITAL TECH. WE DON'T WANT ANY PIPER SCOUTS SNIFFING US.
ALL BOTS AND COMPUTERS ARE OUT COLD. WE'RE RUNNING ON GASOLINE AND TORCHES.
WE'LL BE RIGHT BEHIND YOU.
I'D BETTER GO SHUT OFF MY MACHINES.
YELL AT INBY IF YOU SEE HIM.
WILL DO.
39
BOTH FUEL PODS ARE ATTACHED, MY BROTHERS AND SISTERS ARE ALL POWERED DOWN, AND THE STABILIZER LEGS HAVE BEEN RETRACTED.
WE ARE MOBILE.
CLIMB ABOARD. I NEED TO PUT YOU TO SLEEP. WHERE ARE THE KIDS?
I HAVE NOT SEEN THEM RECENTLY.
WHEN WAS THE LAST TIME YOU SAW THEM?
THIS MORNING. THEY WERE RIDING AWAY ON HORSEBACK.
WHAT!? WHERE?
THEY SAID SOMETHING ABOUT LOOKING FOR SALVAGE.

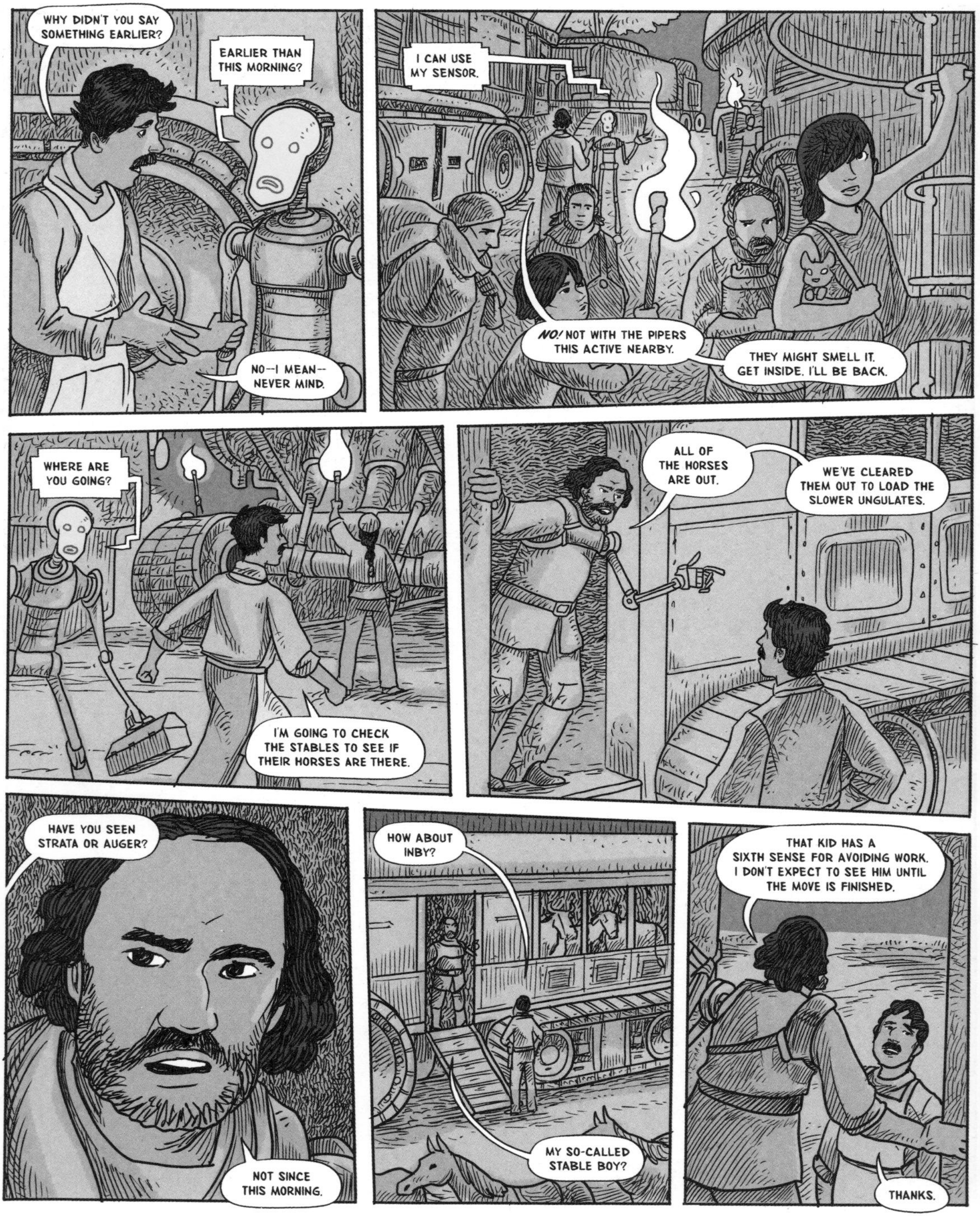
WHY DIDN'T YOU SAY SOMETHING EARLIER?
EARLIER THAN THIS MORNING?
NO--I MEAN--NEVER MIND.
I CAN USE MY SENSOR.
NO! NOT WITH THE PIPERS THIS ACTIVE NEARBY.
THEY MIGHT SMELL IT. GET INSIDE. I'LL BE BACK.
WHERE ARE YOU GOING?
I'M GOING TO CHECK THE STABLES TO SEE IF THEIR HORSES ARE THERE.
ALL OF THE HORSES ARE OUT.
WE'VE CLEARED THEM OUT TO LOAD THE SLOWER UNGULATES.
HAVE YOU SEEN STRATA OR AUGER?
NOT SINCE THIS MORNING.
HOW ABOUT INBY?
MY SO-CALLED STABLE BOY?
THAT KID HAS A SIXTH SENSE FOR AVOIDING WORK. I DON'T EXPECT TO SEE HIM UNTIL THE MOVE IS FINISHED.
THANKS.

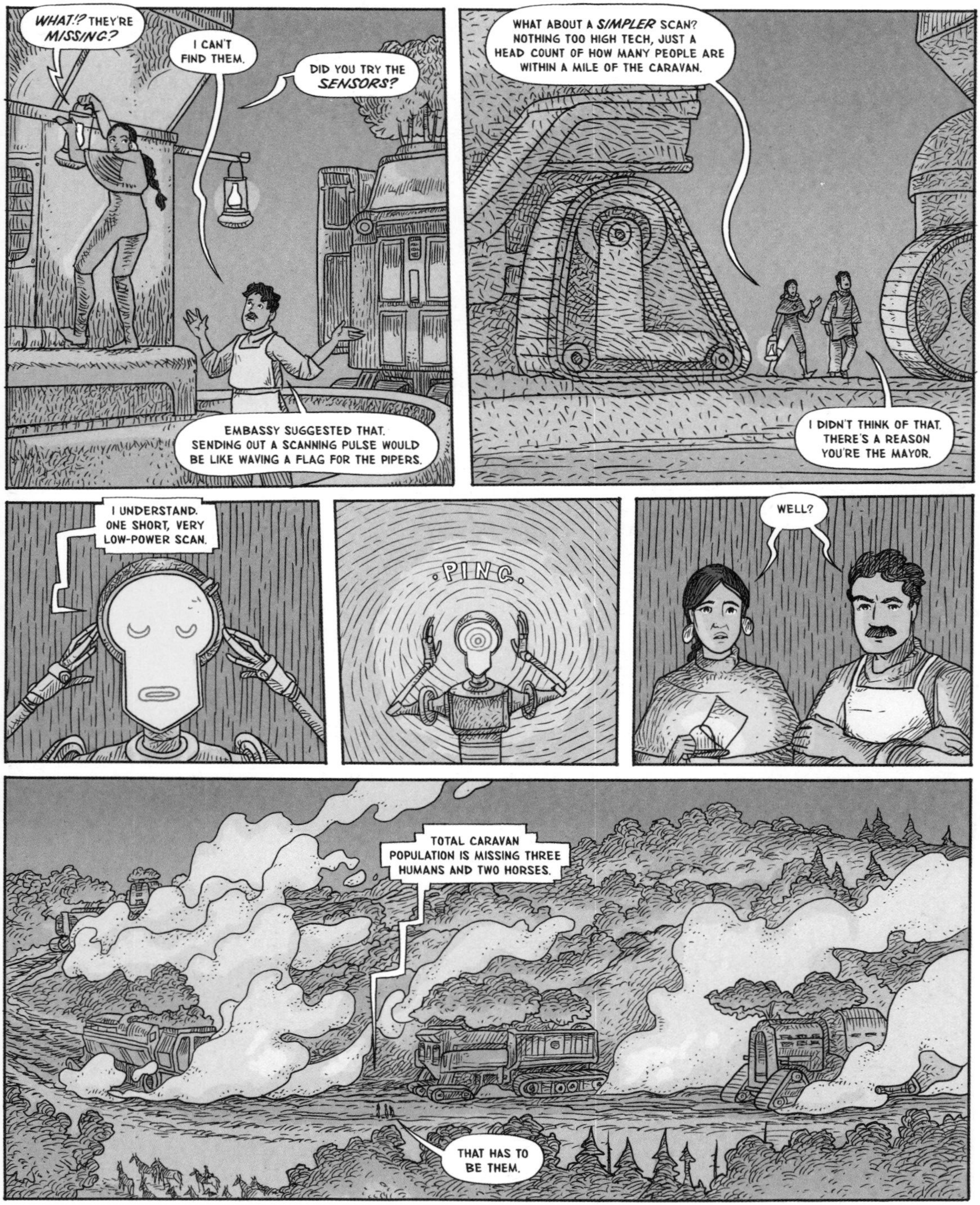

WHAT!? THEY'RE MISSING?
I CAN'T FIND THEM.
DID YOU TRY THE SENSORS?
EMBASSY SUGGESTED THAT. SENDING OUT A SCANNING PULSE WOULD BE LIKE WAVING A FLAG FOR THE PIPERS.
WHAT ABOUT A SIMPLER SCAN? NOTHING TOO HIGH TECH, JUST A HEAD COUNT OF HOW MANY PEOPLE ARE WITHIN A MILE OF THE CARAVAN.
I DIDN'T THINK OF THAT. THERE'S A REASON YOU'RE THE MAYOR.
I UNDERSTAND. ONE SHORT, VERY LOW-POWER SCAN.
PING
WELL?
TOTAL CARAVAN POPULATION IS MISSING THREE HUMANS AND TWO HORSES.
THAT HAS TO BE THEM.

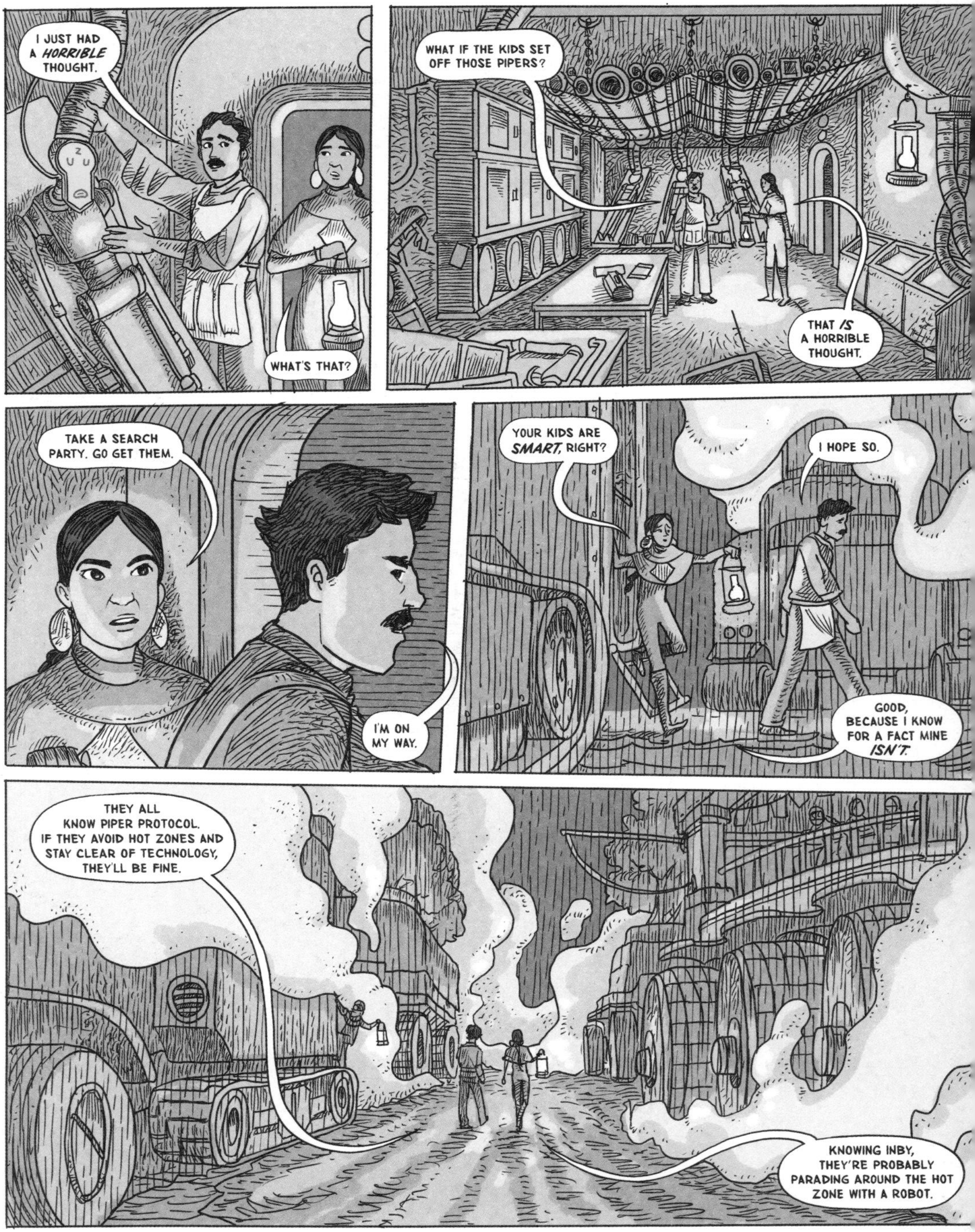
I JUST HAD A *HORRIBLE* THOUGHT.
WHAT'S THAT?
WHAT IF THE KIDS SET OFF THOSE PIPERS?
THAT *IS* A HORRIBLE THOUGHT.
TAKE A SEARCH PARTY. GO GET THEM.
I'M ON MY WAY.
YOUR KIDS ARE *SMART,* RIGHT?
I HOPE SO.
GOOD, BECAUSE I KNOW FOR A FACT MINE *ISN'T.*
THEY ALL KNOW PIPER PROTOCOL. IF THEY AVOID HOT ZONES AND STAY CLEAR OF TECHNOLOGY, THEY'LL BE FINE.
KNOWING INBY, THEY'RE PROBABLY PARADING AROUND THE HOT ZONE WITH A ROBOT.

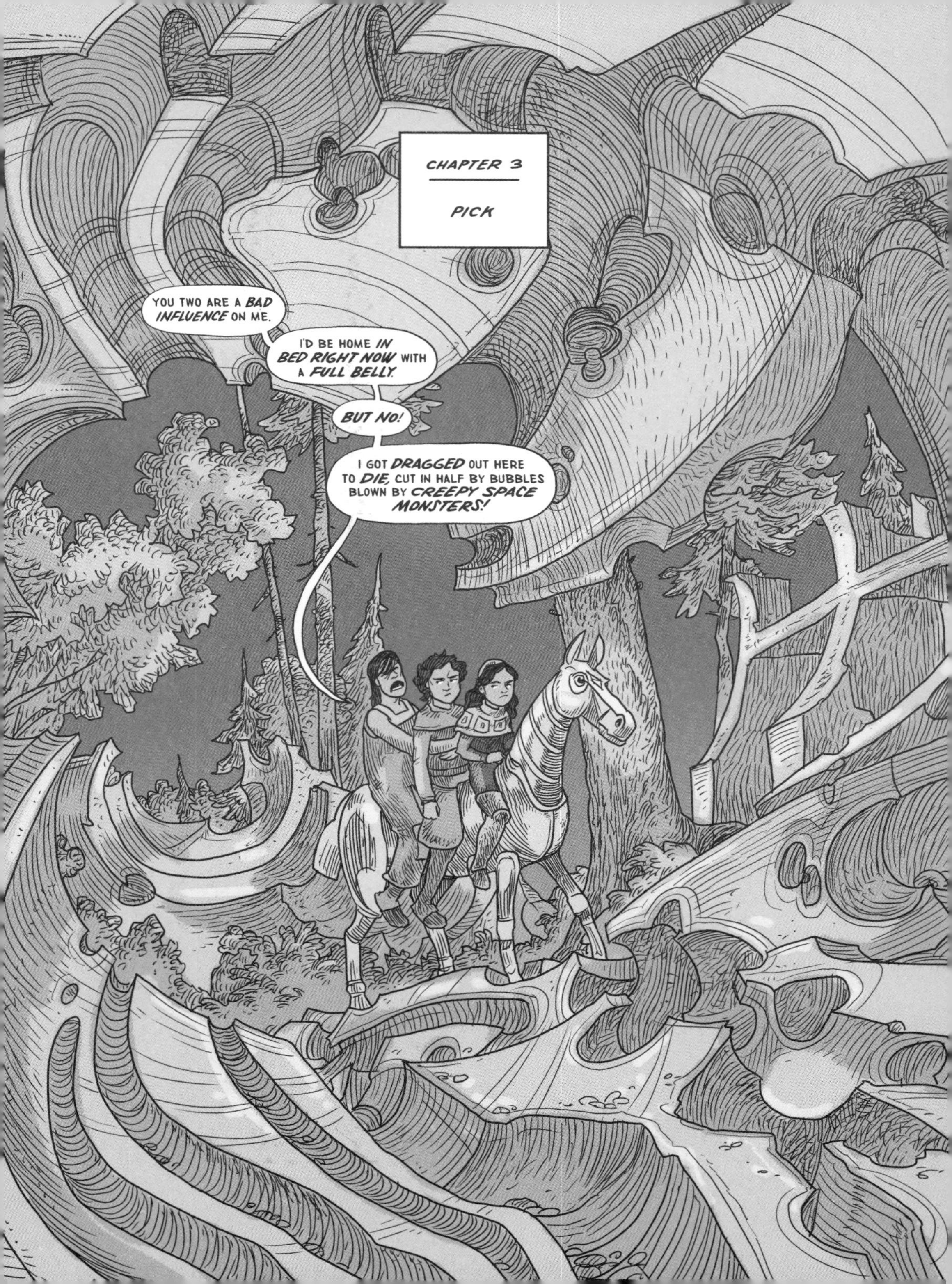
CHAPTER 3
PICK
YOU TWO ARE A BAD INFLUENCE ON ME.
I'D BE HOME IN BED RIGHT NOW WITH A FULL BELLY.
BUT NO!
I GOT DRAGGED OUT HERE TO DIE, CUT IN HALF BY BUBBLES BLOWN BY CREEPY SPACE MONSTERS!

DO THE BUBBLES REALLY *CUT* PEOPLE?

YEAH. HAVEN'T YOU SEEN THE STABLE MASTER'S MISSING ARM?

IT WAS ZAPPED *CLEAN OFF* WHEN HE GOT BETWEEN A PIPER AND SOME OLD COMPUTERS.

THE BUBBLE TURNED HIS ARM INTO SAND!

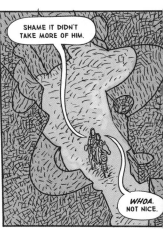

SHAME IT DIDN'T TAKE MORE OF HIM.

WHOA. NOT NICE.

YOU DON'T HAVE TO WORK FOR HIM.

THERE ARE *LIGHTS* UP AHEAD. KLEIDI, STOP.

KLUNG

MAYBE NEXT TIME YOU COULD SAY KLEIDI, *STOP SLOW*

OW!

I CAN'T HELP IT IF SHE OBEYS ME PERFECTLY.

I SEE THE LIGHTS. *SOMETHING'S COMING* TOWARD US!

HIDE! WE NEED TO HIDE!

NO! WE SHOULD RUN!

RUN! GO BACK THE OTHER WAY!

WE CAN'T KEEP TURNING AROUND. WE'LL *NEVER* GET HOME.

WE NEED TO HIDE.

TAKE US UP THERE, KLEIDI.

DO PIPERS EVEN USE LIGHTS?

I DON'T KNOW. HAVE YOU EVER SEEN ONE AT NIGHT?

NO, AND I DON'T WANT TO!

THEY'RE SCARY ENOUGH DURING THE DAYTIME!

THOSE ARE TORCHES. I THINK IT'S *PEOPLE!*

FROM THE CARAVAN? *WE'RE SAVED!* HEY!

SSSH!

I'M FINE WITH PEOPLE—*ANY PEOPLE!*

SSSH!

I DON'T RECOGNIZE THEM.

FERALS!?

OH, WAIT. I *DON'T* LIKE FERALS.

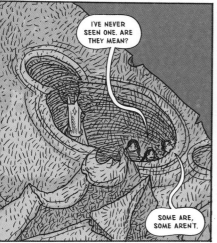

I'VE NEVER SEEN ONE. ARE THEY MEAN?

SOME ARE, SOME AREN'T.

HOW CAN YOU TELL WHICH ONES ARE WHICH?

WHO SAID THAT?

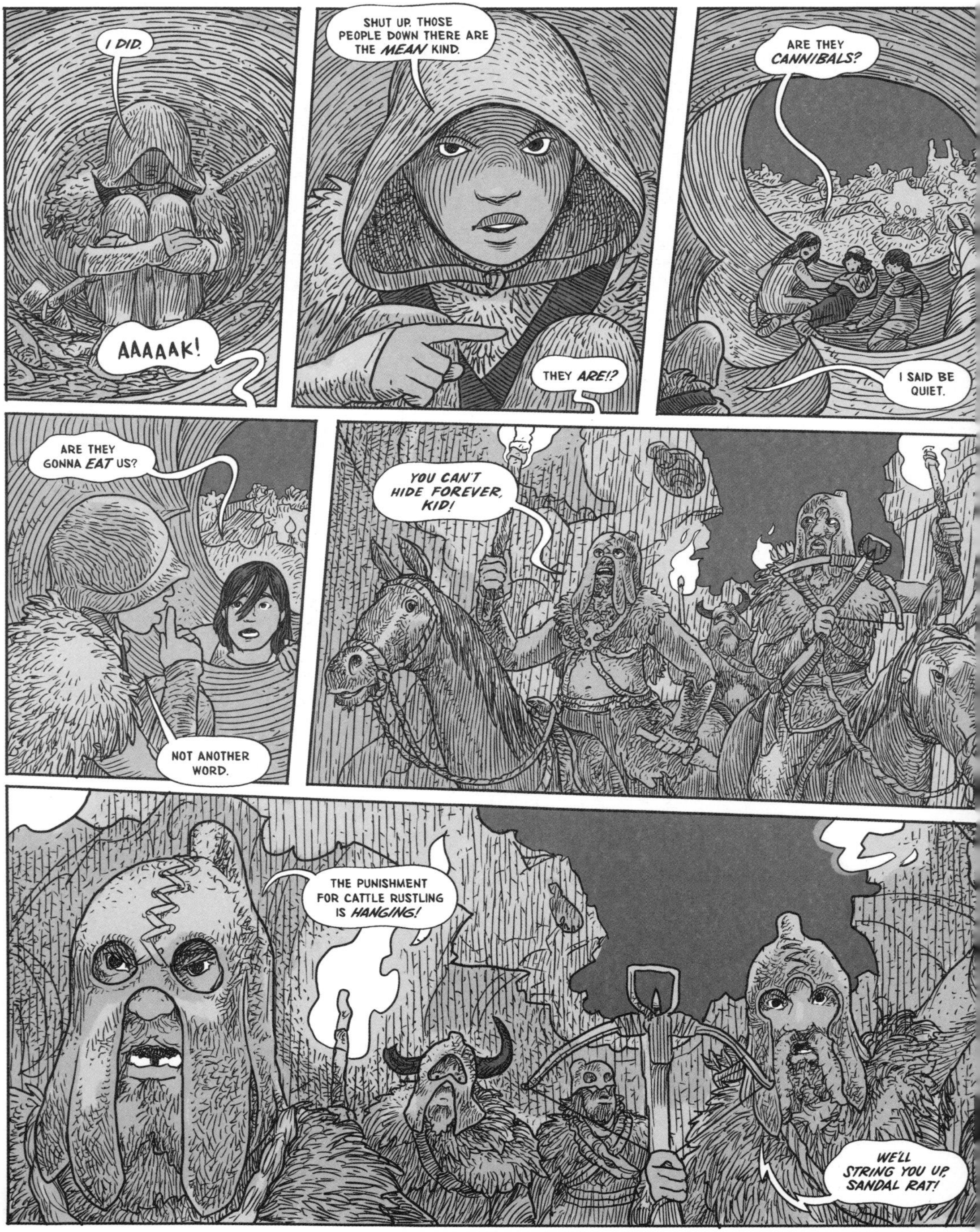

I DID.
AAAAAK!
SHUT UP. THOSE PEOPLE DOWN THERE ARE THE MEAN KIND.
THEY ARE!?
ARE THEY CANNIBALS?
I SAID BE QUIET.
ARE THEY GONNA EAT US?
NOT ANOTHER WORD.
YOU CAN'T HIDE FOREVER, KID!
THE PUNISHMENT FOR CATTLE RUSTLING IS HANGING!
WE'LL STRING YOU UP, SANDAL RAT!

ARE YOU A CATTLE RUSTLER!?

NO.

DO YOU *SEE* ANY CATTLE?

TOO BAD. I COULD EAT A *WHOLE CATTLE* RIGHT NOW.

WHAT *ARE* YOU DOING HERE?

I'M *HIDING*. HAVEN'T YOU BEEN PAYING ATTENTION?

I MEAN IN THE HOT ZONE.

HOT ZONE?

A PIPER-INFESTED AREA.

IF I WERE YOU, I'D BE MORE WORRIED ABOUT BEING IN A *SALT CLAN*-INFESTED AREA.

WOULD THEY REALLY *HANG* YOU?

YES, AND YOU TOO, IF THEY FELT LIKE IT.

THEY DIDN'T SCARE ME. I'M MORE AFRAID OF PIPERS.

PIPERS DON'T BOTHER YOU, UNLESS YOU HAVE SOMETHING THEY WANT.

WELL, WE *DO*.

IS THAT A *ROBOT!?* ARE YOU *CRAZY!?*

YES, HER NAME IS KLEIDI.

STEP AWAY FROM *THE BOT*, LITTLE GIRL.

WHY?

'CAUSE I'M A *GONNA SMASH IT*.

NO!

THAT MUCH *METAL*-- A *WORKING ROBOT!* THE PIPERS WILL BE *ALL OVER US!* WE'VE GOT TO *CRUSH* IT TO *BITS!*

ABSOLUTELY *NOT!* WE JUST RESCUED THIS PONY!

IT'LL BE FINE ONCE WE GET OUT OF THE HOT ZONE.

YOU KEEP SAYING "HOT ZONE." WHAT IS THAT?

THE PLACES WHERE THE PIPERS ARE.

OH, SO, THE *WHOLE PLANET EARTH?*

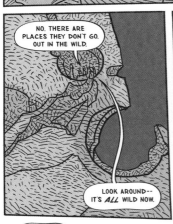

NO. THERE ARE PLACES THEY DON'T GO. OUT IN THE WILD.

LOOK AROUND-- IT'S *ALL* WILD NOW.

AND THAT SILLY HORSE WILL GET YOU *KILLED.*

SHE'S SAVED US SO FAR.

YOU JUST CAN'T *HAVE* THINGS LIKE THAT ANYMORE.

WE HAVE *LOTS* OF ROBOTS!

WHAT? WHERE?

IN THE *CARAVAN.* IT'S LIKE A MOVING TOWN.

A MOVING TOWN FULL OF ROBOTS? ARE YOU COMPLETELY INSANE?

I'M INBY.

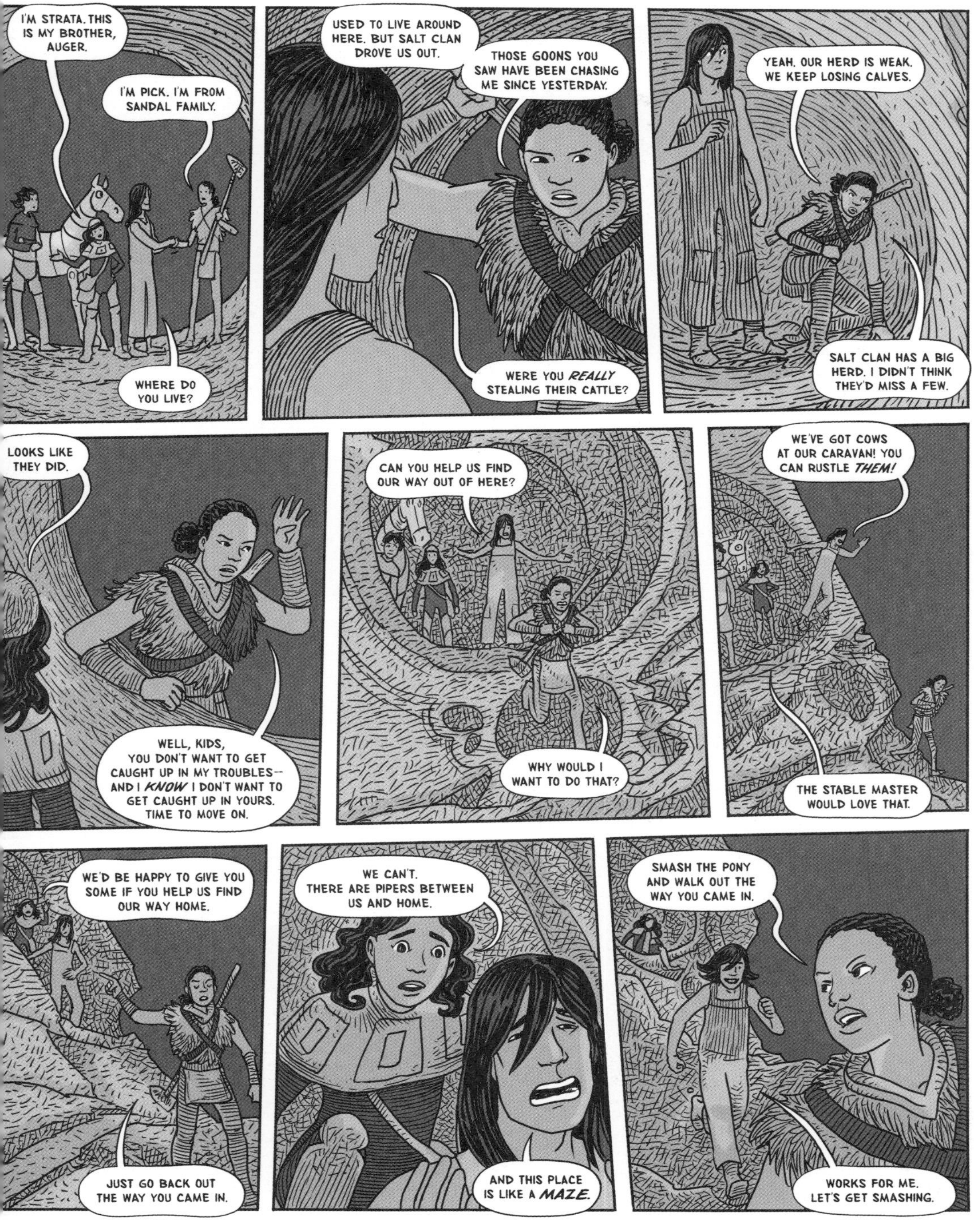
I'M STRATA. THIS IS MY BROTHER, AUGER.
I'M PICK. I'M FROM SANDAL FAMILY.
WHERE DO YOU LIVE?
USED TO LIVE AROUND HERE. BUT SALT CLAN DROVE US OUT.
THOSE GOONS YOU SAW HAVE BEEN CHASING ME SINCE YESTERDAY.
WERE YOU REALLY STEALING THEIR CATTLE?
YEAH. OUR HERD IS WEAK. WE KEEP LOSING CALVES.
SALT CLAN HAS A BIG HERD. I DIDN'T THINK THEY'D MISS A FEW.
LOOKS LIKE THEY DID.
WELL, KIDS, YOU DON'T WANT TO GET CAUGHT UP IN MY TROUBLES-- AND I KNOW I DON'T WANT TO GET CAUGHT UP IN YOURS. TIME TO MOVE ON.
CAN YOU HELP US FIND OUR WAY OUT OF HERE?
WHY WOULD I WANT TO DO THAT?
WE'VE GOT COWS AT OUR CARAVAN! YOU CAN RUSTLE THEM!
THE STABLE MASTER WOULD LOVE THAT.
WE'D BE HAPPY TO GIVE YOU SOME IF YOU HELP US FIND OUR WAY HOME.
JUST GO BACK OUT THE WAY YOU CAME IN.
WE CAN'T. THERE ARE PIPERS BETWEEN US AND HOME.
AND THIS PLACE IS LIKE A MAZE.
SMASH THE PONY AND WALK OUT THE WAY YOU CAME IN.
WORKS FOR ME. LET'S GET SMASHING.

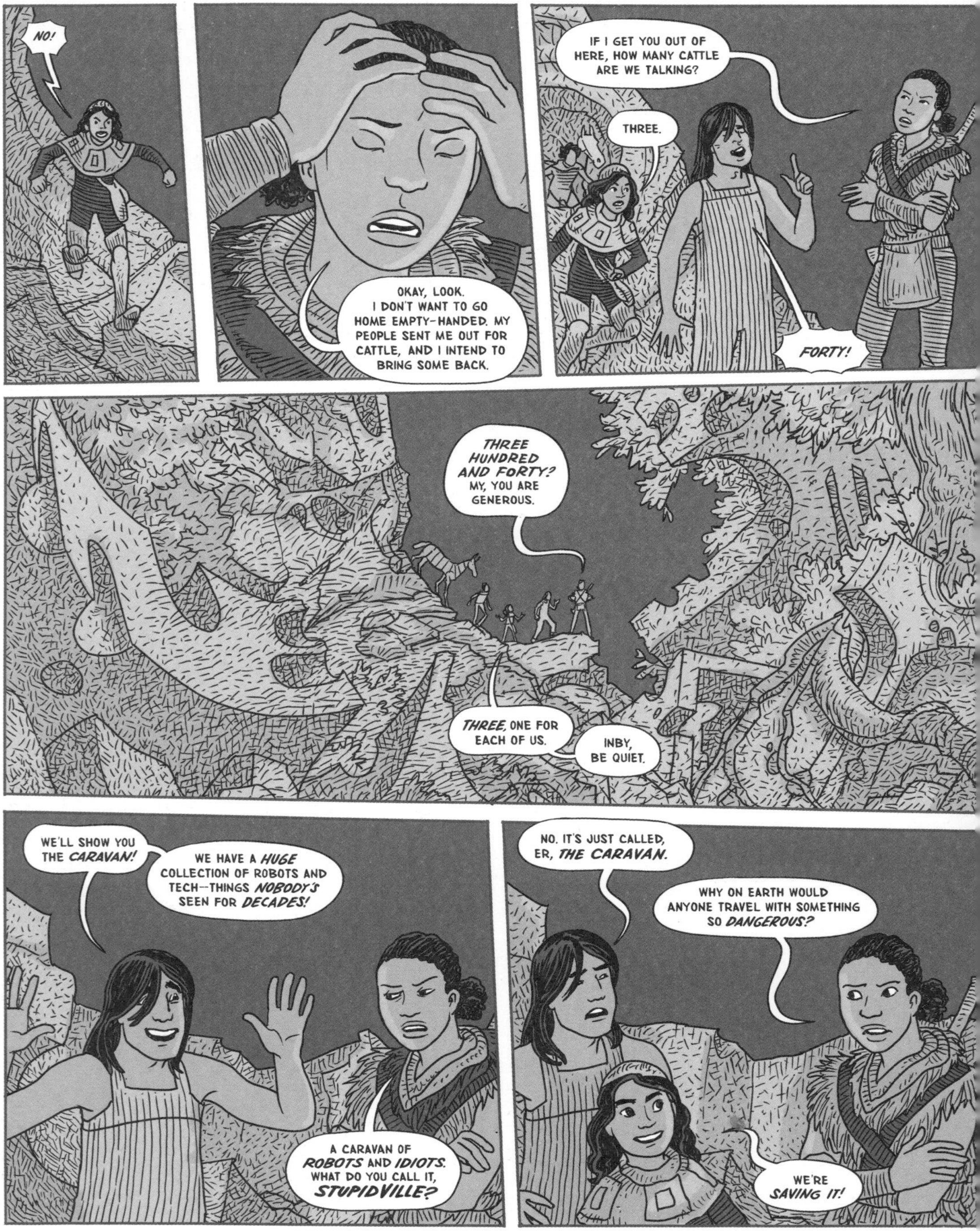
NO!
OKAY, LOOK. I DON'T WANT TO GO HOME EMPTY-HANDED. MY PEOPLE SENT ME OUT FOR CATTLE, AND I INTEND TO BRING SOME BACK.
IF I GET YOU OUT OF HERE, HOW MANY CATTLE ARE WE TALKING?
THREE.
FORTY!
THREE HUNDRED AND FORTY? MY, YOU ARE GENEROUS.
THREE, ONE FOR EACH OF US.
INBY, BE QUIET.
WE'LL SHOW YOU THE CARAVAN!
WE HAVE A HUGE COLLECTION OF ROBOTS AND TECH--THINGS NOBODY'S SEEN FOR DECADES!
A CARAVAN OF ROBOTS AND IDIOTS. WHAT DO YOU CALL IT, STUPIDVILLE?
NO. IT'S JUST CALLED, ER, THE CARAVAN.
WHY ON EARTH WOULD ANYONE TRAVEL WITH SOMETHING SO DANGEROUS?
WE'RE SAVING IT!

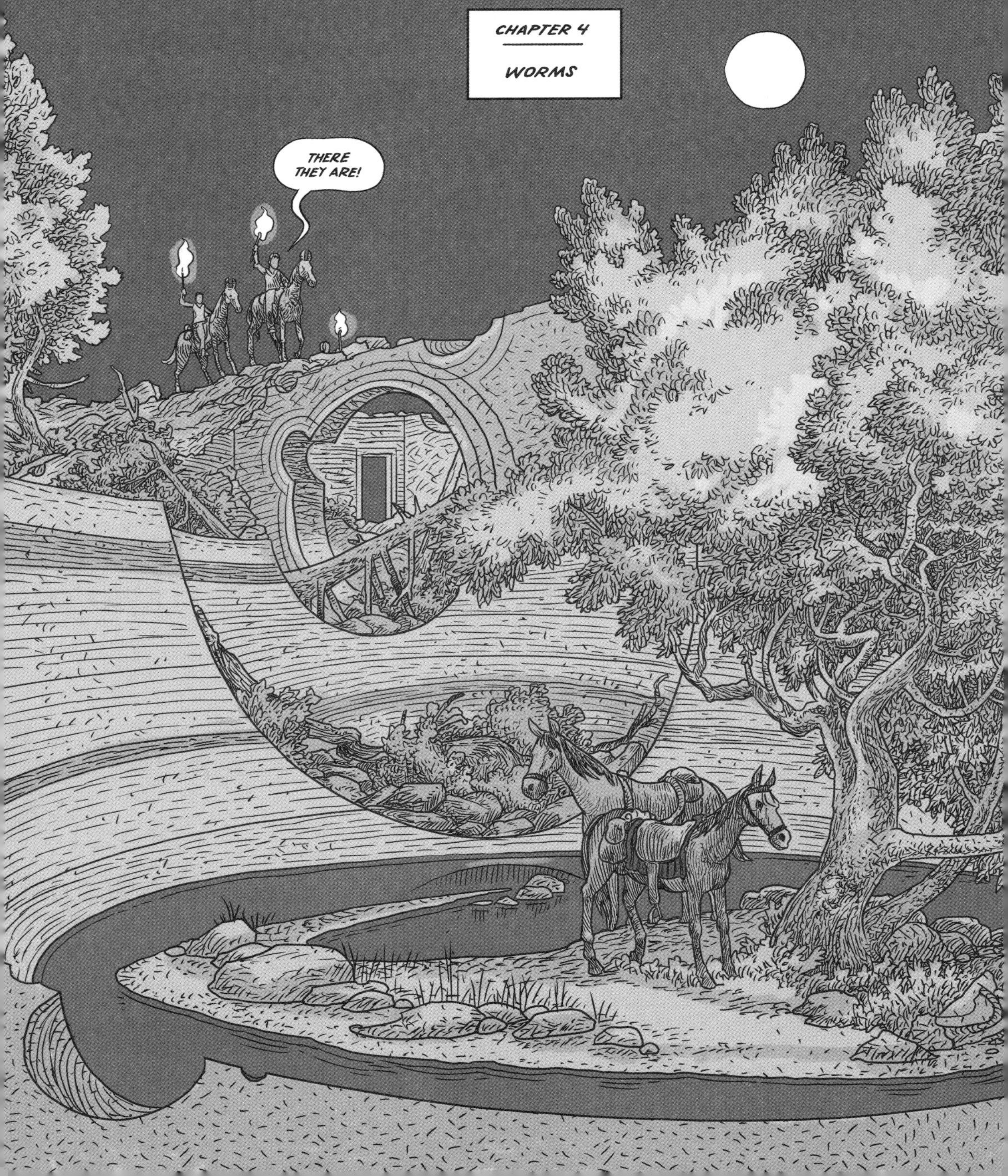
CHAPTER 4
WORMS
THERE THEY ARE!

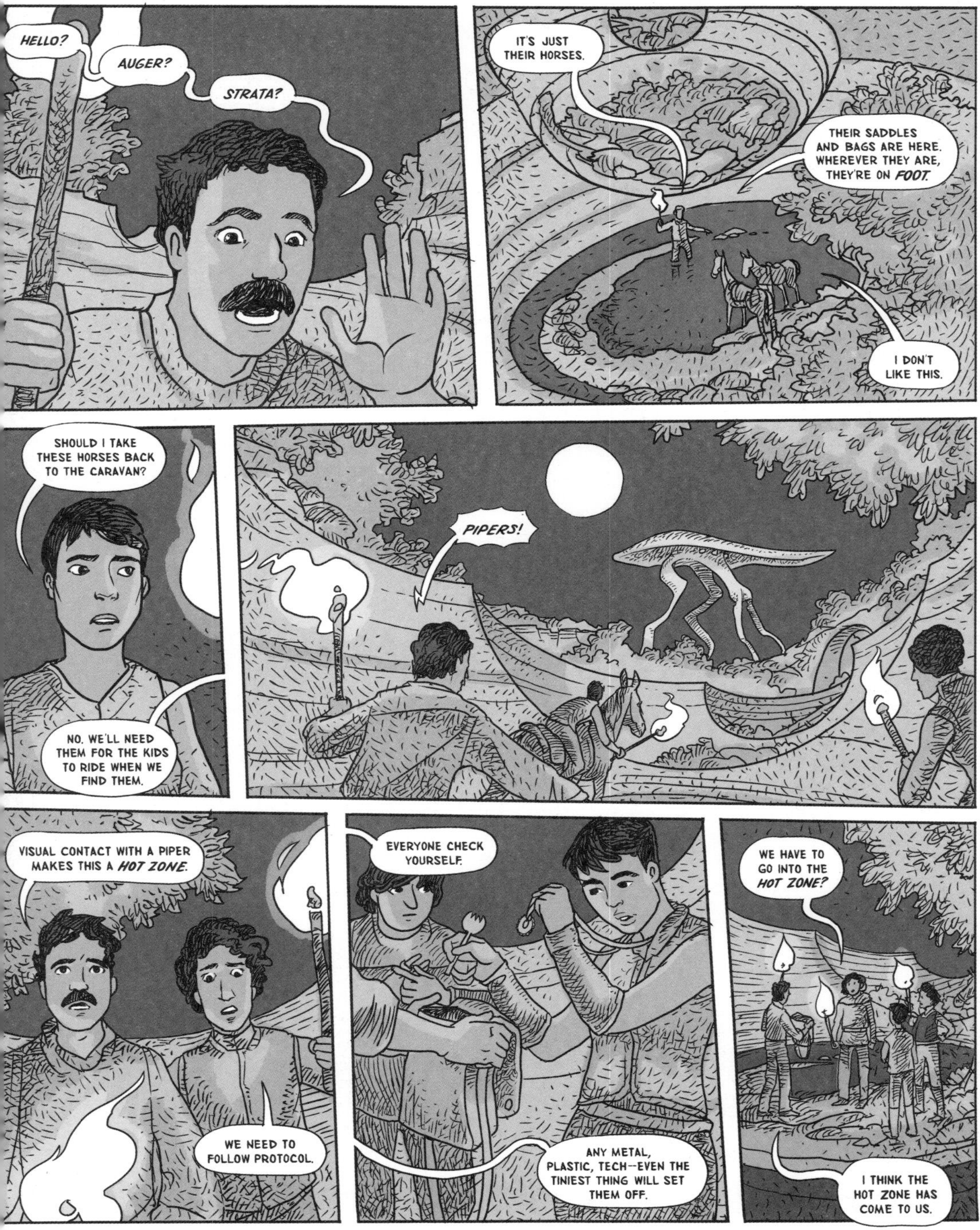
HELLO?
AUGER?
STRATA?
IT'S JUST THEIR HORSES.
THEIR SADDLES AND BAGS ARE HERE. WHEREVER THEY ARE, THEY'RE ON FOOT.
I DON'T LIKE THIS.
SHOULD I TAKE THESE HORSES BACK TO THE CARAVAN?
NO. WE'LL NEED THEM FOR THE KIDS TO RIDE WHEN WE FIND THEM.
PIPERS!
VISUAL CONTACT WITH A PIPER MAKES THIS A HOT ZONE.
WE NEED TO FOLLOW PROTOCOL.
EVERYONE CHECK YOURSELF.
ANY METAL, PLASTIC, TECH--EVEN THE TINIEST THING WILL SET THEM OFF.
WE HAVE TO GO INTO THE HOT ZONE?
I THINK THE HOT ZONE HAS COME TO US.

I'LL HANG IT ON THIS BRANCH.

THIS TREE SHOULD BE EASY TO SPOT ON OUR RETURN.

I'LL TIE THIS BANDANA ON SO WE DON'T MISS IT.

OKAY, LET'S GO.

PIPIPIPIPIPIPIPIP

PIPIP,

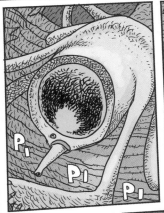

PI
PI
PI

BWAP

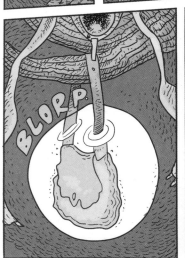

BLORP

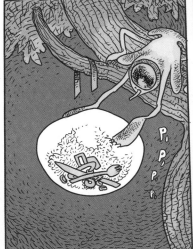

PI
P,
P,
P,

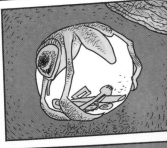

PIPIPIPIPIP

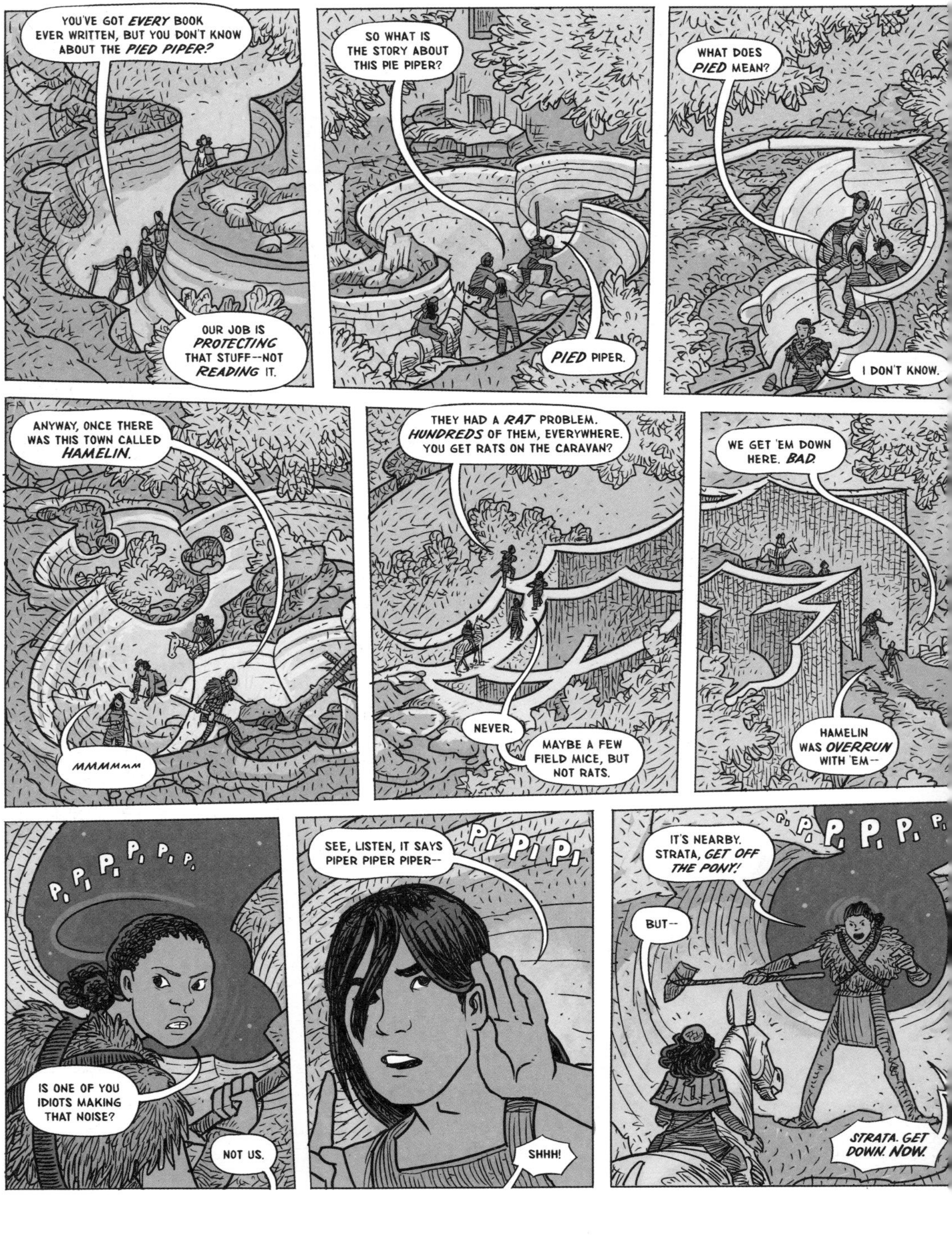
YOU'VE GOT EVERY BOOK EVER WRITTEN, BUT YOU DON'T KNOW ABOUT THE PIED PIPER?
OUR JOB IS PROTECTING THAT STUFF--NOT READING IT.
SO WHAT IS THE STORY ABOUT THIS PIE PIPER?
PIED PIPER.
WHAT DOES PIED MEAN?
I DON'T KNOW.
ANYWAY, ONCE THERE WAS THIS TOWN CALLED HAMELIN.
MMMMMM
THEY HAD A RAT PROBLEM. HUNDREDS OF THEM, EVERYWHERE. YOU GET RATS ON THE CARAVAN?
NEVER.
MAYBE A FEW FIELD MICE, BUT NOT RATS.
WE GET 'EM DOWN HERE. BAD.
HAMELIN WAS OVERRUN WITH 'EM--
P P P P P P
IS ONE OF YOU IDIOTS MAKING THAT NOISE?
NOT US.
SEE, LISTEN, IT SAYS PIPER PIPER PIPER--
PI PI PI PI
SHHH!
P P P P P P
IT'S NEARBY. STRATA, GET OFF THE PONY!
BUT--
STRATA. GET DOWN. NOW.

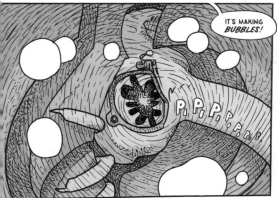

IT'S MAKING *BUBBLES!*

P.P.P.P.P.

IT'S COMING *THROUGH!*

BWAP

BWAP

BWAAP

CLIMB UP! IT'S COMING!

YOU'RE ALMOST THERE.

I CAN'T *REACH!*

I'M SO *SORRY,* KLEIDI!

I THOUGHT WE COULD *GET AWAY!*

CRUMP

OOOF!

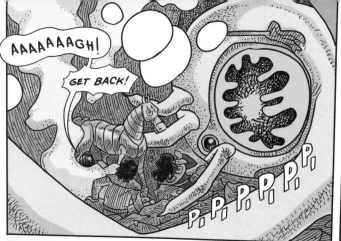

AAAAAAGH!

GET BACK!

P.P.P.P.P.P.

KLEIDI, STAY RIGHT THERE!

SHE'S SAVING US!

DUCK AND COVER!

P.P.P.P.P.P.

KRUNK

SKRAAAAAAAAAA~

WHAT!?

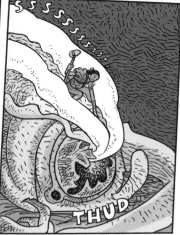

SSSSSSSSSS

THUD

THESE MOVIES BETTER BE WORTH IT.

S

HOLY CATS! YOU *KILLED* A *PIPER*!

STAY WHERE YOU ARE!

HOLD STILL!

S P L O O R T

HUH?

WHAT?

B L O O R P

IT'S FULL OF *WORMS!?*

STAY BACK! THE PIPER'S DOWN, BUT THAT BUBBLE'S STILL *DEADLY!*

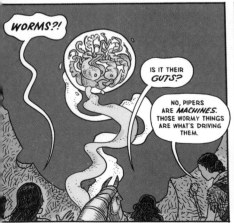

WORMS?!

IS IT THEIR *GUTS?*

NO, PIPERS ARE *MACHINES.* THOSE WORMY THINGS ARE WHAT'S DRIVING THEM.

YOU SAVED US!

NOT QUITE YET.

WE'LL BE *SAFE* WHEN THAT PONY'S IN *PIECES.*

NO!

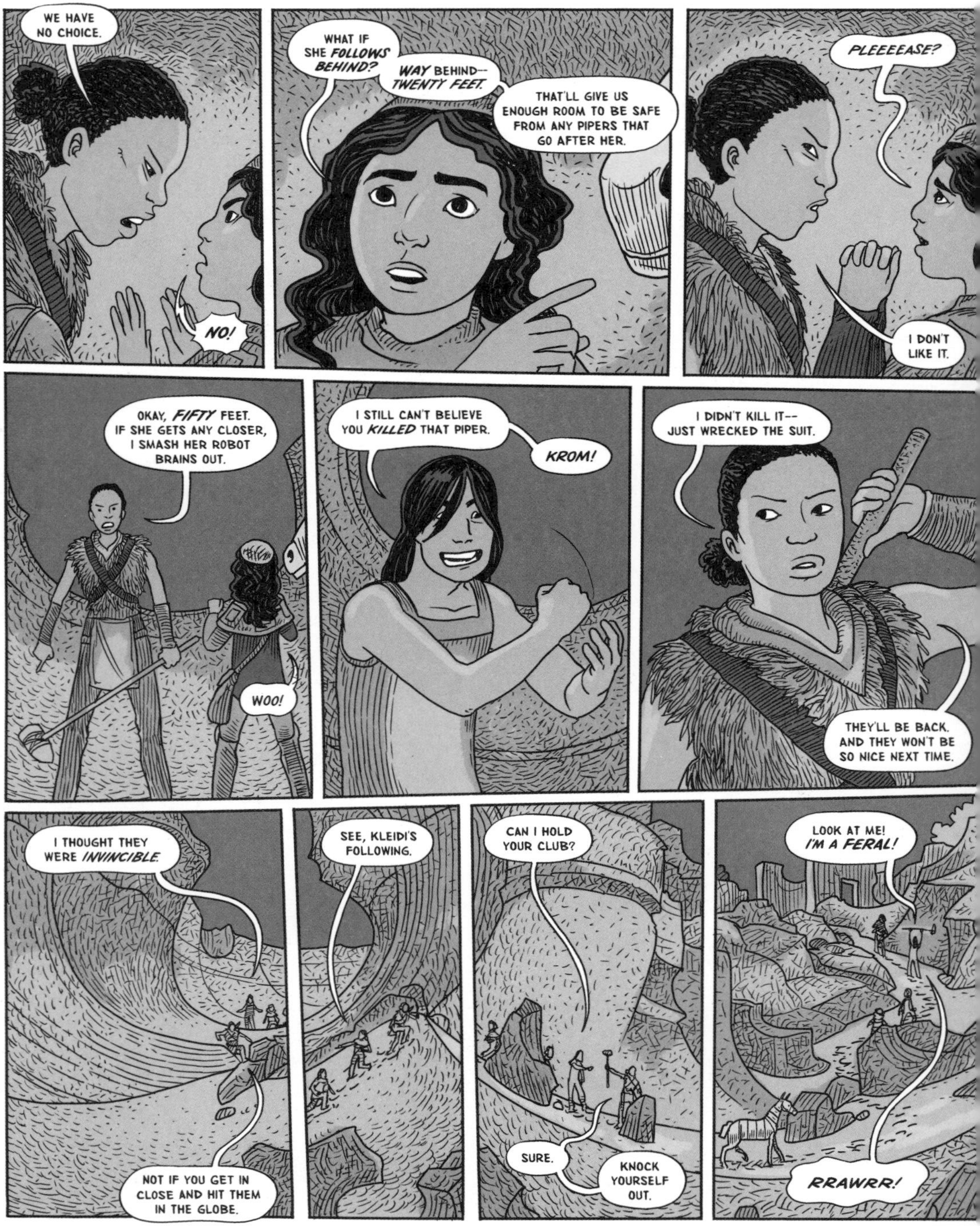
WE HAVE NO CHOICE.
NO!
WHAT IF SHE *FOLLOWS BEHIND?*
WAY BEHIND-- *TWENTY FEET.*
THAT'LL GIVE US ENOUGH ROOM TO BE SAFE FROM ANY PIPERS THAT GO AFTER HER.
PLEEEEASE?
I DON'T LIKE IT.
OKAY, *FIFTY* FEET. IF SHE GETS ANY CLOSER, I SMASH HER ROBOT BRAINS OUT.
WOO!
I STILL CAN'T BELIEVE YOU *KILLED* THAT PIPER.
KROM!
I DIDN'T KILL IT-- JUST WRECKED THE SUIT.
THEY'LL BE BACK. AND THEY WON'T BE SO NICE NEXT TIME.
I THOUGHT THEY WERE *INVINCIBLE.*
NOT IF YOU GET IN CLOSE AND HIT THEM IN THE GLOBE.
SEE, KLEIDI'S FOLLOWING.
CAN I HOLD YOUR CLUB?
SURE.
KNOCK YOURSELF OUT.
LOOK AT ME! *I'M A FERAL!*
RRAWRR!

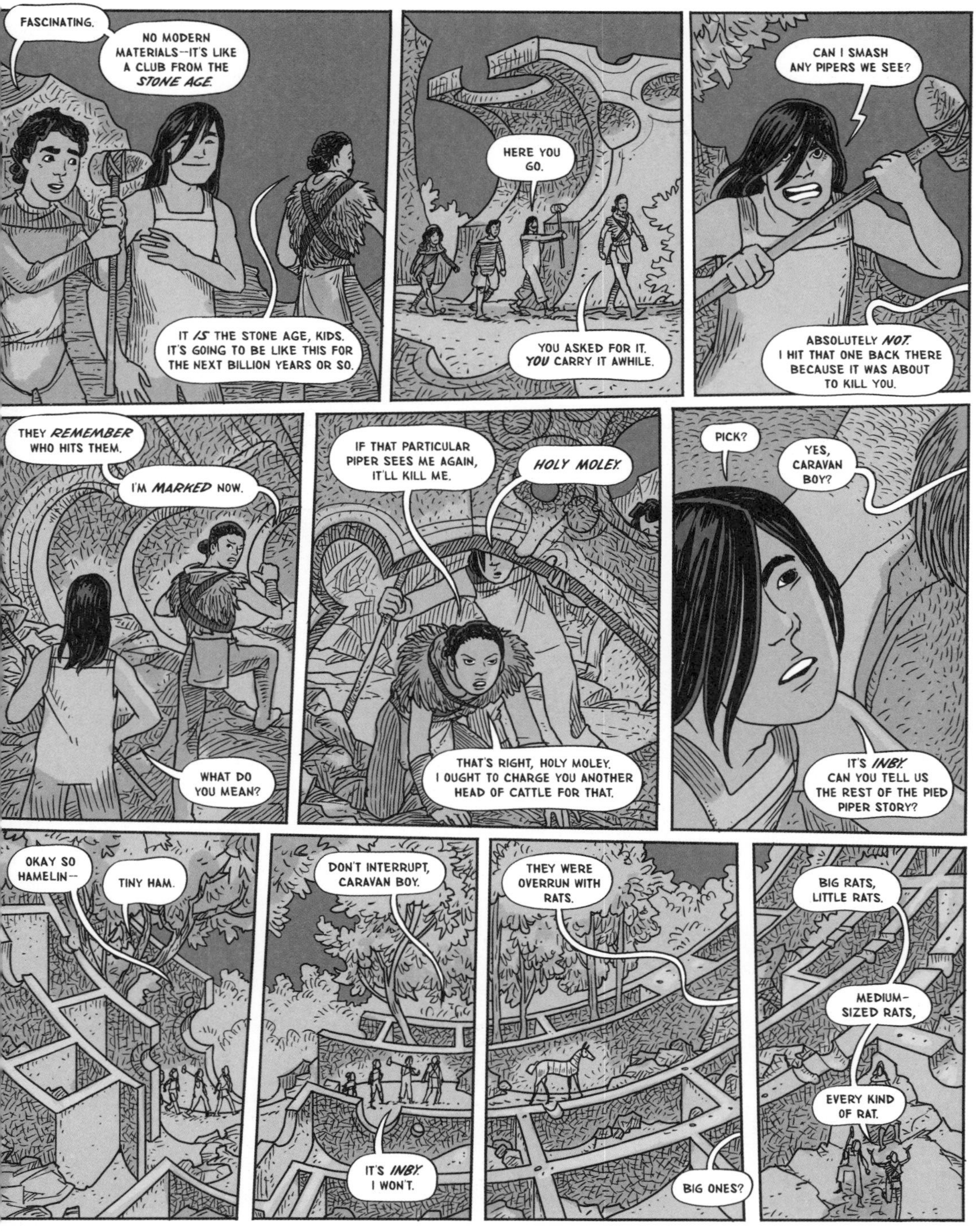

FASCINATING.
NO MODERN MATERIALS--IT'S LIKE A CLUB FROM THE *STONE AGE.*
IT *IS* THE STONE AGE, KIDS. IT'S GOING TO BE LIKE THIS FOR THE NEXT BILLION YEARS OR SO.
HERE YOU GO.
YOU ASKED FOR IT. *YOU* CARRY IT AWHILE.
CAN I SMASH ANY PIPERS WE SEE?
ABSOLUTELY *NOT.* I HIT THAT ONE BACK THERE BECAUSE IT WAS ABOUT TO KILL YOU.
THEY *REMEMBER* WHO HITS THEM.
I'M *MARKED* NOW.
WHAT DO YOU MEAN?
IF THAT PARTICULAR PIPER SEES ME AGAIN, IT'LL KILL ME.
HOLY MOLEY.
THAT'S RIGHT, HOLY MOLEY. I OUGHT TO CHARGE YOU ANOTHER HEAD OF CATTLE FOR THAT.
PICK?
YES, CARAVAN BOY?
IT'S *INBY.* CAN YOU TELL US THE REST OF THE PIED PIPER STORY?
OKAY SO HAMELIN--
TINY HAM.
DON'T INTERRUPT, CARAVAN BOY.
IT'S *INBY.* I WON'T.
THEY WERE OVERRUN WITH RATS.
BIG ONES?
BIG RATS, LITTLE RATS.
MEDIUM-SIZED RATS,
EVERY KIND OF RAT.

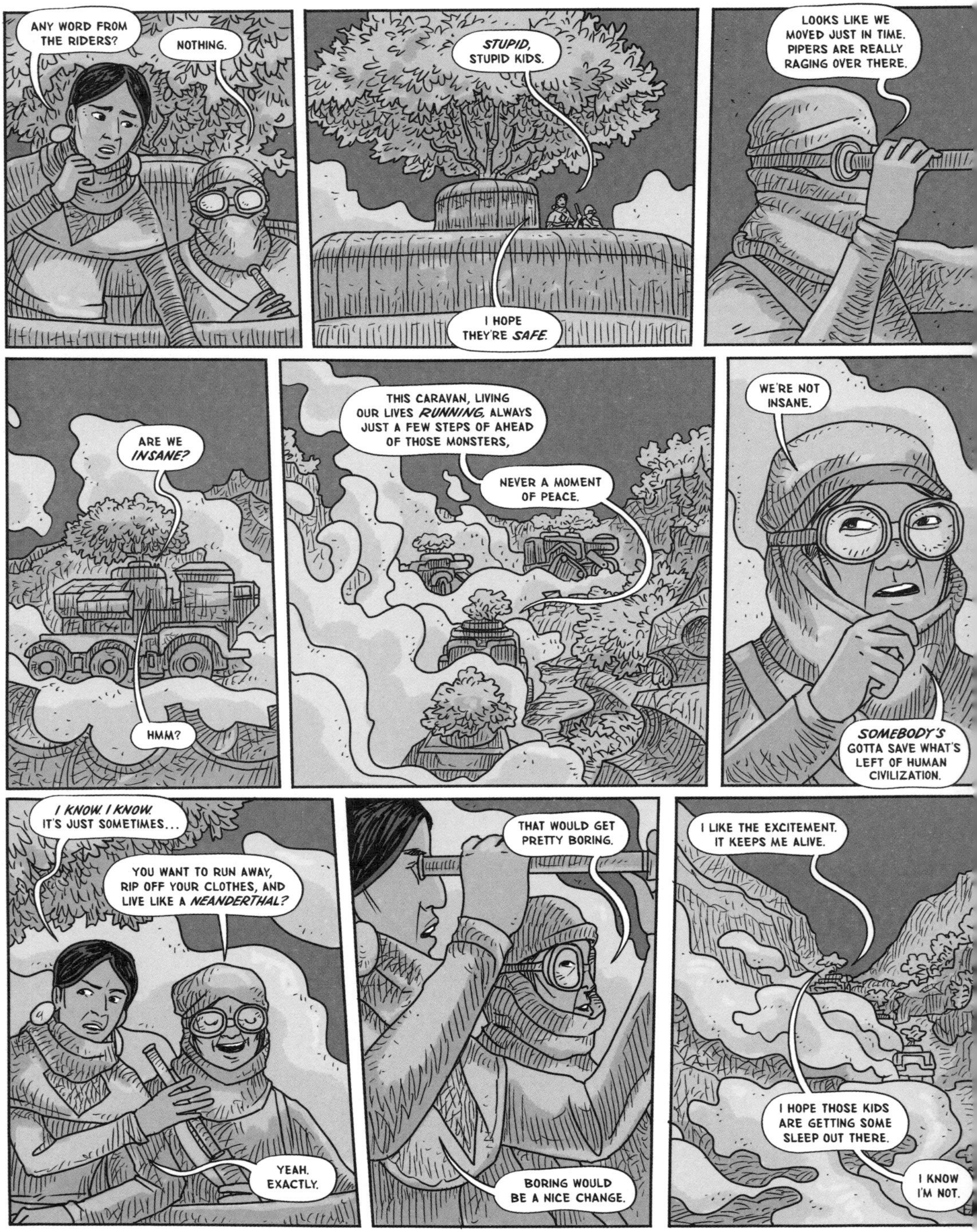
ANY WORD FROM THE RIDERS?
NOTHING.
STUPID, STUPID KIDS.
I HOPE THEY'RE SAFE.
LOOKS LIKE WE MOVED JUST IN TIME. PIPERS ARE REALLY RAGING OVER THERE.
ARE WE INSANE?
HMM?
THIS CARAVAN, LIVING OUR LIVES RUNNING, ALWAYS JUST A FEW STEPS OF AHEAD OF THOSE MONSTERS,
NEVER A MOMENT OF PEACE.
WE'RE NOT INSANE.
SOMEBODY'S GOTTA SAVE WHAT'S LEFT OF HUMAN CIVILIZATION.
I KNOW. I KNOW. IT'S JUST SOMETIMES...
YOU WANT TO RUN AWAY, RIP OFF YOUR CLOTHES, AND LIVE LIKE A NEANDERTHAL?
YEAH. EXACTLY.
THAT WOULD GET PRETTY BORING.
BORING WOULD BE A NICE CHANGE.
I LIKE THE EXCITEMENT. IT KEEPS ME ALIVE.
I HOPE THOSE KIDS ARE GETTING SOME SLEEP OUT THERE.
I KNOW I'M NOT.

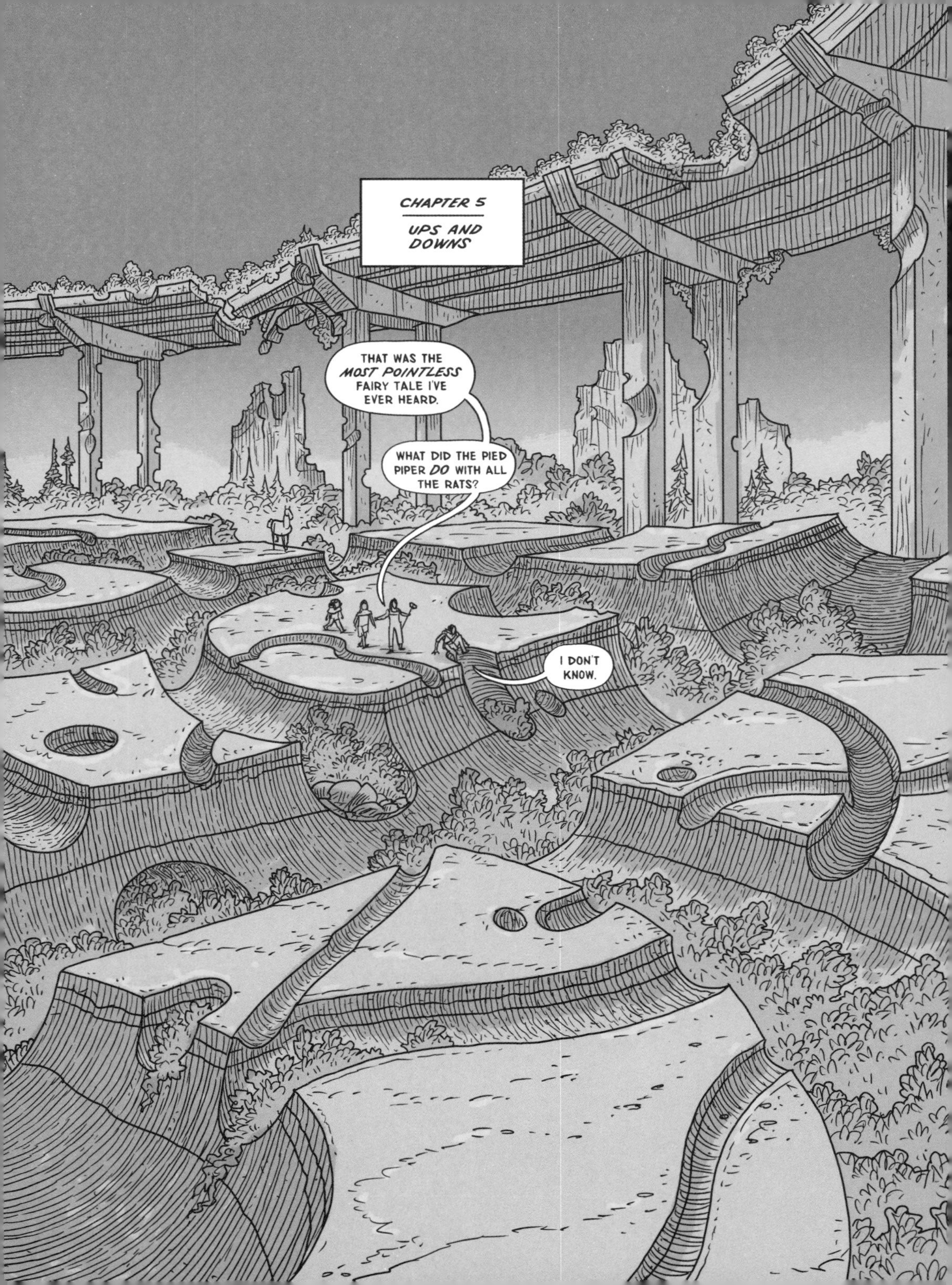
CHAPTER 5
UPS AND DOWNS
THAT WAS THE MOST POINTLESS FAIRY TALE I'VE EVER HEARD.
WHAT DID THE PIED PIPER DO WITH ALL THE RATS?
I DON'T KNOW.

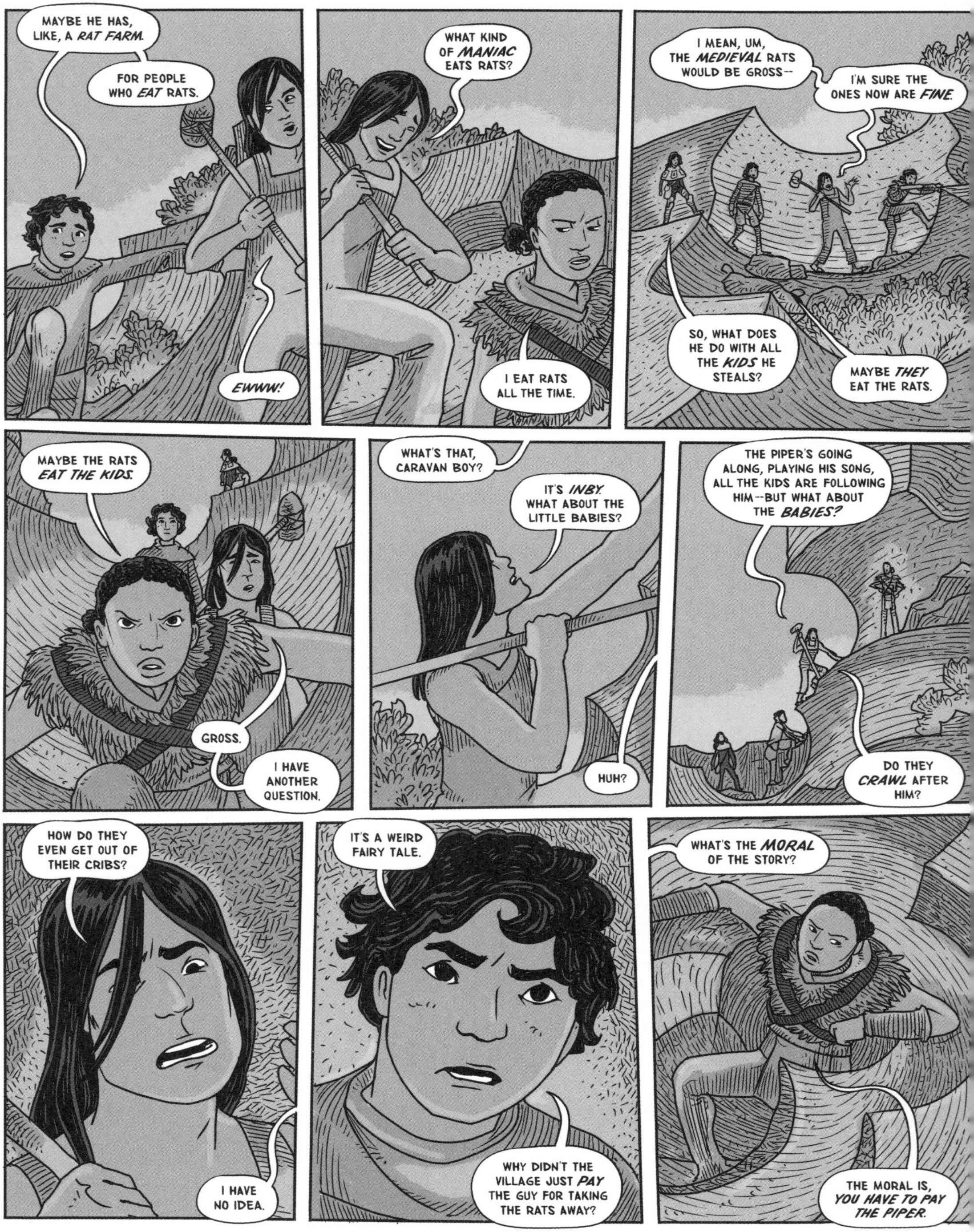
MAYBE HE HAS, LIKE, A RAT FARM.
FOR PEOPLE WHO EAT RATS.
EWWW!
WHAT KIND OF MANIAC EATS RATS?
I EAT RATS ALL THE TIME.
I MEAN, UM, THE MEDIEVAL RATS WOULD BE GROSS--
I'M SURE THE ONES NOW ARE FINE.
SO, WHAT DOES HE DO WITH ALL THE KIDS HE STEALS?
MAYBE THEY EAT THE RATS.
MAYBE THE RATS EAT THE KIDS.
GROSS.
I HAVE ANOTHER QUESTION.
WHAT'S THAT, CARAVAN BOY?
IT'S INBY. WHAT ABOUT THE LITTLE BABIES?
HUH?
THE PIPER'S GOING ALONG, PLAYING HIS SONG, ALL THE KIDS ARE FOLLOWING HIM--BUT WHAT ABOUT THE BABIES?
DO THEY CRAWL AFTER HIM?
HOW DO THEY EVEN GET OUT OF THEIR CRIBS?
I HAVE NO IDEA.
IT'S A WEIRD FAIRY TALE.
WHY DIDN'T THE VILLAGE JUST PAY THE GUY FOR TAKING THE RATS AWAY?
WHAT'S THE MORAL OF THE STORY?
THE MORAL IS, YOU HAVE TO PAY THE PIPER.

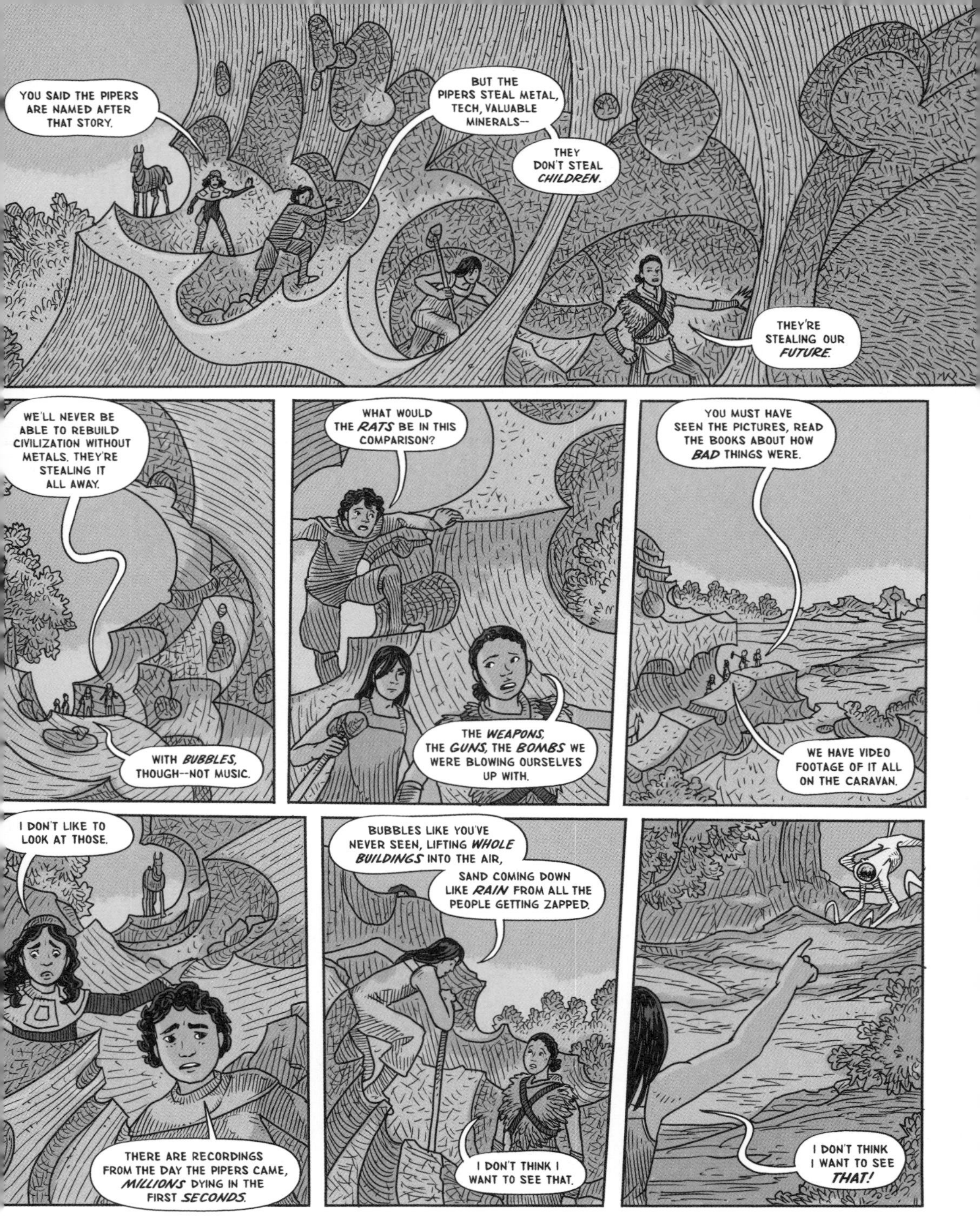
YOU SAID THE PIPERS ARE NAMED AFTER THAT STORY.
BUT THE PIPERS STEAL METAL, TECH, VALUABLE MINERALS--
THEY DON'T STEAL *CHILDREN.*
THEY'RE STEALING OUR *FUTURE.*
WE'LL NEVER BE ABLE TO REBUILD CIVILIZATION WITHOUT METALS. THEY'RE STEALING IT ALL AWAY.
WITH *BUBBLES,* THOUGH--NOT MUSIC.
WHAT WOULD THE *RATS* BE IN THIS COMPARISON?
THE *WEAPONS,* THE *GUNS,* THE *BOMBS* WE WERE BLOWING OURSELVES UP WITH.
YOU MUST HAVE SEEN THE PICTURES, READ THE BOOKS ABOUT HOW *BAD* THINGS WERE.
WE HAVE VIDEO FOOTAGE OF IT ALL ON THE CARAVAN.
I DON'T LIKE TO LOOK AT THOSE.
THERE ARE RECORDINGS FROM THE DAY THE PIPERS CAME, *MILLIONS* DYING IN THE FIRST *SECONDS.*
BUBBLES LIKE YOU'VE NEVER SEEN, LIFTING *WHOLE BUILDINGS* INTO THE AIR,
SAND COMING DOWN LIKE *RAIN* FROM ALL THE PEOPLE GETTING ZAPPED.
I DON'T THINK I WANT TO SEE THAT.
I DON'T THINK I WANT TO SEE *THAT!*

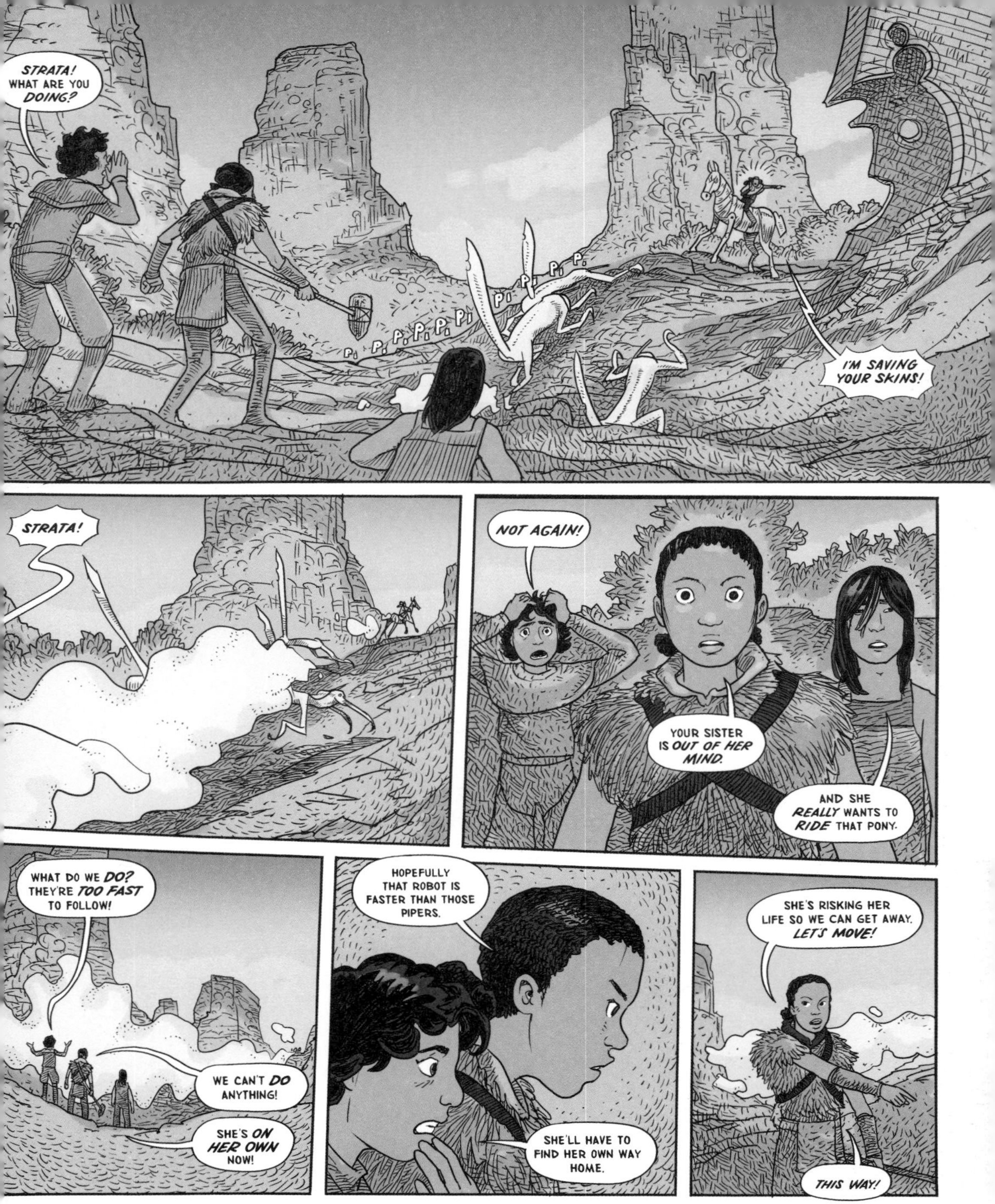
STRATA! WHAT ARE YOU DOING?
PI PI PI PI PI PI PI PI PI PI PI
I'M SAVING YOUR SKINS!
STRATA!
NOT AGAIN!
YOUR SISTER IS OUT OF HER MIND.
AND SHE REALLY WANTS TO RIDE THAT PONY.
WHAT DO WE DO? THEY'RE TOO FAST TO FOLLOW!
WE CAN'T DO ANYTHING!
SHE'S ON HER OWN NOW!
HOPEFULLY THAT ROBOT IS FASTER THAN THOSE PIPERS.
SHE'LL HAVE TO FIND HER OWN WAY HOME.
SHE'S RISKING HER LIFE SO WE CAN GET AWAY. LET'S MOVE!
THIS WAY!

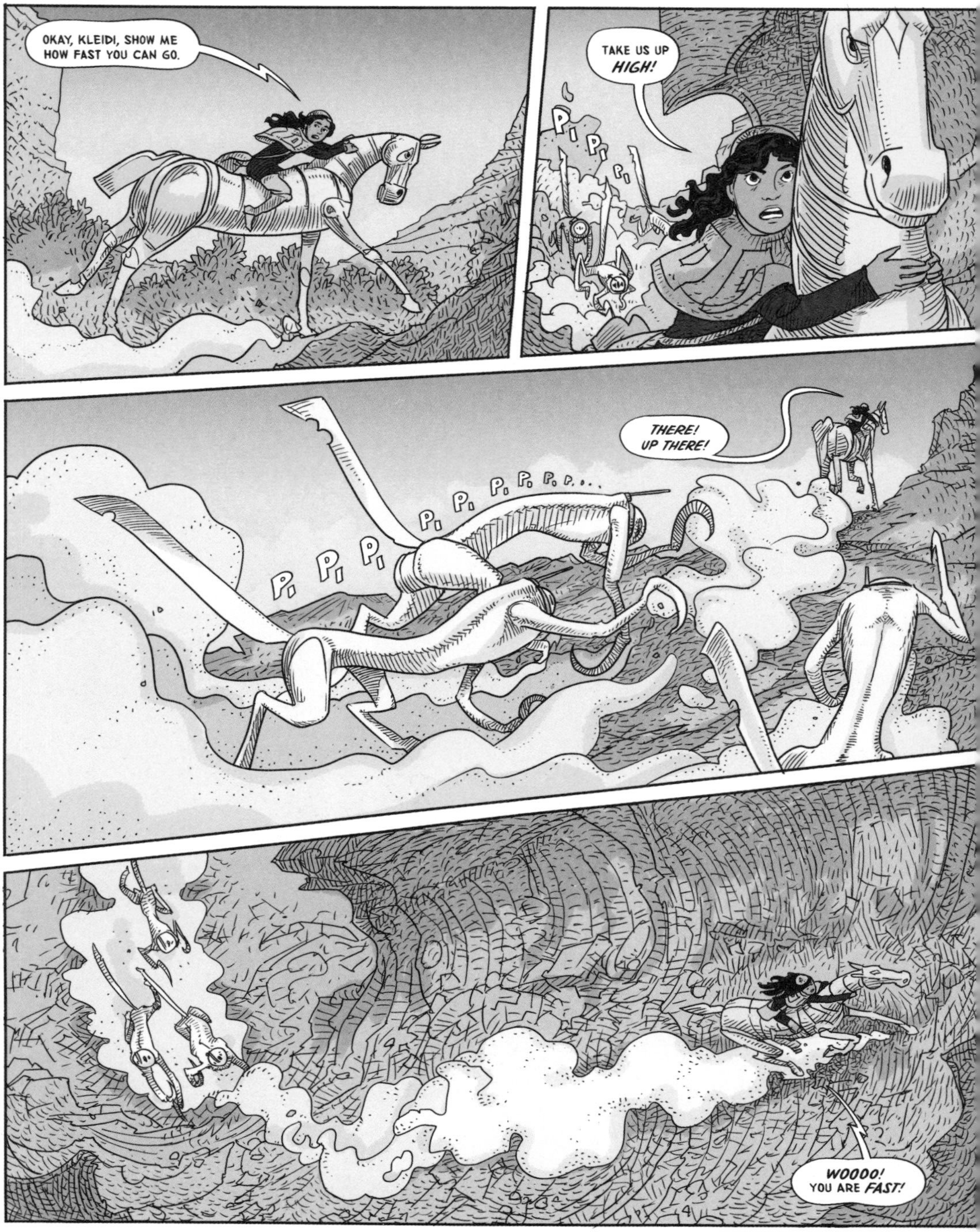
OKAY, KLEIDI, SHOW ME HOW FAST YOU CAN GO.
TAKE US UP HIGH!
THERE! UP THERE!
WOOOO! YOU ARE FAST!

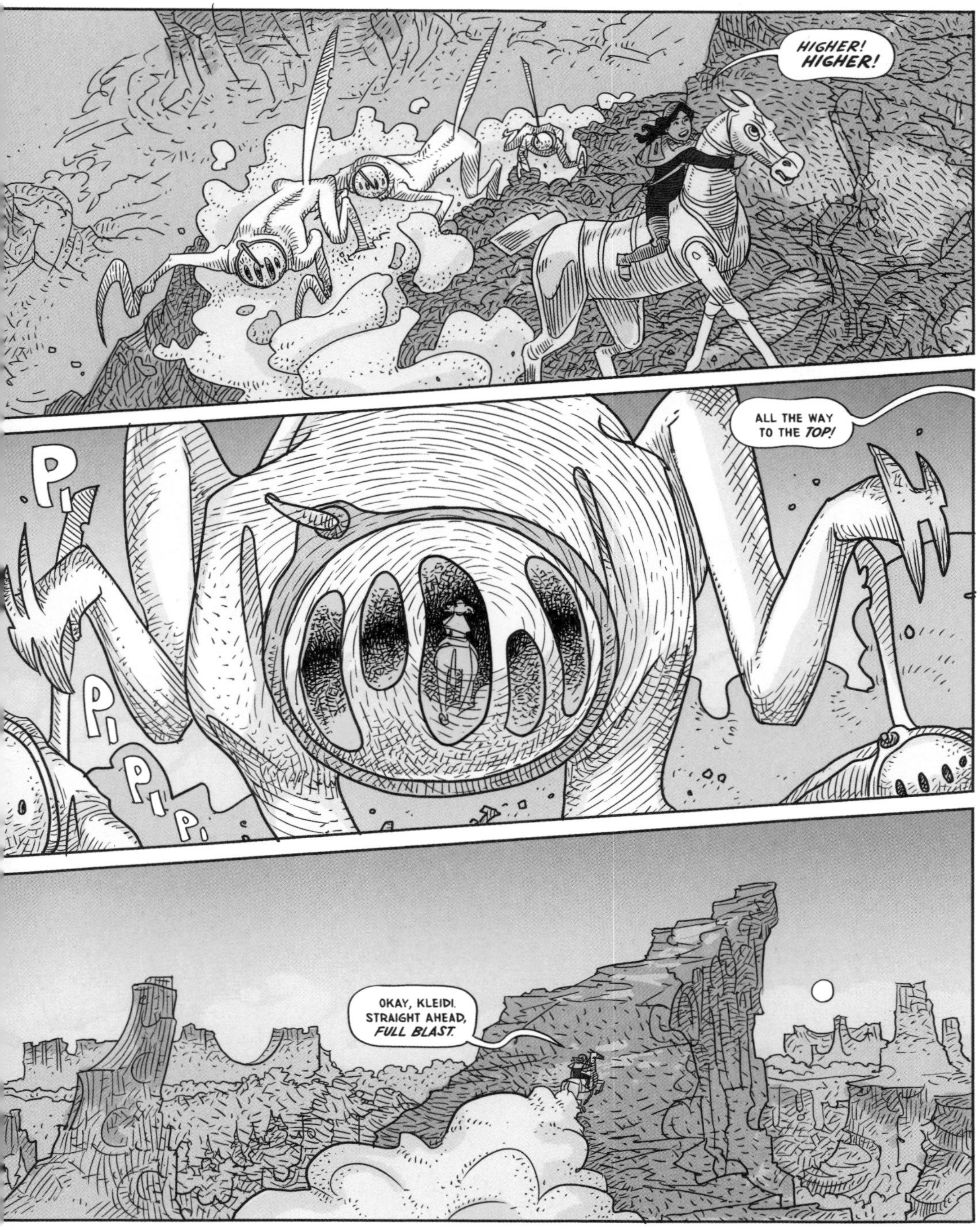
HIGHER! HIGHER!
ALL THE WAY TO THE *TOP!*
PI PI PI PI PI
OKAY, KLEIDI. STRAIGHT AHEAD, *FULL BLAST.*

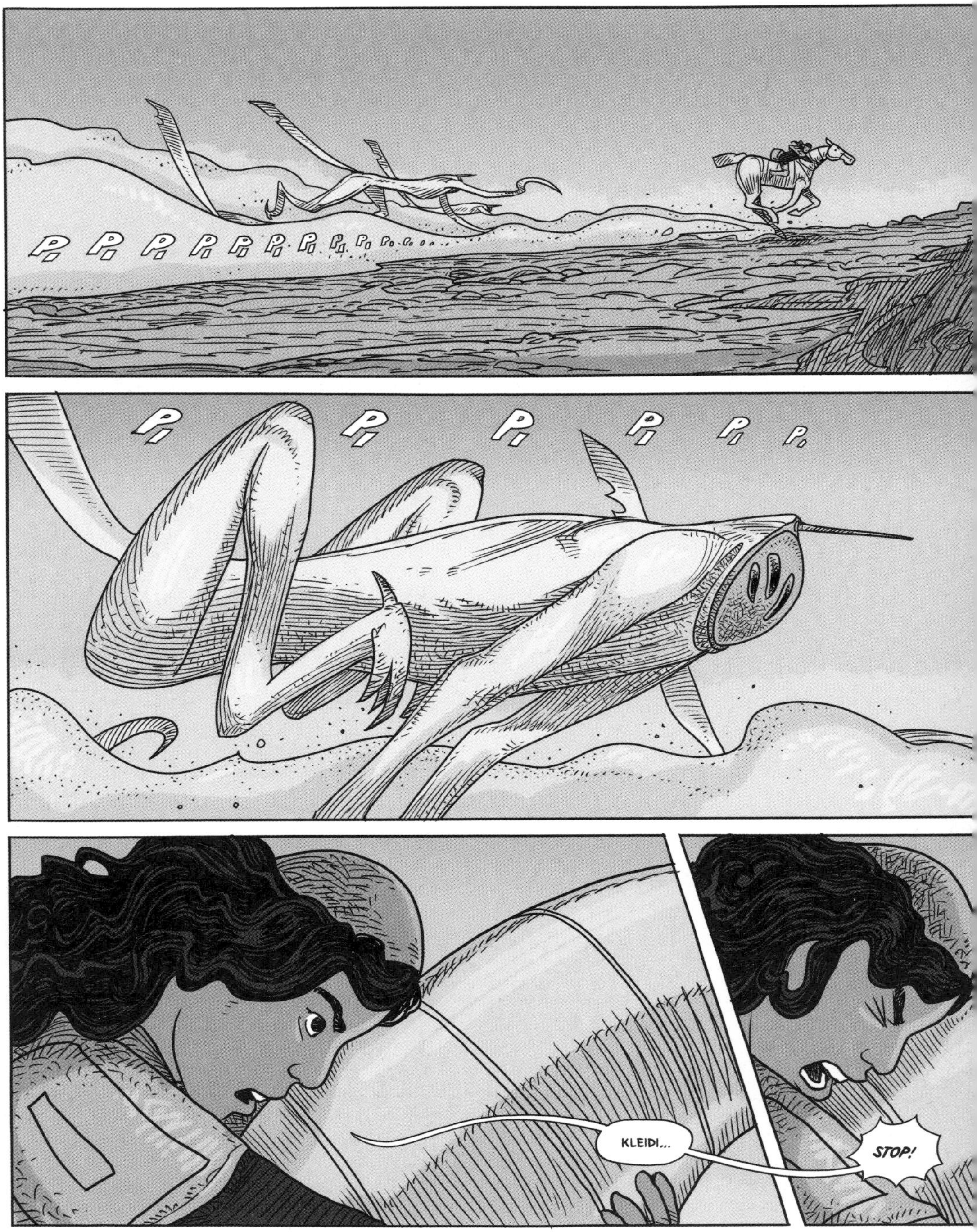
PI PI PI PI PI PI PI PI PI PI PI PI
PI PI PI PI PI PI
KLEIDI...
STOP!

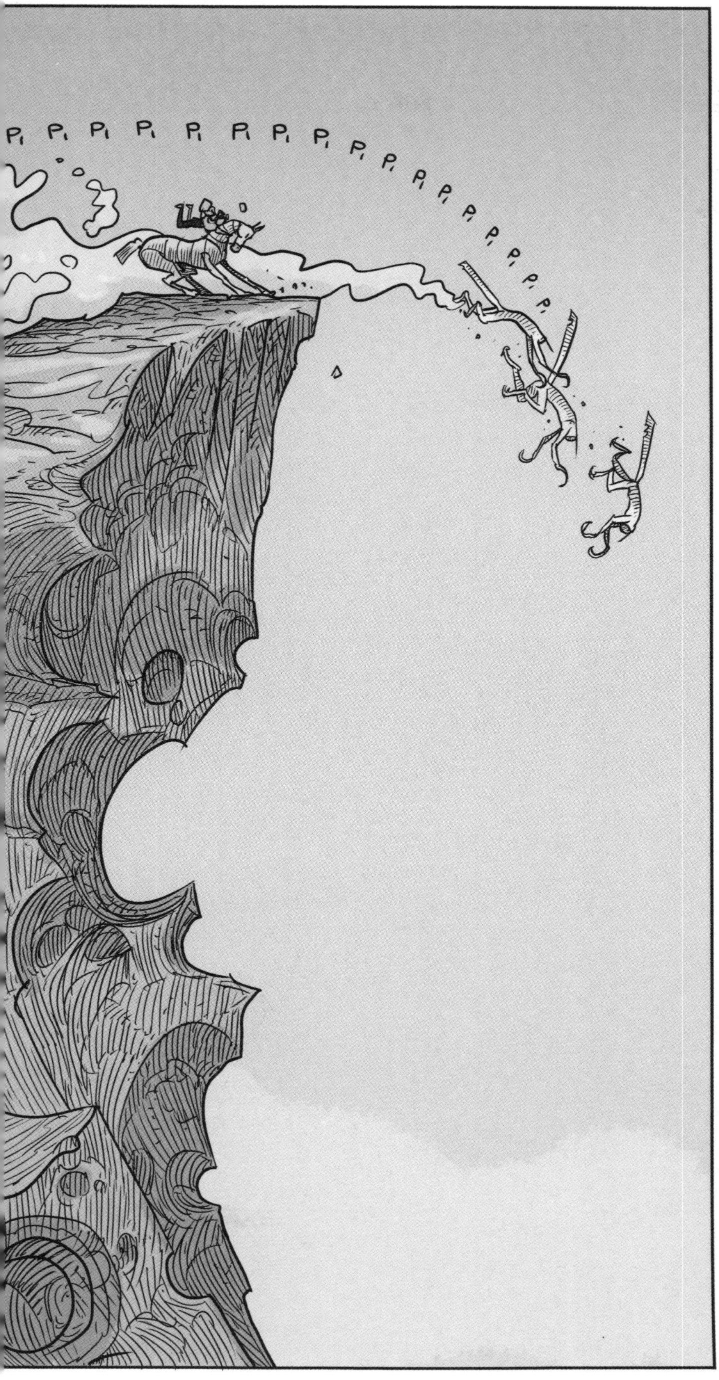
P P P P P P P P P P P P P P P P P P P P P

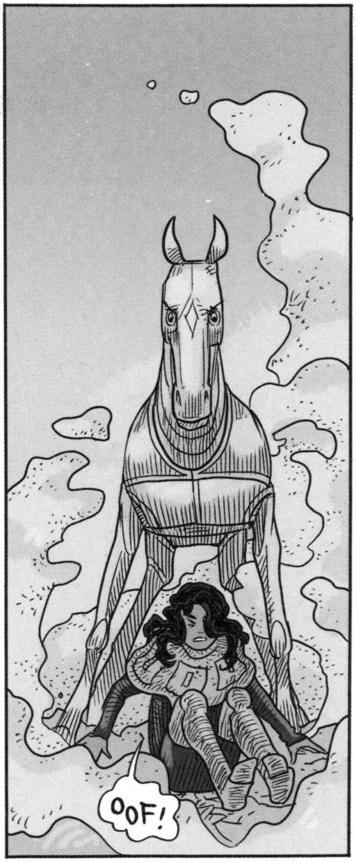
OOF!

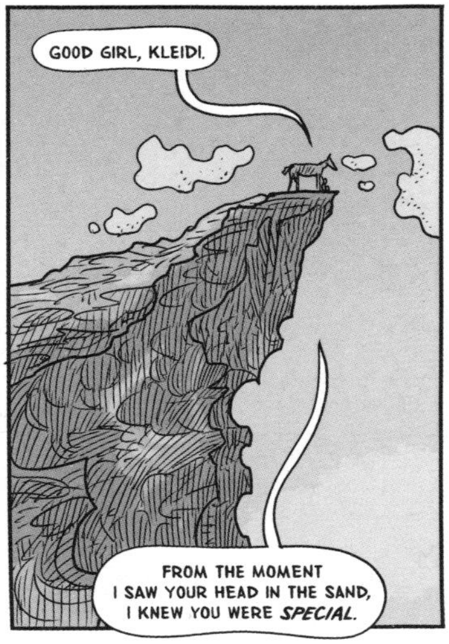
GOOD GIRL, KLEIDI.
FROM THE MOMENT I SAW YOUR HEAD IN THE SAND, I KNEW YOU WERE *SPECIAL.*

SHH! *FREEZE.*

PIPERS?

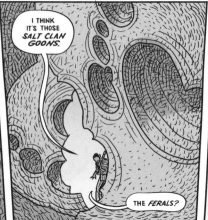

I THINK IT'S THOSE *SALT CLAN GOONS.*

RIDERS?

THE *FERALS?*

IS THERE ANYTHING OUT HERE THAT *ISN'T* TRYING TO KILL YOU?

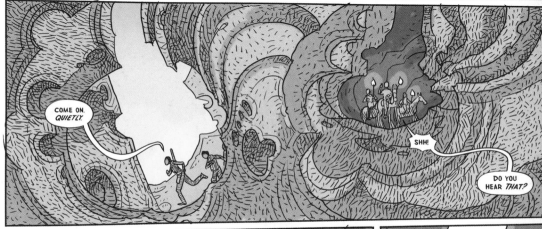

COME ON. *QUIETLY.*

SHH!

DO YOU HEAR *THAT?*

WHAT?

SOUNDED LIKE *VOICES.*

IT'S ALL THE ECHOES IN HERE. C'MON.

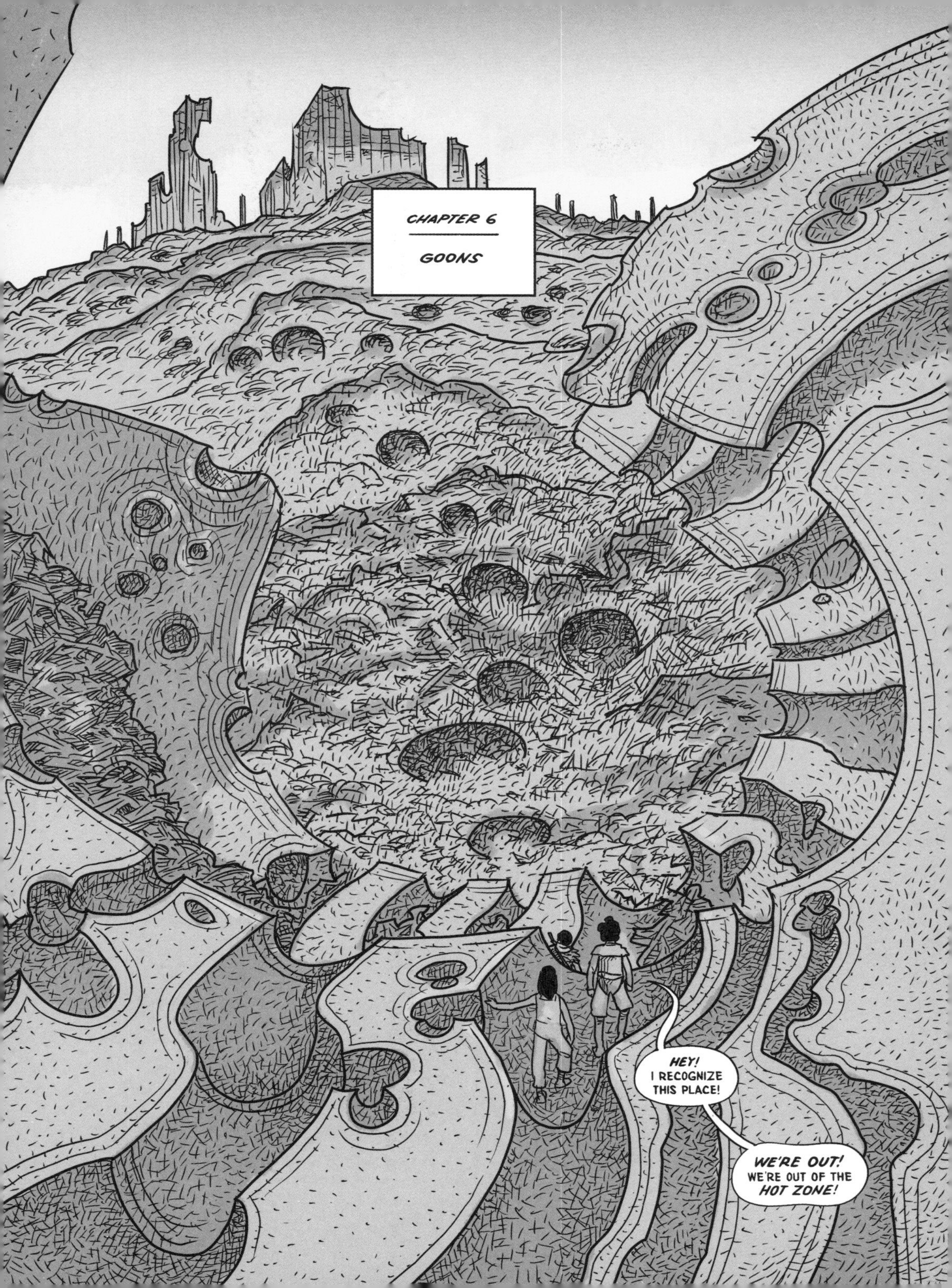
CHAPTER 6
GOONS
HEY! I RECOGNIZE THIS PLACE!
WE'RE OUT! WE'RE OUT OF THE HOT ZONE!

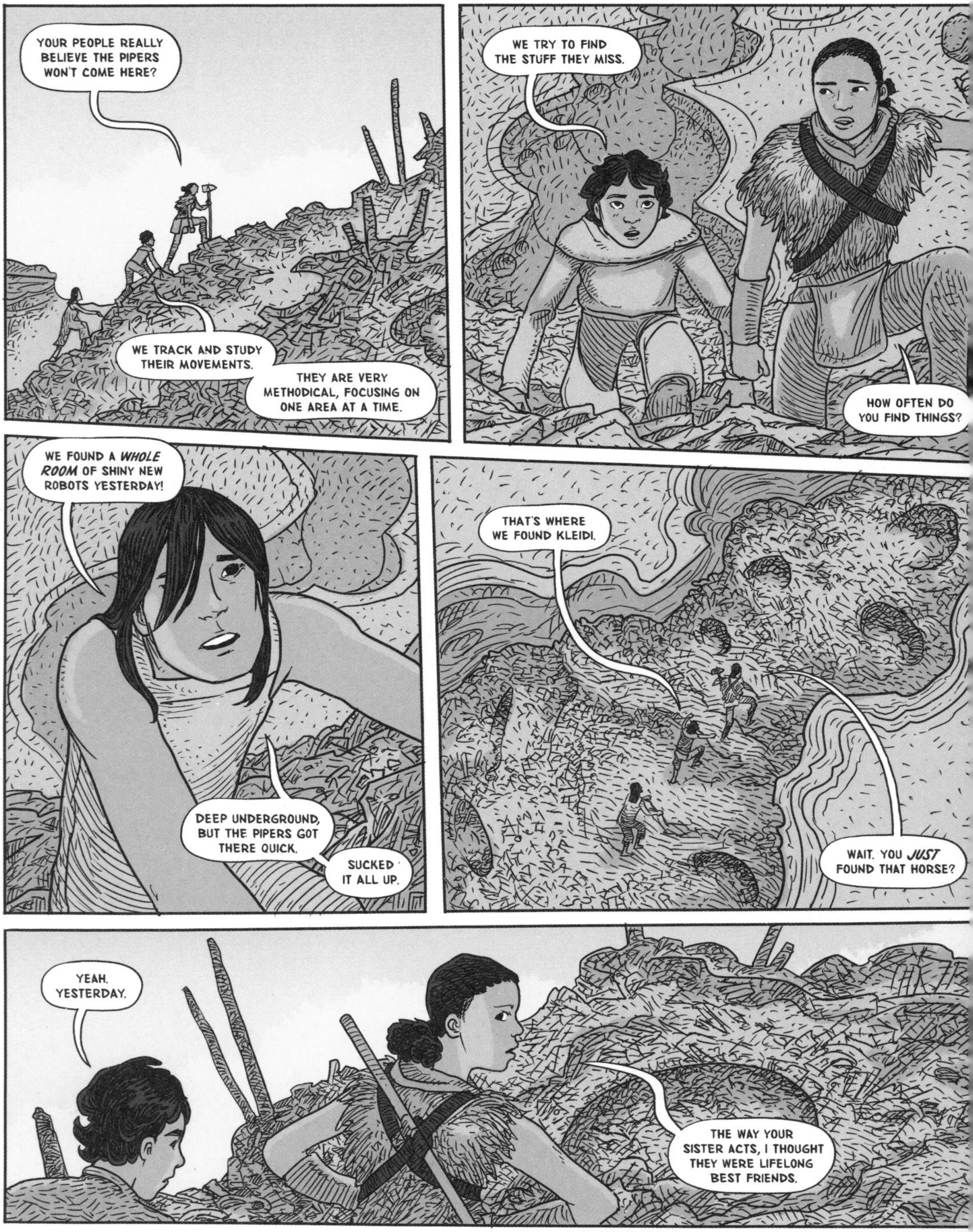
YOUR PEOPLE REALLY BELIEVE THE PIPERS WON'T COME HERE?
WE TRACK AND STUDY THEIR MOVEMENTS.
THEY ARE VERY METHODICAL, FOCUSING ON ONE AREA AT A TIME.
WE TRY TO FIND THE STUFF THEY MISS.
HOW OFTEN DO YOU FIND THINGS?
WE FOUND A *WHOLE ROOM* OF SHINY NEW ROBOTS YESTERDAY!
DEEP UNDERGROUND, BUT THE PIPERS GOT THERE QUICK.
SUCKED IT ALL UP.
THAT'S WHERE WE FOUND KLEIDI.
WAIT. YOU *JUST* FOUND THAT HORSE?
YEAH. YESTERDAY.
THE WAY YOUR SISTER ACTS, I THOUGHT THEY WERE LIFELONG BEST FRIENDS.

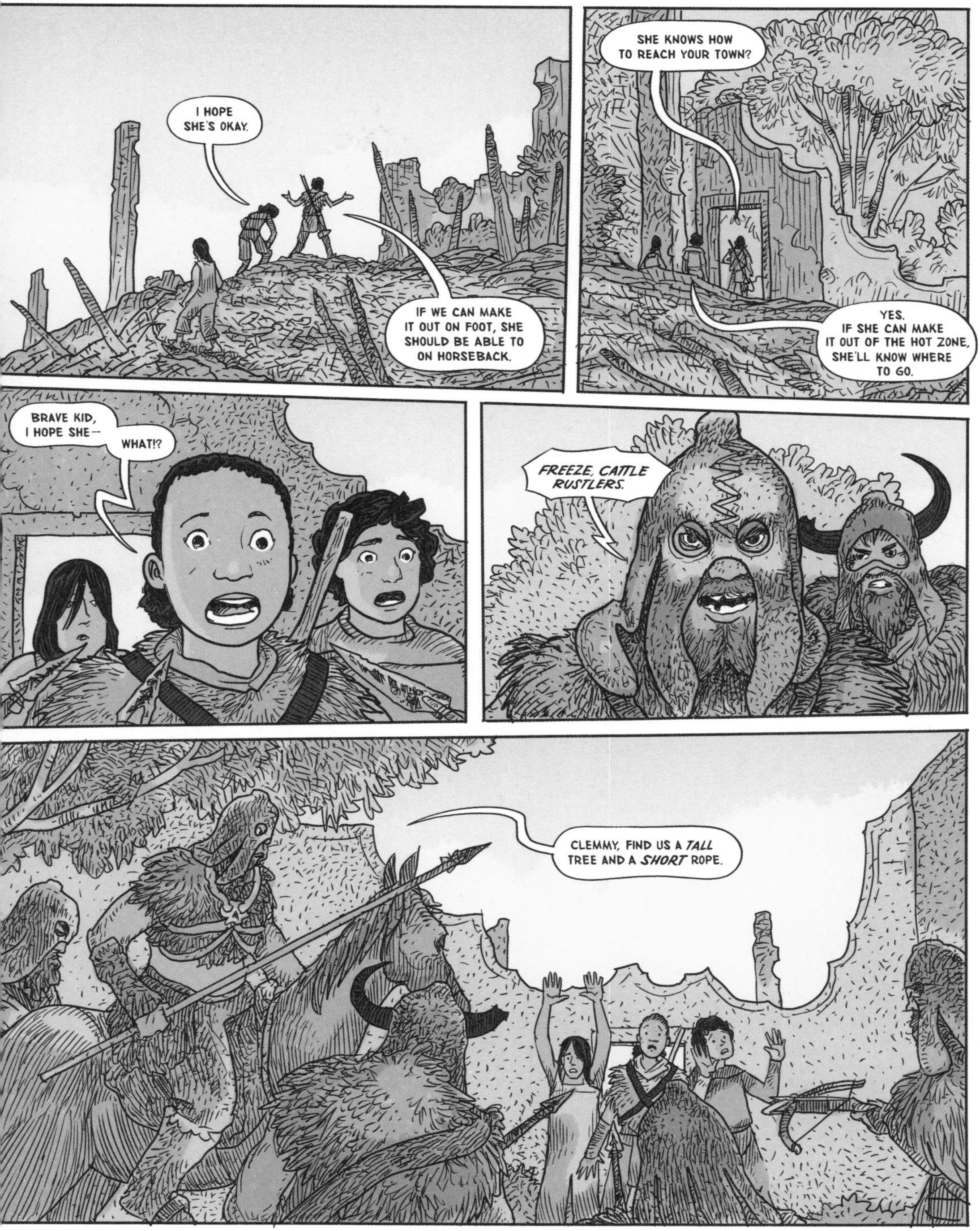
I HOPE SHE'S OKAY.
IF WE CAN MAKE IT OUT ON FOOT, SHE SHOULD BE ABLE TO ON HORSEBACK.
SHE KNOWS HOW TO REACH YOUR TOWN?
YES. IF SHE CAN MAKE IT OUT OF THE HOT ZONE, SHE'LL KNOW WHERE TO GO.
BRAVE KID, I HOPE SHE--
WHAT!?
FREEZE, CATTLE RUSTLERS.
CLEMMY, FIND US A TALL TREE AND A SHORT ROPE.

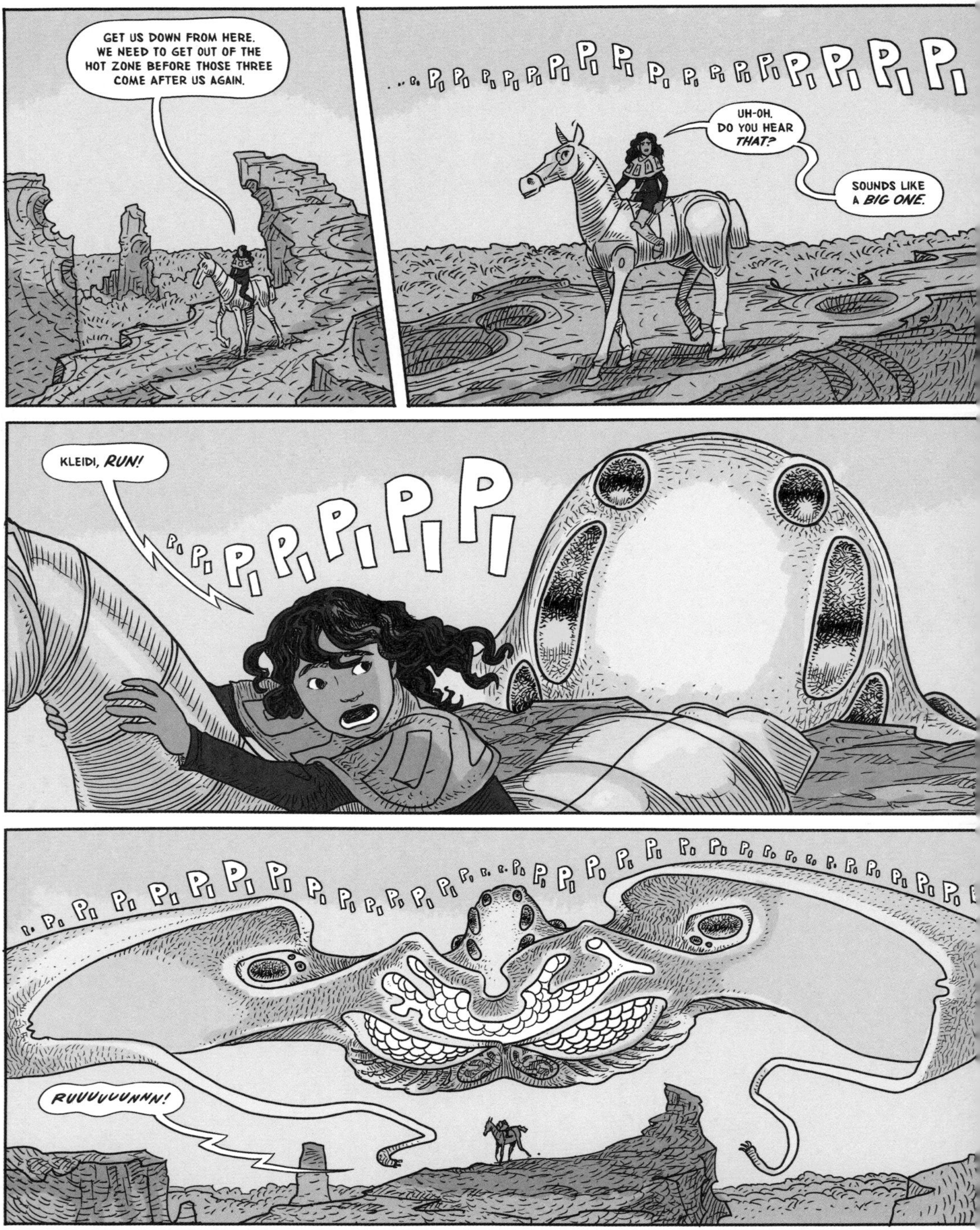
GET US DOWN FROM HERE. WE NEED TO GET OUT OF THE HOT ZONE BEFORE THOSE THREE COME AFTER US AGAIN.
UH-OH. DO YOU HEAR *THAT?*
SOUNDS LIKE A *BIG ONE*.
KLEIDI, *RUN!*
RUUUUUUNNN!

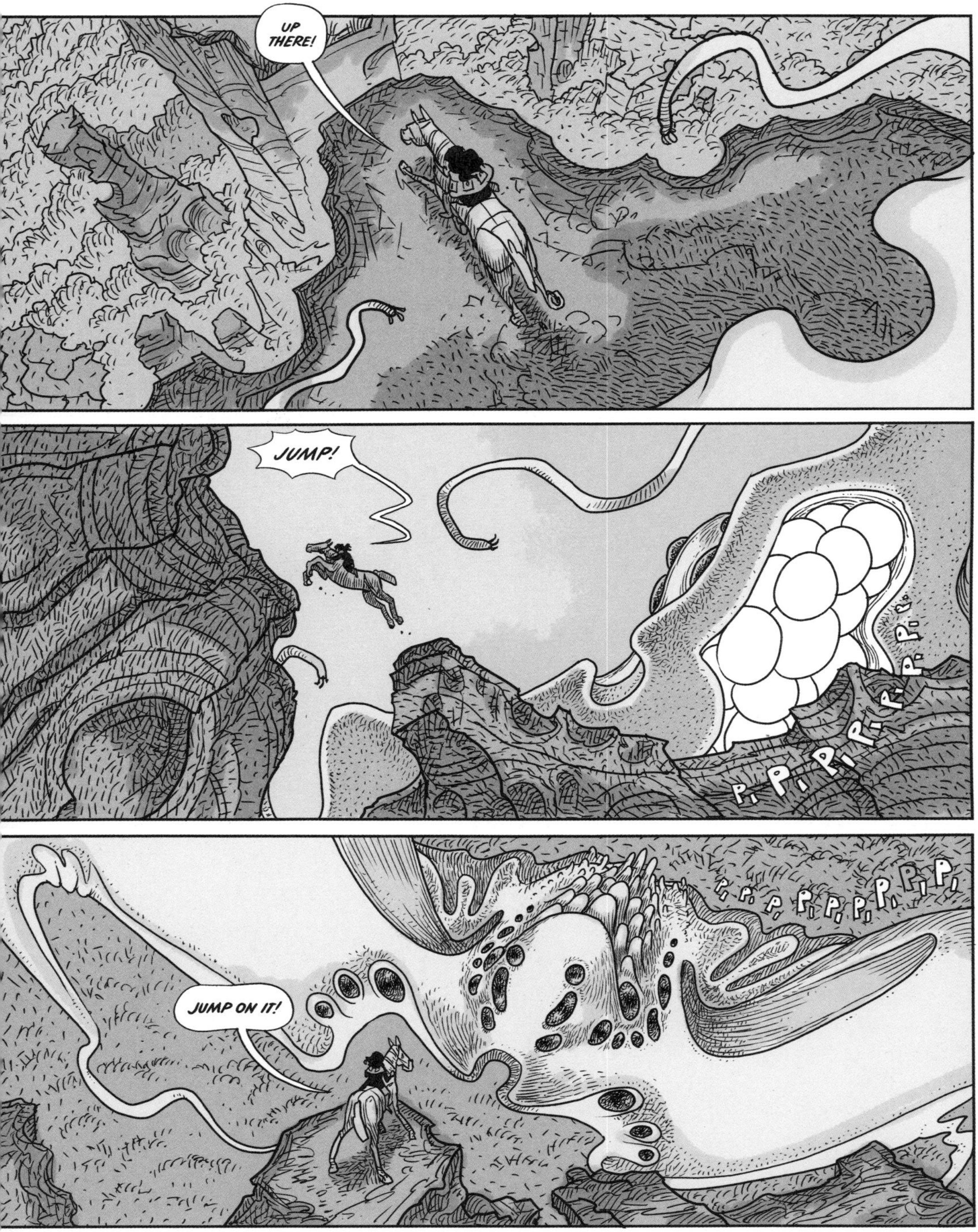
UP THERE!
JUMP!
JUMP ON IT!

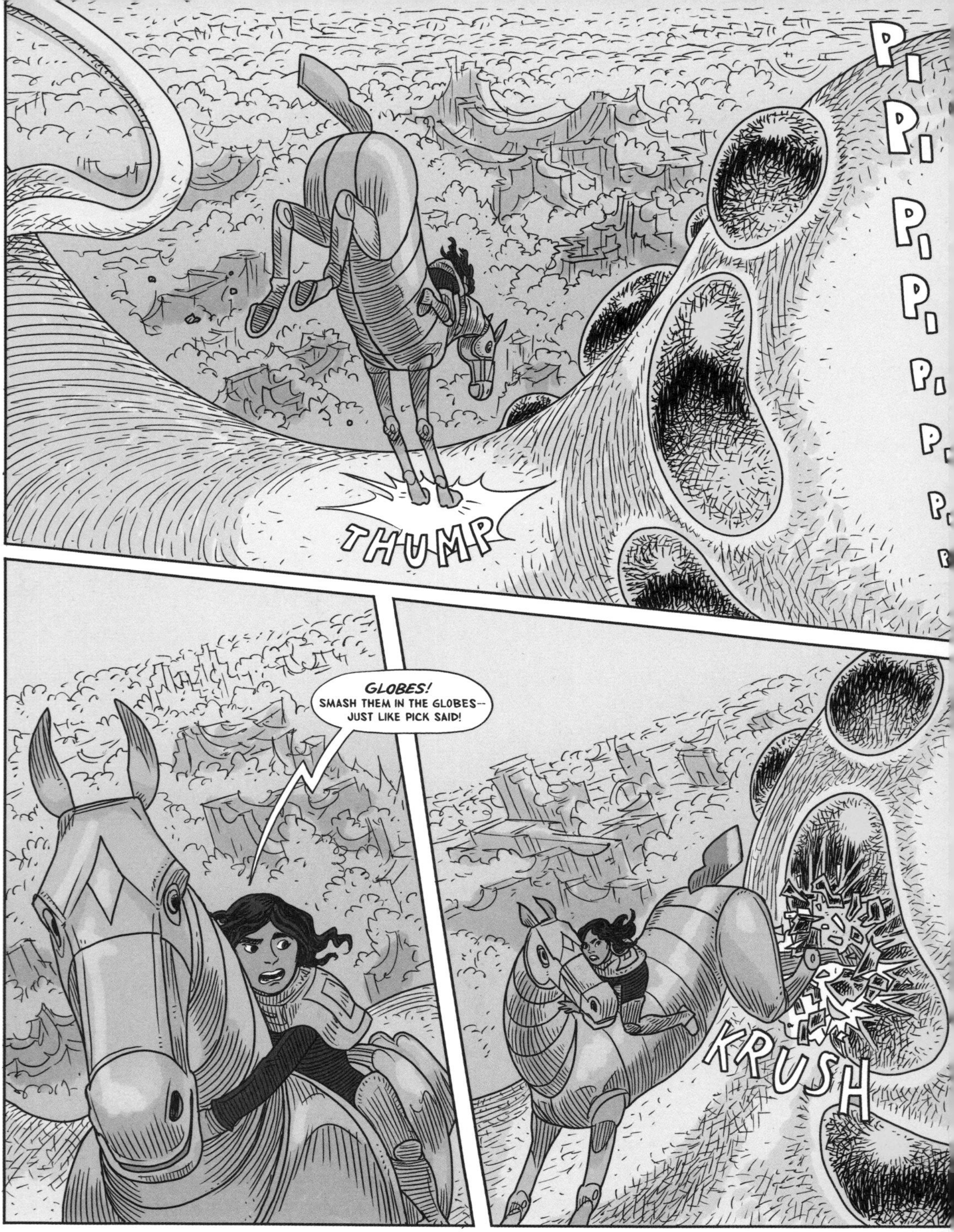
PI PI PI PI PI PI PI P
THUMP
GLOBES!
SMASH THEM IN THE GLOBES--
JUST LIKE PICK SAID!
KRUSH

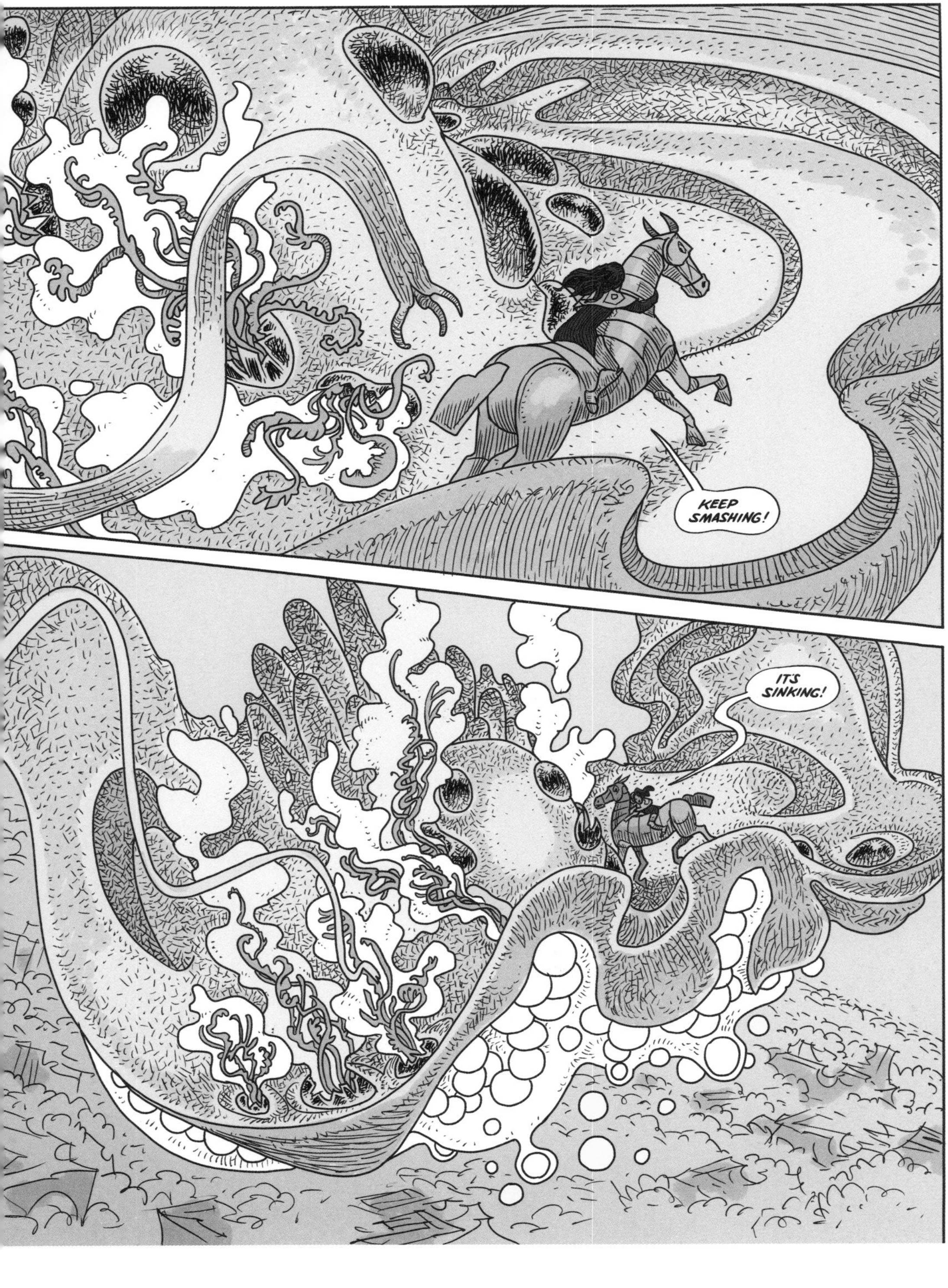
KEEP SMASHING!
IT'S SINKING!

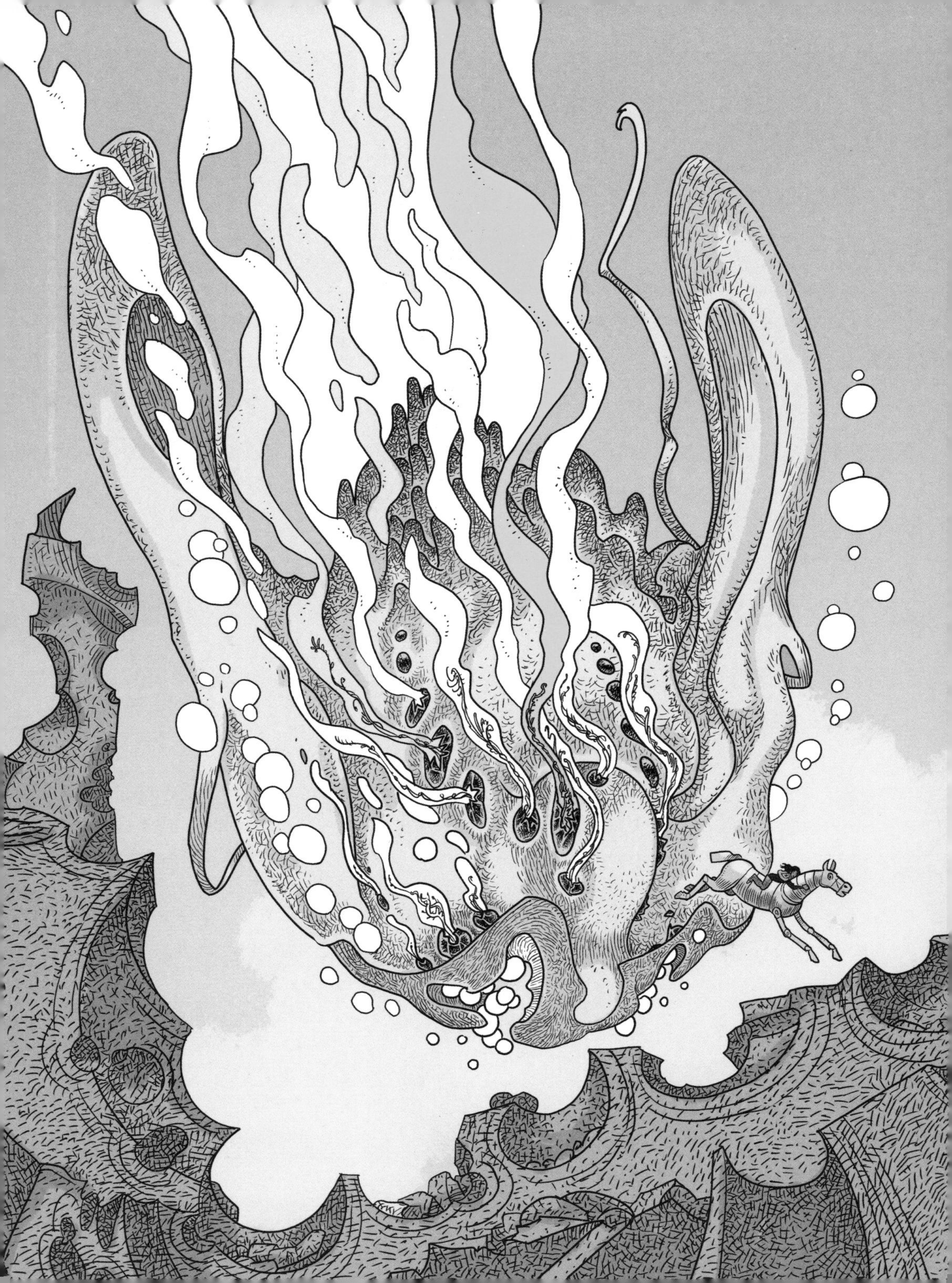

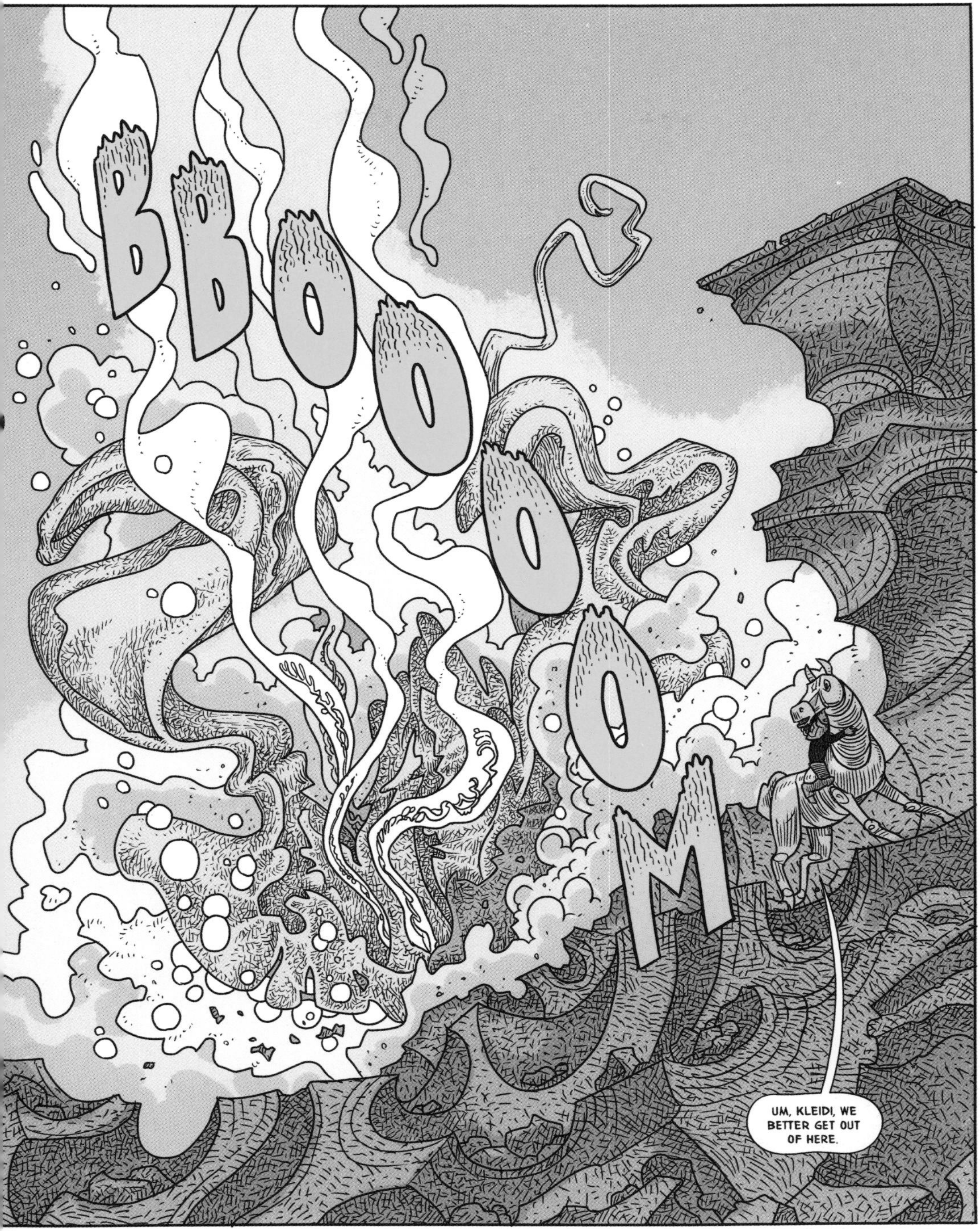
BBOOOOOM
UM, KLEIDI, WE BETTER GET OUT OF HERE.

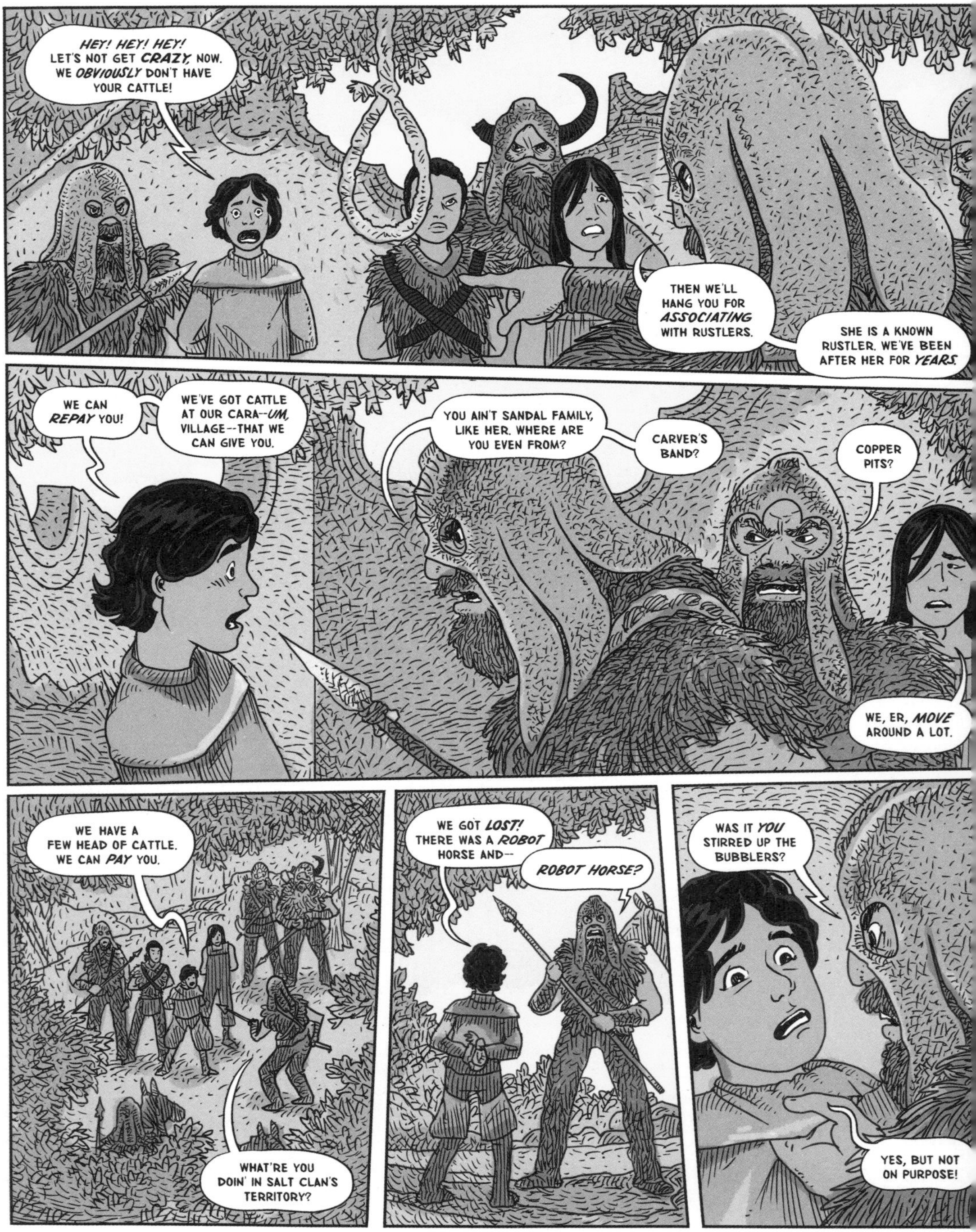
HEY! HEY! HEY! LET'S NOT GET CRAZY, NOW. WE OBVIOUSLY DON'T HAVE YOUR CATTLE!
THEN WE'LL HANG YOU FOR ASSOCIATING WITH RUSTLERS.
SHE IS A KNOWN RUSTLER. WE'VE BEEN AFTER HER FOR YEARS.
WE CAN REPAY YOU!
WE'VE GOT CATTLE AT OUR CARA--UM, VILLAGE--THAT WE CAN GIVE YOU.
YOU AIN'T SANDAL FAMILY, LIKE HER. WHERE ARE YOU EVEN FROM?
CARVER'S BAND?
COPPER PITS?
WE, ER, MOVE AROUND A LOT.
WE HAVE A FEW HEAD OF CATTLE. WE CAN PAY YOU.
WHAT'RE YOU DOIN' IN SALT CLAN'S TERRITORY?
WE GOT LOST! THERE WAS A ROBOT HORSE AND--
ROBOT HORSE?
WAS IT YOU STIRRED UP THE BUBBLERS?
YES, BUT NOT ON PURPOSE!

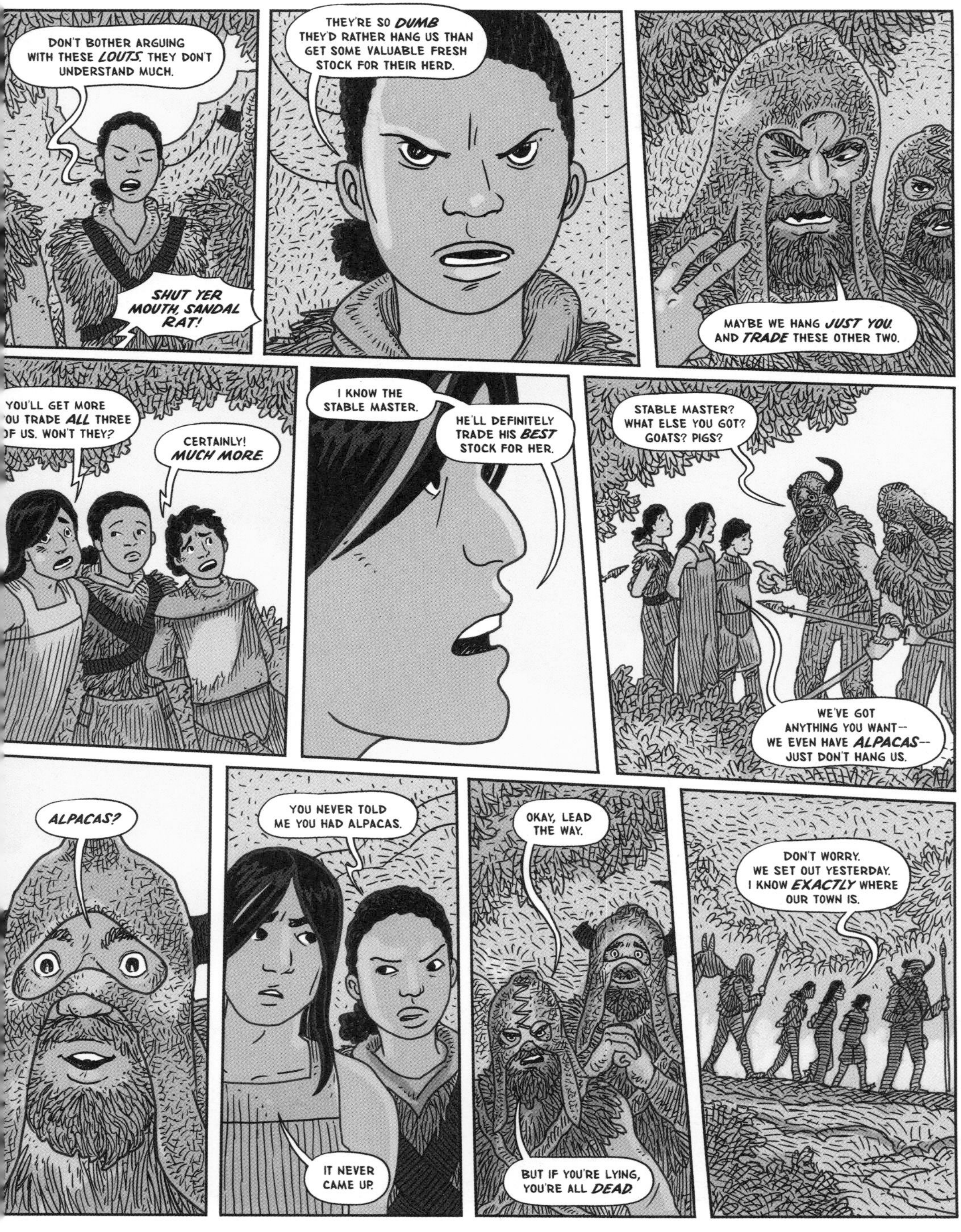
DON'T BOTHER ARGUING WITH THESE LOUTS. THEY DON'T UNDERSTAND MUCH.
SHUT YER MOUTH, SANDAL RAT!
THEY'RE SO DUMB THEY'D RATHER HANG US THAN GET SOME VALUABLE FRESH STOCK FOR THEIR HERD.
MAYBE WE HANG JUST YOU. AND TRADE THESE OTHER TWO.
YOU'LL GET MORE YOU TRADE ALL THREE OF US. WON'T THEY?
CERTAINLY! MUCH MORE.
I KNOW THE STABLE MASTER.
HE'LL DEFINITELY TRADE HIS BEST STOCK FOR HER.
STABLE MASTER? WHAT ELSE YOU GOT? GOATS? PIGS?
WE'VE GOT ANYTHING YOU WANT-- WE EVEN HAVE ALPACAS-- JUST DON'T HANG US.
ALPACAS?
YOU NEVER TOLD ME YOU HAD ALPACAS.
IT NEVER CAME UP.
OKAY, LEAD THE WAY.
BUT IF YOU'RE LYING, YOU'RE ALL DEAD.
DON'T WORRY. WE SET OUT YESTERDAY. I KNOW EXACTLY WHERE OUR TOWN IS.

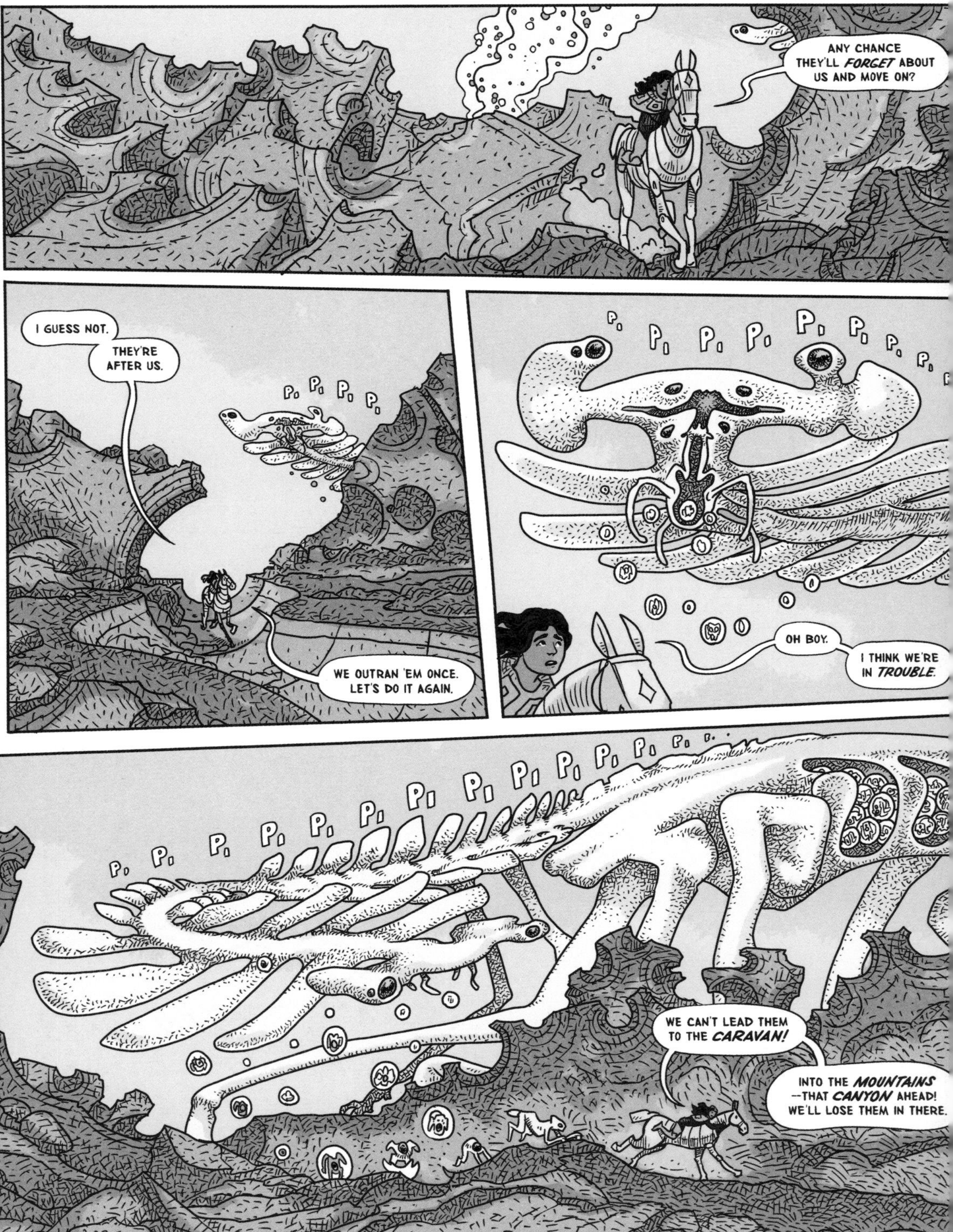
ANY CHANCE THEY'LL *FORGET* ABOUT US AND MOVE ON?
I GUESS NOT.
THEY'RE AFTER US.
WE OUTRAN 'EM ONCE. LET'S DO IT AGAIN.
OH BOY.
I THINK WE'RE IN *TROUBLE*.
WE CAN'T LEAD THEM TO THE *CARAVAN!*
INTO THE *MOUNTAINS* --THAT *CANYON* AHEAD! WE'LL LOSE THEM IN THERE.

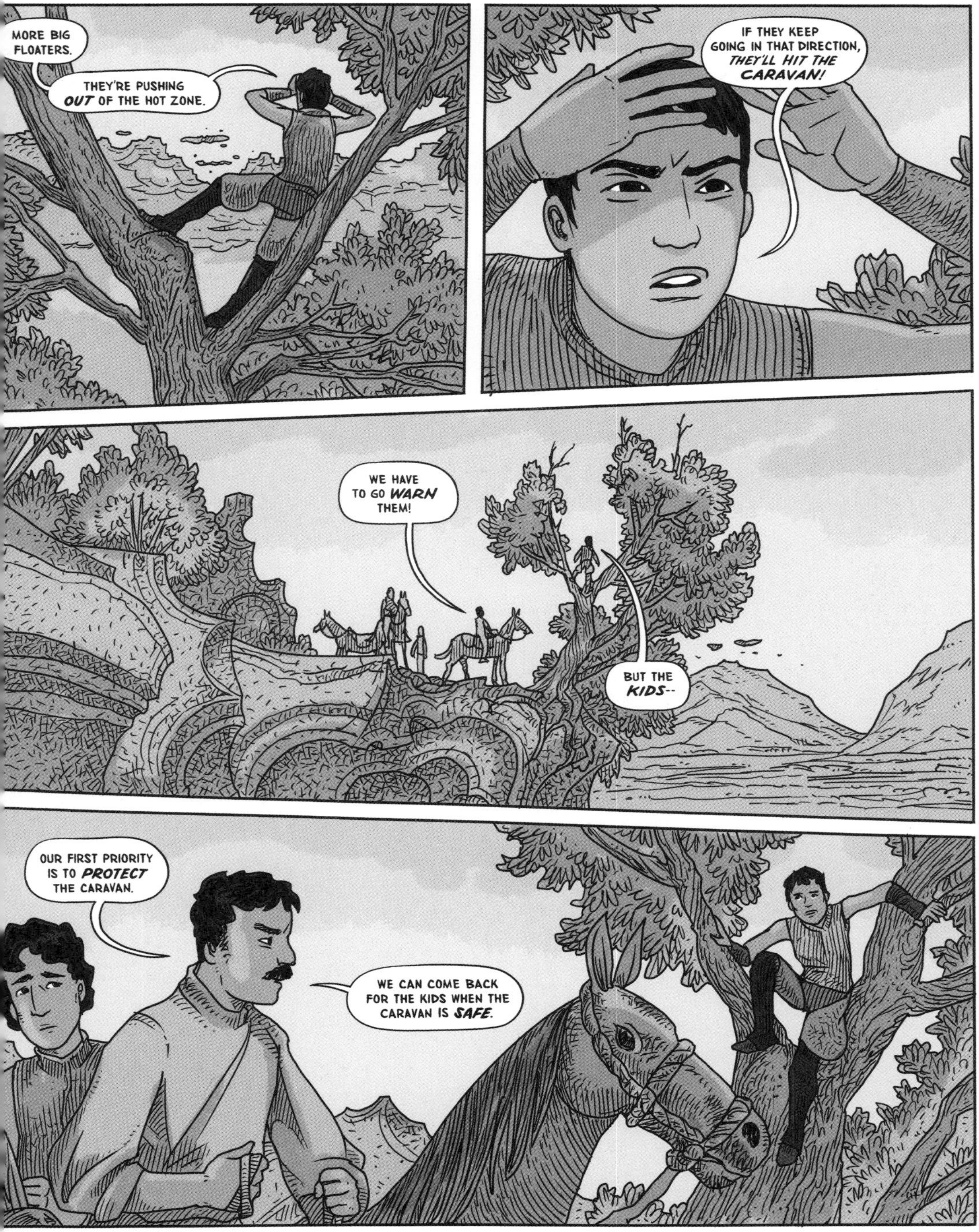
MORE BIG FLOATERS.
THEY'RE PUSHING OUT OF THE HOT ZONE.
IF THEY KEEP GOING IN THAT DIRECTION, THEY'LL HIT THE CARAVAN!
WE HAVE TO GO WARN THEM!
BUT THE KIDS--
OUR FIRST PRIORITY IS TO PROTECT THE CARAVAN.
WE CAN COME BACK FOR THE KIDS WHEN THE CARAVAN IS SAFE.

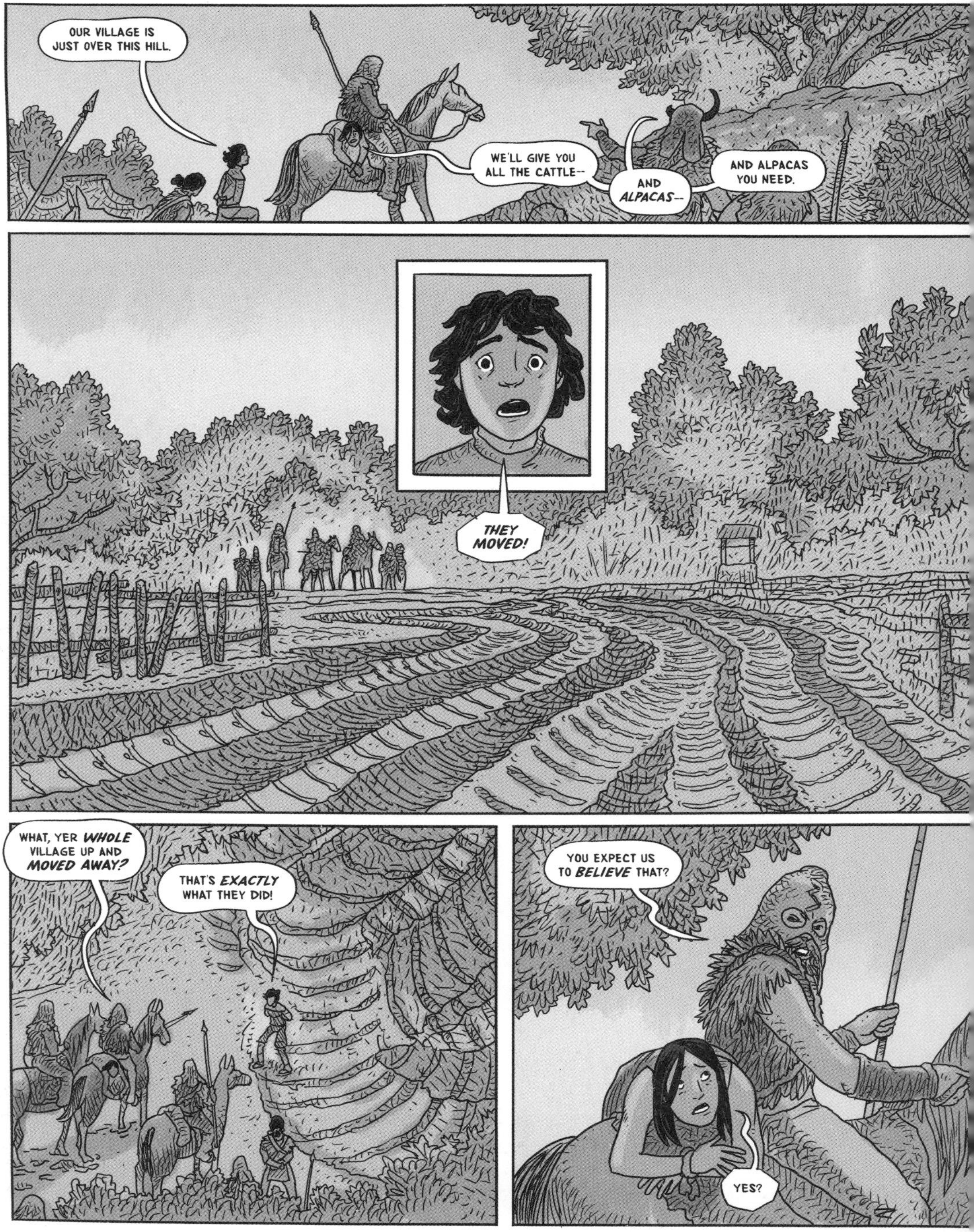
OUR VILLAGE IS JUST OVER THIS HILL.
WE'LL GIVE YOU ALL THE CATTLE--
AND ALPACAS--
AND ALPACAS YOU NEED.
THEY MOVED!
WHAT, YER WHOLE VILLAGE UP AND MOVED AWAY?
THAT'S EXACTLY WHAT THEY DID!
YOU EXPECT US TO BELIEVE THAT?
YES?

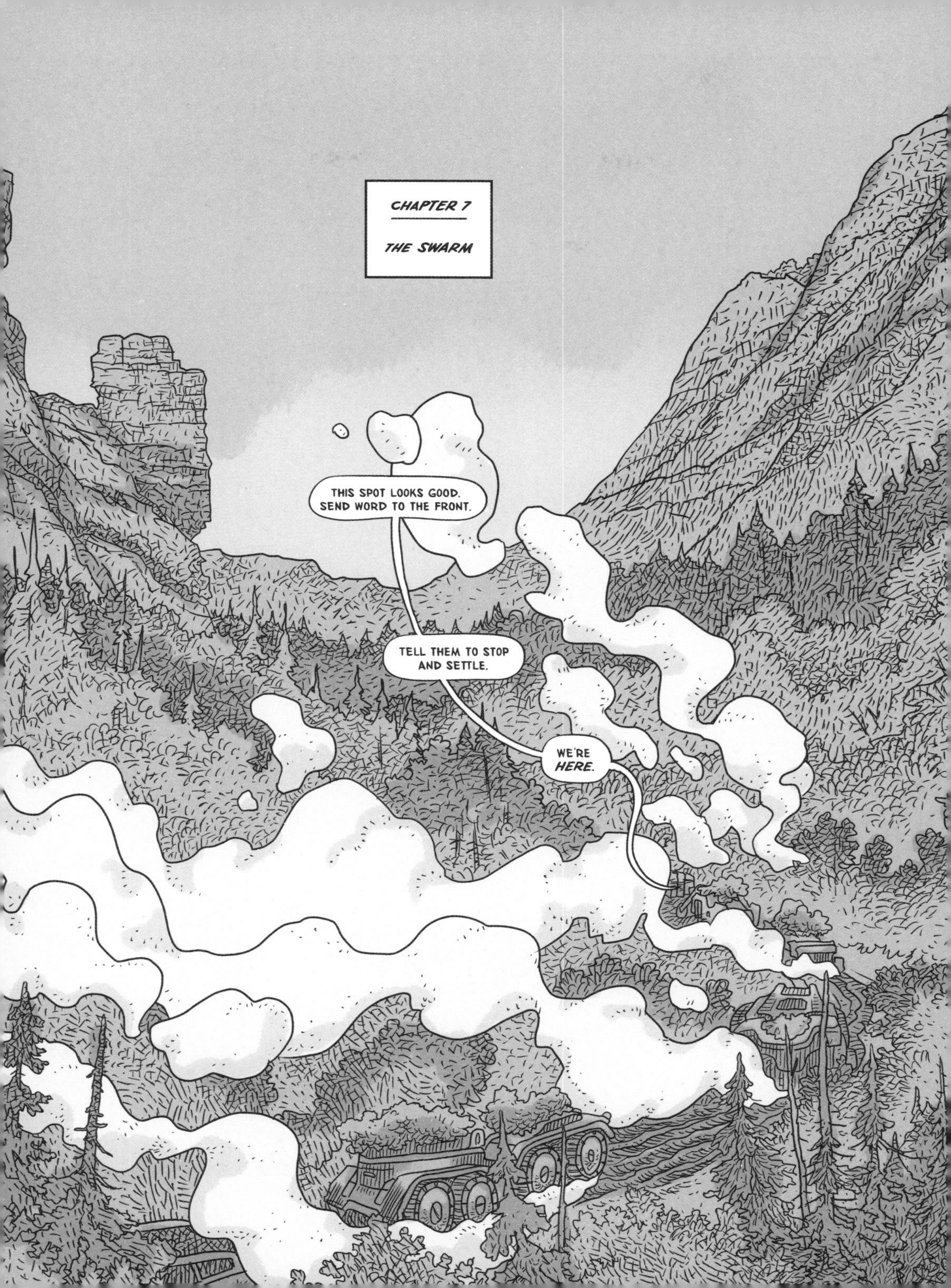
CHAPTER 7
THE SWARM
THIS SPOT LOOKS GOOD. SEND WORD TO THE FRONT.
TELL THEM TO STOP AND SETTLE.
WE'RE HERE.

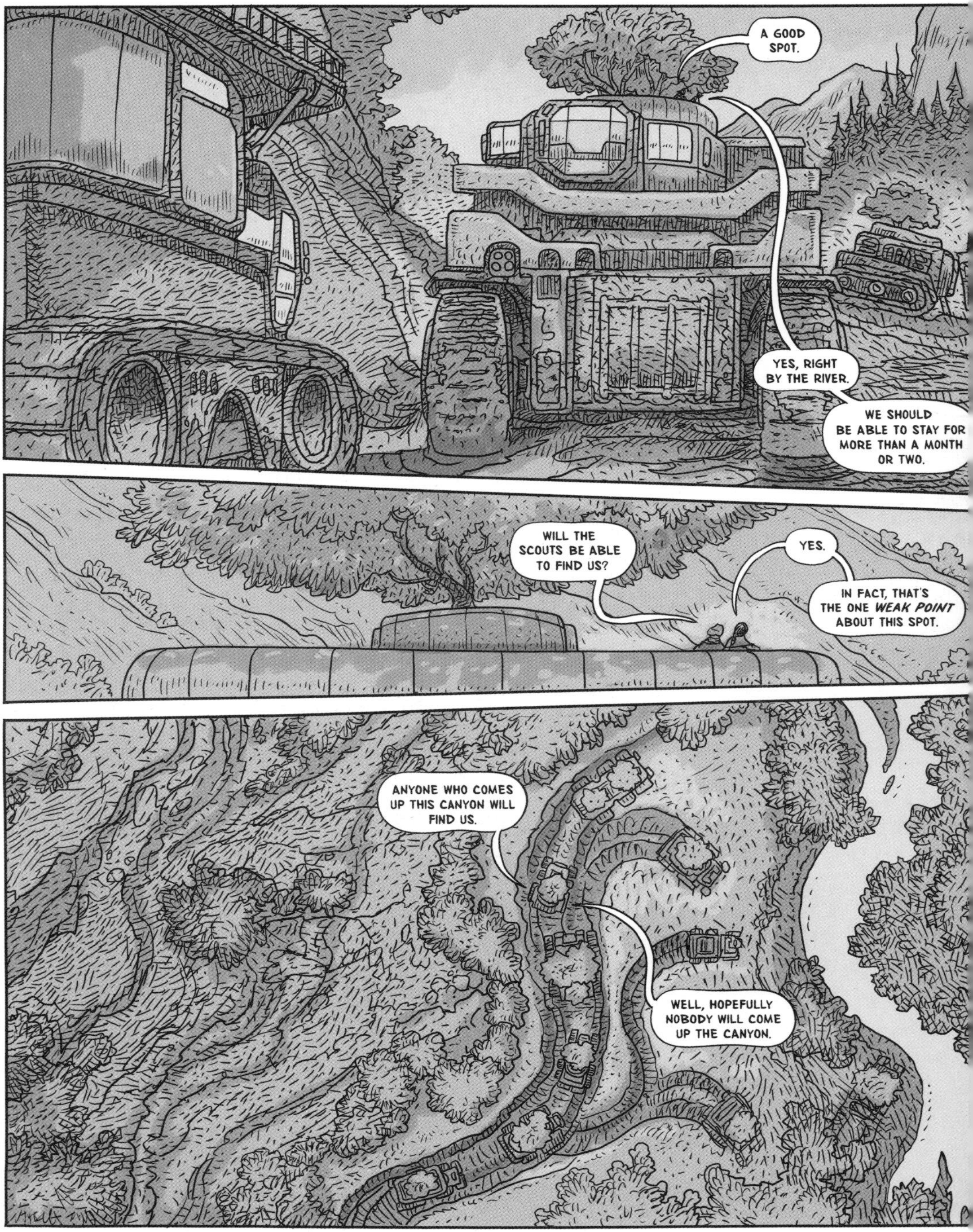
A GOOD SPOT.
YES, RIGHT BY THE RIVER.
WE SHOULD BE ABLE TO STAY FOR MORE THAN A MONTH OR TWO.
WILL THE SCOUTS BE ABLE TO FIND US?
YES.
IN FACT, THAT'S THE ONE *WEAK POINT* ABOUT THIS SPOT.
ANYONE WHO COMES UP THIS CANYON WILL FIND US.
WELL, HOPEFULLY NOBODY WILL COME UP THE CANYON.

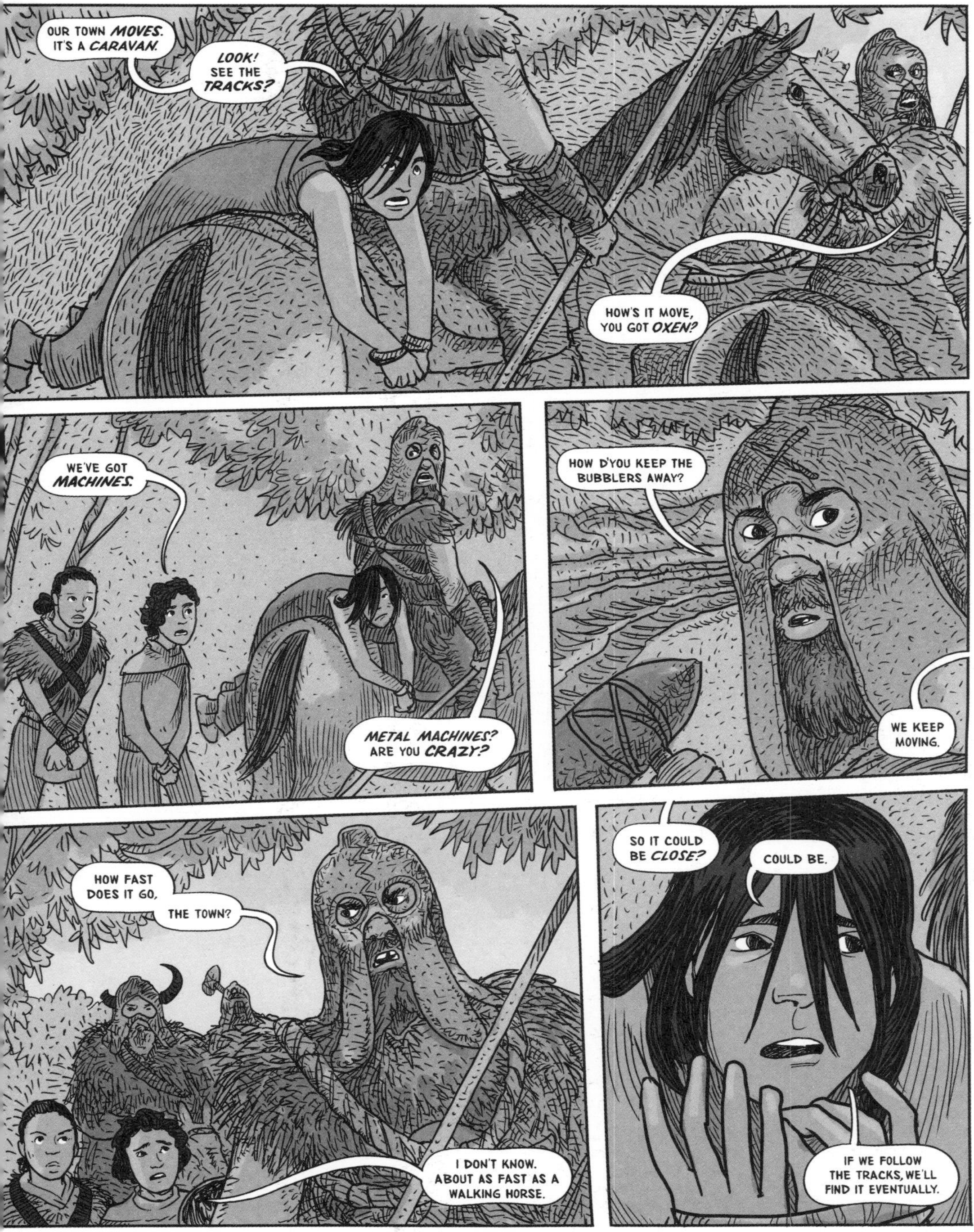
OUR TOWN *MOVES.* IT'S A *CARAVAN.*
LOOK! SEE THE *TRACKS?*
HOW'S IT MOVE, YOU GOT *OXEN?*
WE'VE GOT *MACHINES.*
METAL MACHINES? ARE YOU *CRAZY?*
HOW D'YOU KEEP THE BUBBLERS AWAY?
WE KEEP MOVING.
HOW FAST DOES IT GO,
THE TOWN?
I DON'T KNOW. ABOUT AS FAST AS A WALKING HORSE.
SO IT COULD BE *CLOSE?*
COULD BE.
IF WE FOLLOW THE TRACKS, WE'LL FIND IT EVENTUALLY.

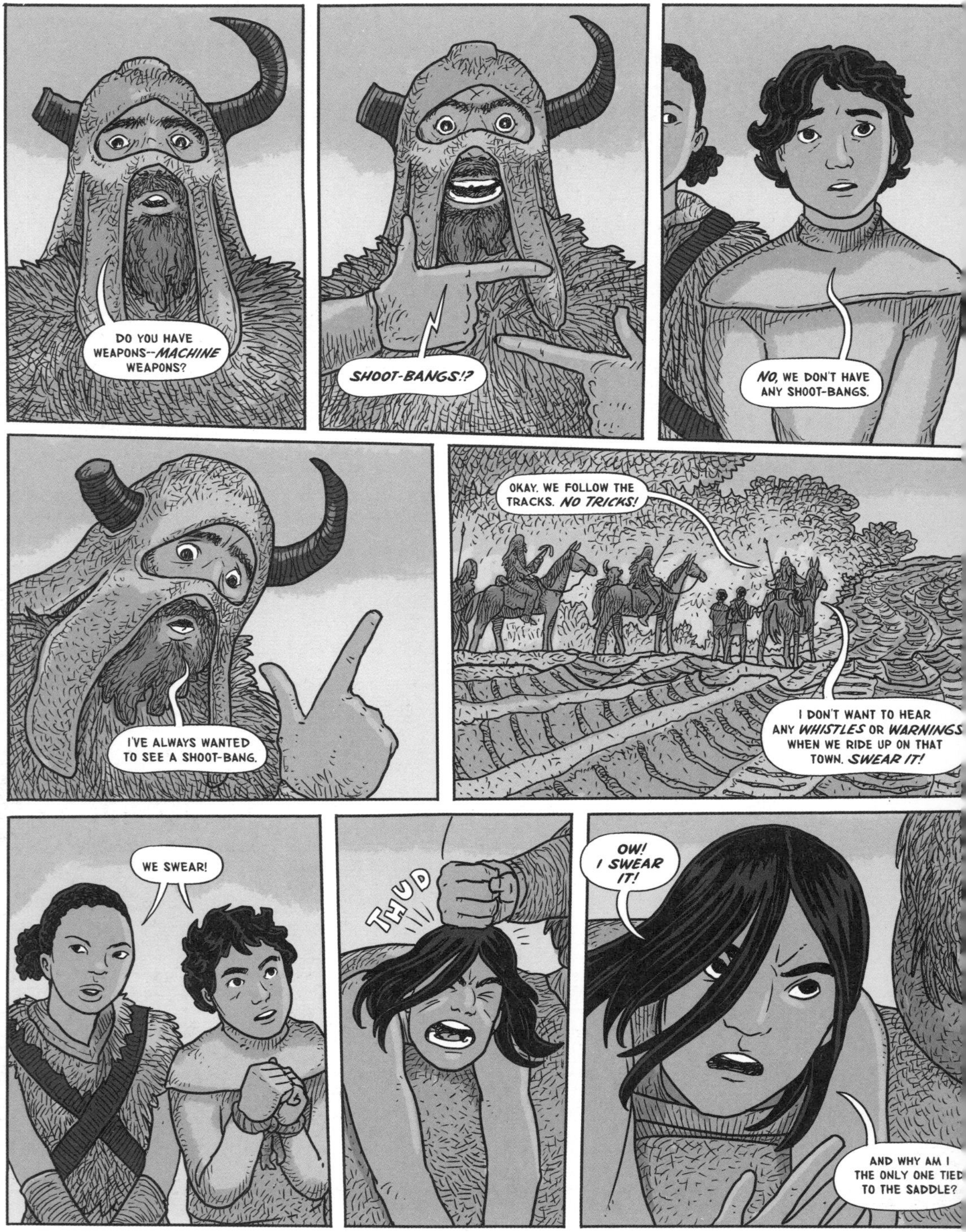
DO YOU HAVE WEAPONS--MACHINE WEAPONS?
SHOOT-BANGS!?
NO, WE DON'T HAVE ANY SHOOT-BANGS.
I'VE ALWAYS WANTED TO SEE A SHOOT-BANG.
OKAY. WE FOLLOW THE TRACKS. NO TRICKS!
I DON'T WANT TO HEAR ANY WHISTLES OR WARNINGS WHEN WE RIDE UP ON THAT TOWN. SWEAR IT!
WE SWEAR!
THUD
OW! I SWEAR IT!
AND WHY AM I THE ONLY ONE TIED TO THE SADDLE?

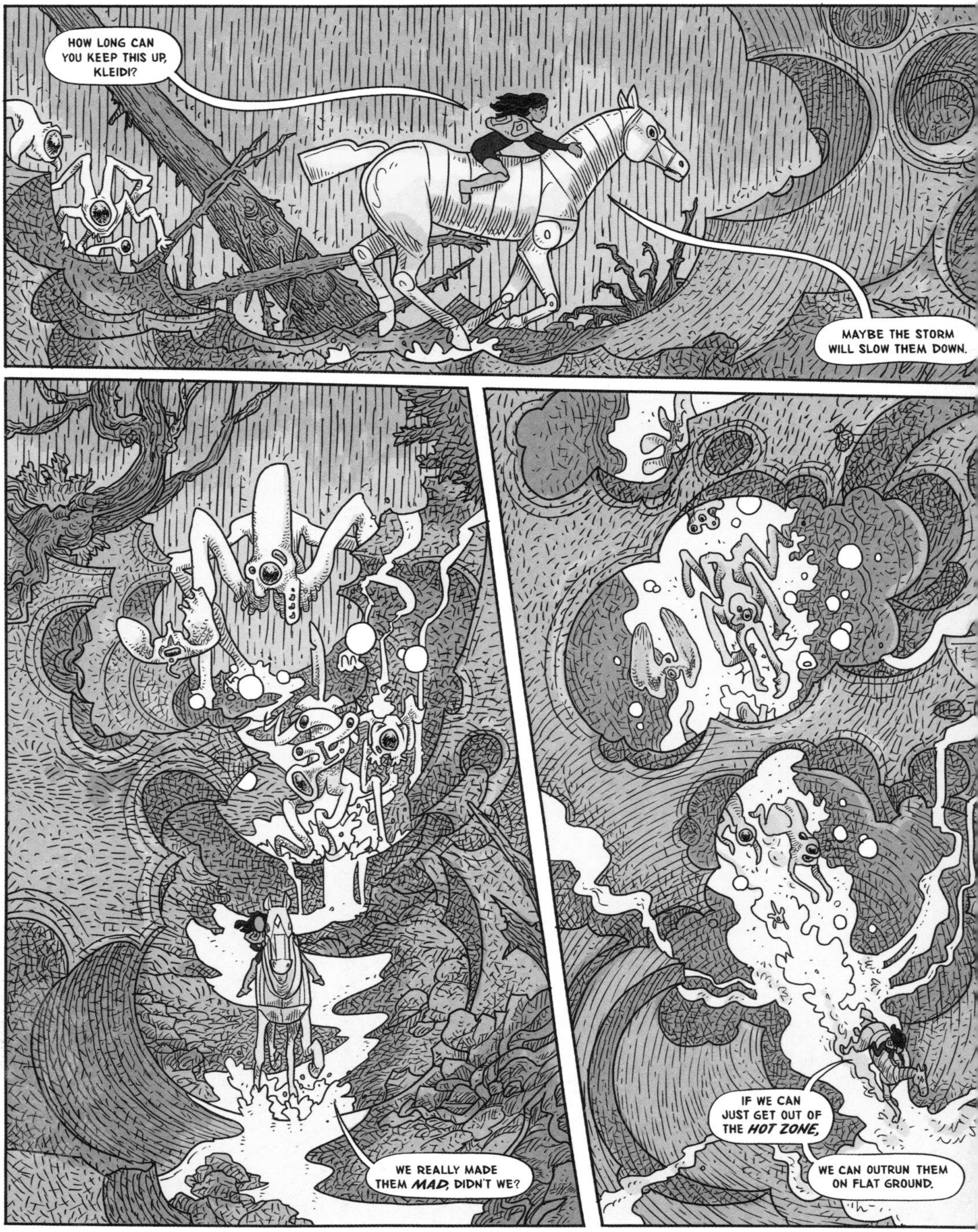
HOW LONG CAN YOU KEEP THIS UP, KLEIDI?
MAYBE THE STORM WILL SLOW THEM DOWN.
WE REALLY MADE THEM *MAD*, DIDN'T WE?
IF WE CAN JUST GET OUT OF THE *HOT ZONE*,
WE CAN OUTRUN THEM ON FLAT GROUND.

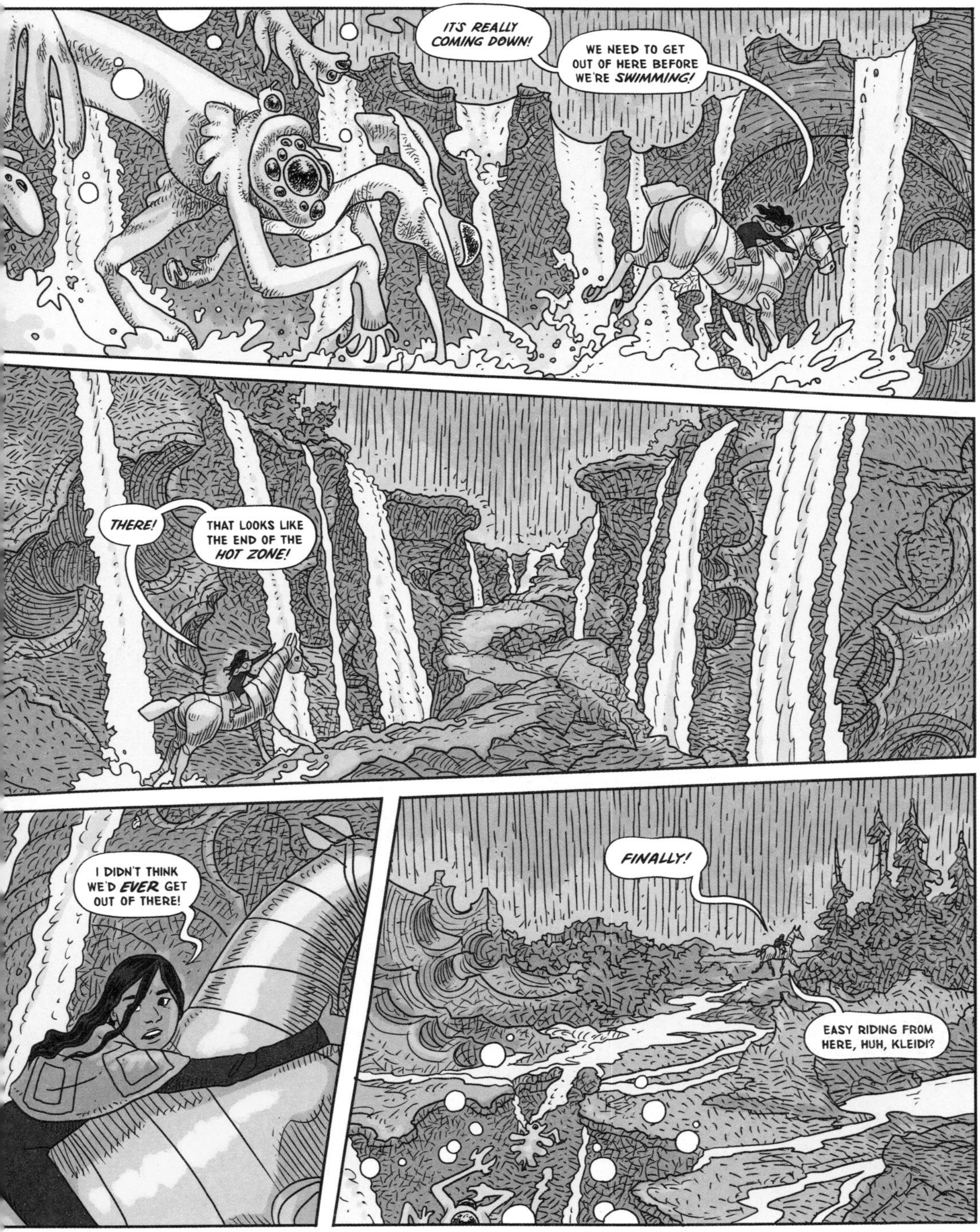
IT'S REALLY COMING DOWN!
WE NEED TO GET OUT OF HERE BEFORE WE'RE SWIMMING!
THERE!
THAT LOOKS LIKE THE END OF THE HOT ZONE!
I DIDN'T THINK WE'D EVER GET OUT OF THERE!
FINALLY!
EASY RIDING FROM HERE, HUH, KLEIDI?

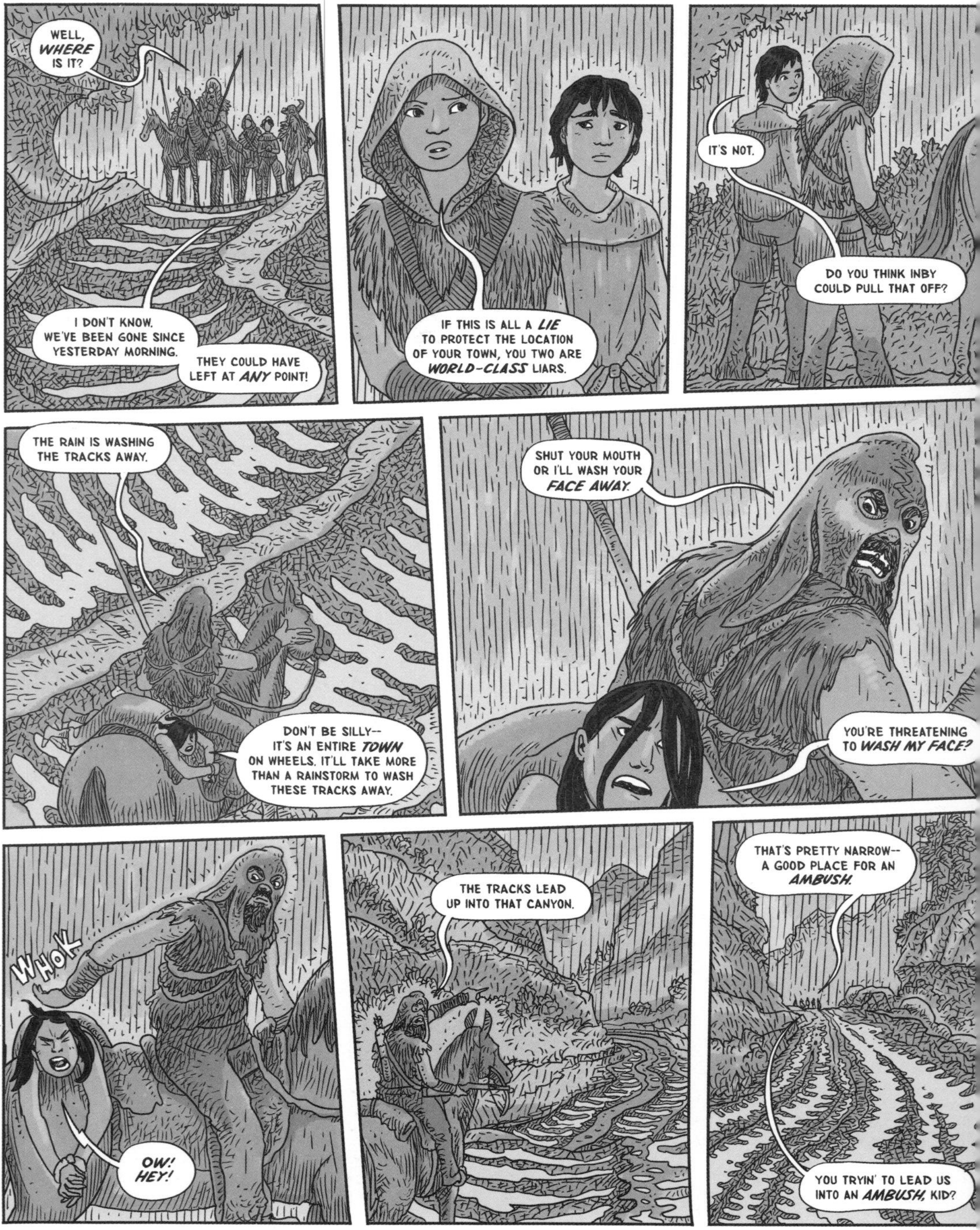

WELL, *WHERE* IS IT?
I DON'T KNOW. WE'VE BEEN GONE SINCE YESTERDAY MORNING.
THEY COULD HAVE LEFT AT *ANY* POINT!
IF THIS IS ALL A *LIE* TO PROTECT THE LOCATION OF YOUR TOWN, YOU TWO ARE *WORLD-CLASS* LIARS.
IT'S NOT.
DO YOU THINK INBY COULD PULL THAT OFF?
THE RAIN IS WASHING THE TRACKS AWAY.
DON'T BE SILLY-- IT'S AN ENTIRE *TOWN* ON WHEELS. IT'LL TAKE MORE THAN A RAINSTORM TO WASH THESE TRACKS AWAY.
SHUT YOUR MOUTH OR I'LL WASH YOUR *FACE AWAY.*
YOU'RE THREATENING TO *WASH MY FACE?*
WHOK
OW! HEY!
THE TRACKS LEAD UP INTO THAT CANYON.
THAT'S PRETTY NARROW-- A GOOD PLACE FOR AN *AMBUSH.*
YOU TRYIN' TO LEAD US INTO AN *AMBUSH,* KID?

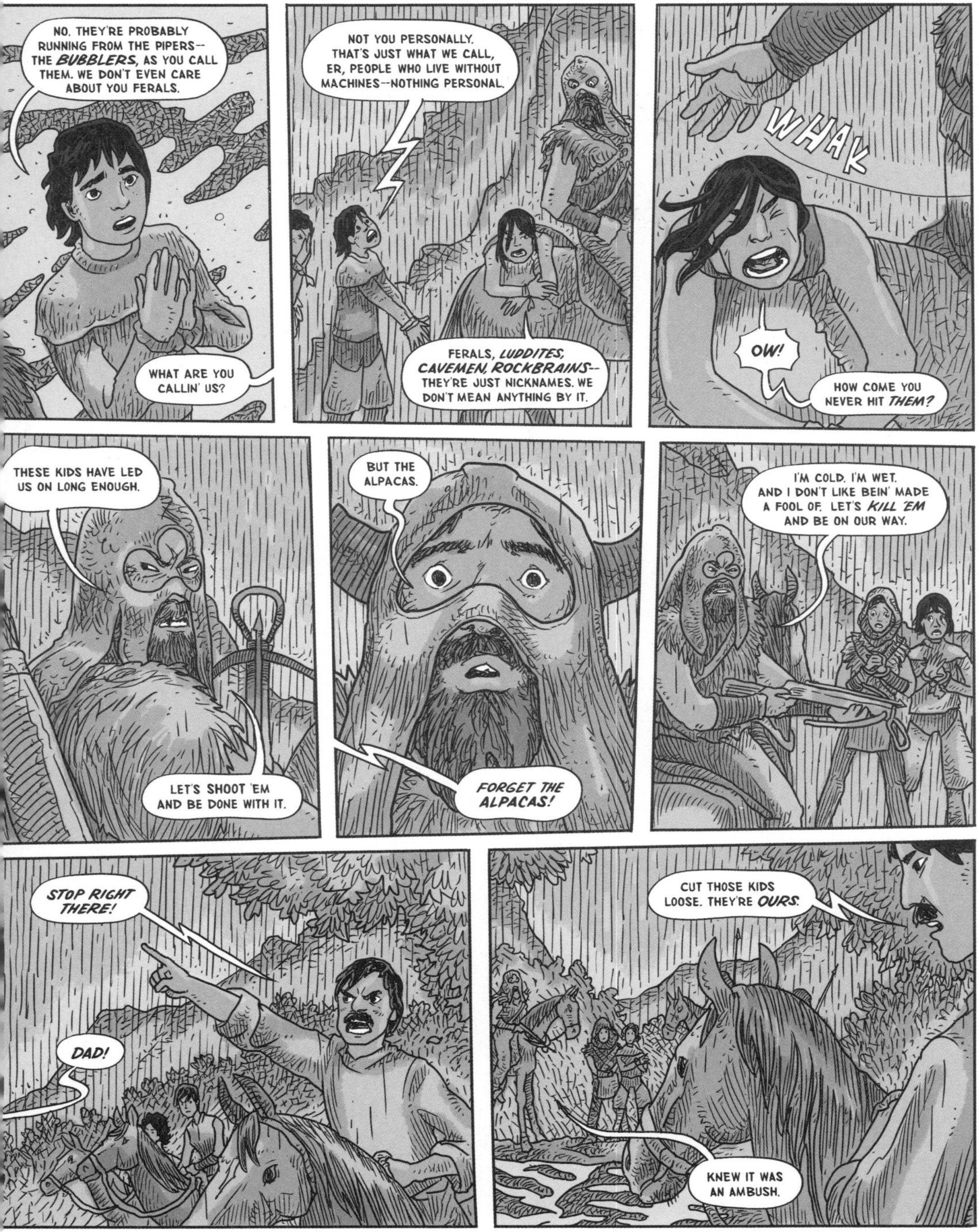
NO. THEY'RE PROBABLY RUNNING FROM THE PIPERS-- THE *BUBBLERS*, AS YOU CALL THEM. WE DON'T EVEN CARE ABOUT YOU FERALS.
WHAT ARE YOU CALLIN' US?
NOT YOU PERSONALLY. THAT'S JUST WHAT WE CALL, ER, PEOPLE WHO LIVE WITHOUT MACHINES--NOTHING PERSONAL.
FERALS, *LUDDITES, CAVEMEN, ROCKBRAINS*-- THEY'RE JUST NICKNAMES. WE DON'T MEAN ANYTHING BY IT.
WHAK
OW!
HOW COME YOU NEVER HIT *THEM?*
THESE KIDS HAVE LED US ON LONG ENOUGH.
LET'S SHOOT 'EM AND BE DONE WITH IT.
BUT THE ALPACAS.
FORGET THE ALPACAS!
I'M COLD. I'M WET. AND I DON'T LIKE BEIN' MADE A FOOL OF. LET'S *KILL 'EM* AND BE ON OUR WAY.
STOP RIGHT THERE!
DAD!
CUT THOSE KIDS LOOSE. THEY'RE *OURS*.
KNEW IT WAS AN AMBUSH.

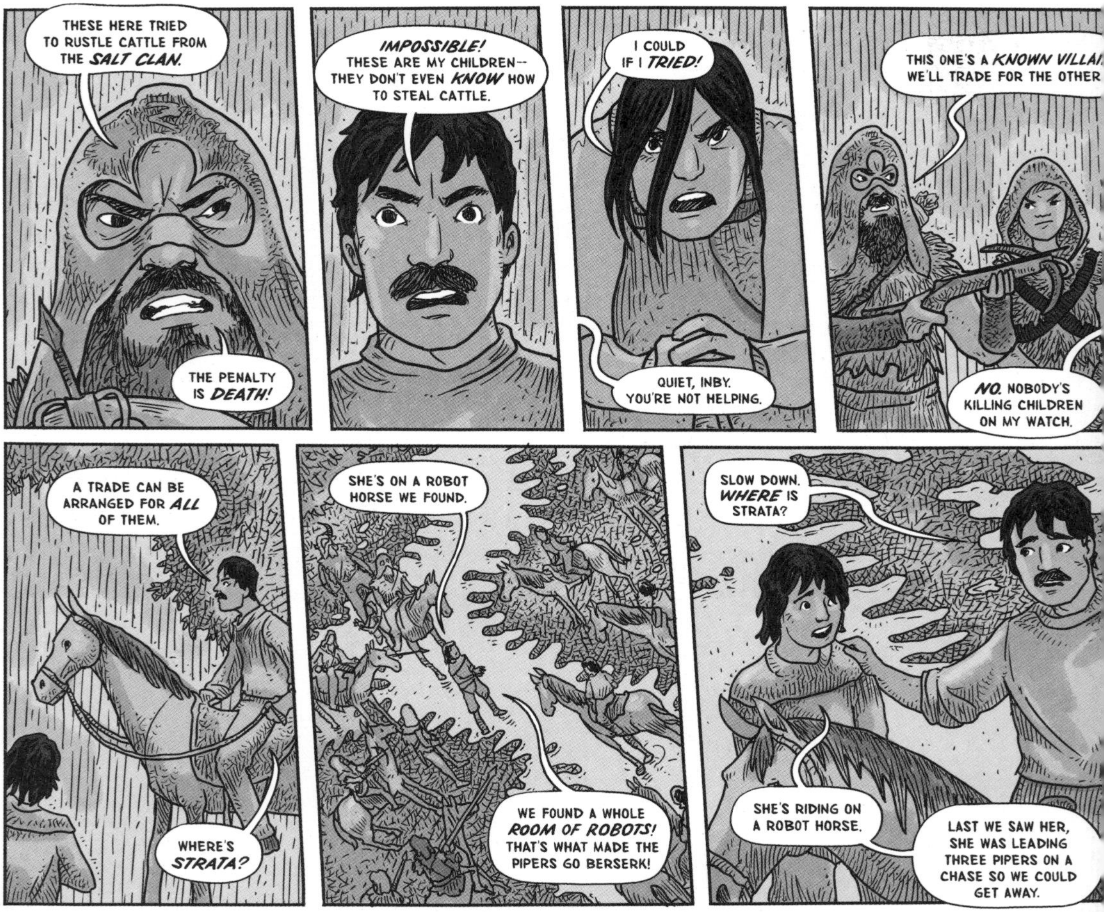

THESE HERE TRIED TO RUSTLE CATTLE FROM THE SALT CLAN.
THE PENALTY IS DEATH!
IMPOSSIBLE! THESE ARE MY CHILDREN-- THEY DON'T EVEN KNOW HOW TO STEAL CATTLE.
I COULD IF I TRIED!
QUIET, INBY. YOU'RE NOT HELPING.
THIS ONE'S A KNOWN VILLAI WE'LL TRADE FOR THE OTHER
NO. NOBODY'S KILLING CHILDREN ON MY WATCH.
A TRADE CAN BE ARRANGED FOR ALL OF THEM.
WHERE'S STRATA?
SHE'S ON A ROBOT HORSE WE FOUND.
WE FOUND A WHOLE ROOM OF ROBOTS! THAT'S WHAT MADE THE PIPERS GO BERSERK!
SLOW DOWN. WHERE IS STRATA?
SHE'S RIDING ON A ROBOT HORSE.
LAST WE SAW HER, SHE WAS LEADING THREE PIPERS ON A CHASE SO WE COULD GET AWAY.
SHE'S ON A ROBOT IN THE HOT ZONE!?
YOU CAN SORT OUT YOUR FAMILY TROUBLES LATER.
WHAT'S THE TRADE FOR THESE THREE?
SHUT UP! MY DAUGHTER IS OUT THERE BEING CHASED BY SOMETHING BIGGER, UGLIER, AND WEIRDER THAN YOU GOONS!
GOONS?!
MAYBE WE JUST SLAUGHTER YOU ALL RIGHT NOW.

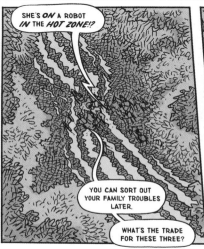

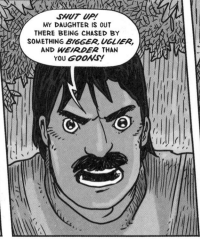

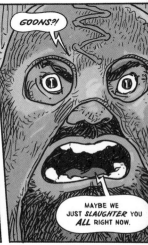

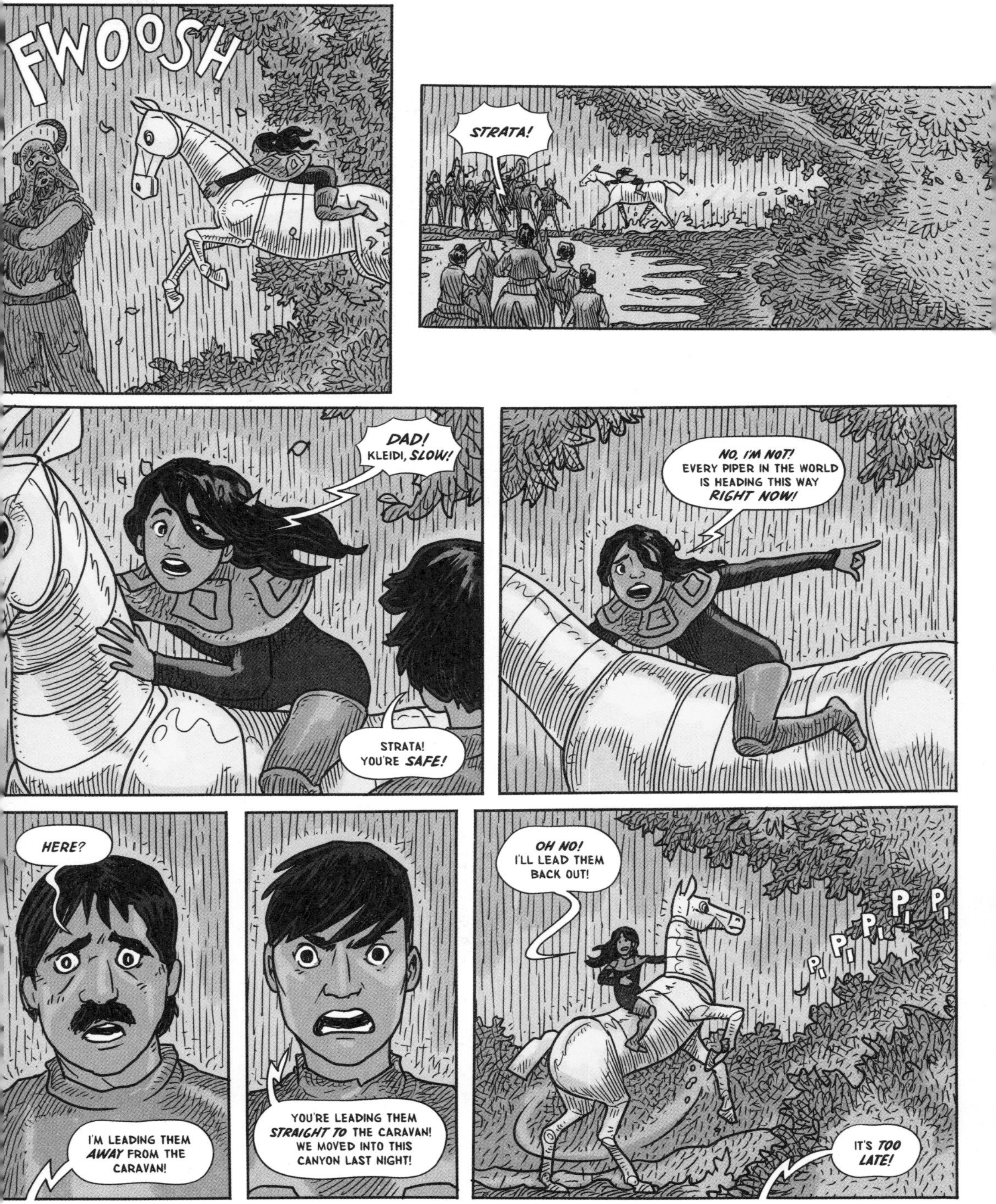
FWOOSH
STRATA!
DAD! KLEIDI, SLOW!
STRATA! YOU'RE SAFE!
NO, I'M NOT! EVERY PIPER IN THE WORLD IS HEADING THIS WAY RIGHT NOW!
HERE?
I'M LEADING THEM AWAY FROM THE CARAVAN!
YOU'RE LEADING THEM STRAIGHT TO THE CARAVAN! WE MOVED INTO THIS CANYON LAST NIGHT!
OH NO! I'LL LEAD THEM BACK OUT!
PI PI PI PI PI PI
IT'S TOO LATE!

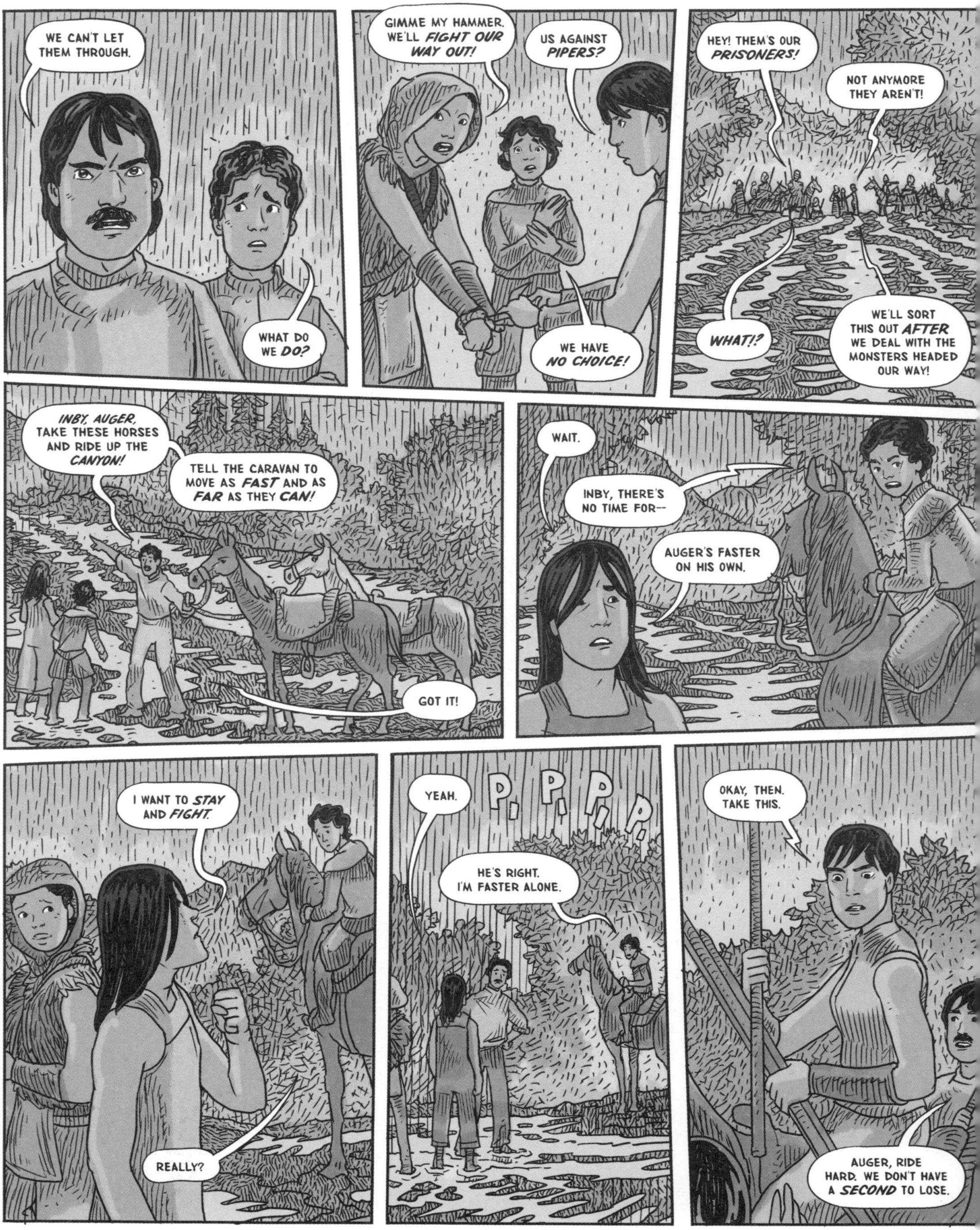
WE CAN'T LET THEM THROUGH.
WHAT DO WE *DO?*
GIMME MY HAMMER. WE'LL *FIGHT OUR WAY OUT!*
US AGAINST *PIPERS?*
WE HAVE *NO CHOICE!*
HEY! THEM'S OUR *PRISONERS!*
NOT ANYMORE THEY AREN'T!
WHAT!?
WE'LL SORT THIS OUT *AFTER* WE DEAL WITH THE MONSTERS HEADED OUR WAY!
INBY, AUGER, TAKE THESE HORSES AND RIDE UP THE *CANYON!*
TELL THE CARAVAN TO MOVE AS *FAST* AND AS *FAR* AS THEY *CAN!*
GOT IT!
WAIT.
INBY, THERE'S NO TIME FOR--
AUGER'S FASTER ON HIS OWN.
I WANT TO *STAY* AND *FIGHT.*
REALLY?
YEAH.
P P P P P
HE'S RIGHT. I'M FASTER ALONE.
OKAY, THEN. TAKE THIS.
AUGER, RIDE HARD. WE DON'T HAVE A *SECOND* TO LOSE.

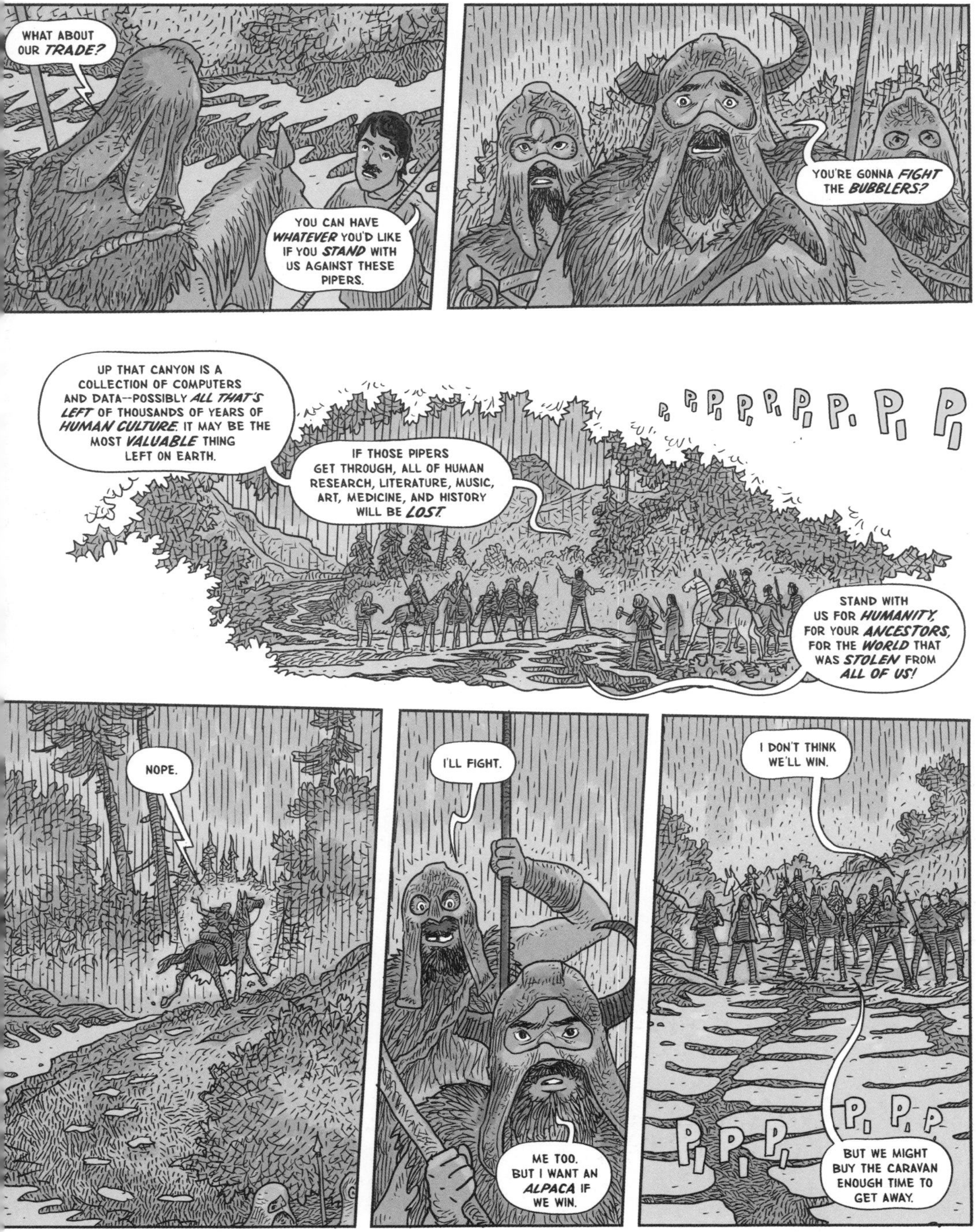
WHAT ABOUT OUR TRADE?
YOU CAN HAVE WHATEVER YOU'D LIKE IF YOU STAND WITH US AGAINST THESE PIPERS.
YOU'RE GONNA FIGHT THE BUBBLERS?
UP THAT CANYON IS A COLLECTION OF COMPUTERS AND DATA--POSSIBLY ALL THAT'S LEFT OF THOUSANDS OF YEARS OF HUMAN CULTURE. IT MAY BE THE MOST VALUABLE THING LEFT ON EARTH.
IF THOSE PIPERS GET THROUGH, ALL OF HUMAN RESEARCH, LITERATURE, MUSIC, ART, MEDICINE, AND HISTORY WILL BE LOST.
PI PI PI PI PI PI PI PI PI
STAND WITH US FOR HUMANITY, FOR YOUR ANCESTORS, FOR THE WORLD THAT WAS STOLEN FROM ALL OF US!
NOPE.
I'LL FIGHT.
ME TOO. BUT I WANT AN ALPACA IF WE WIN.
I DON'T THINK WE'LL WIN.
PI PI PI PI PI PI
BUT WE MIGHT BUY THE CARAVAN ENOUGH TIME TO GET AWAY.

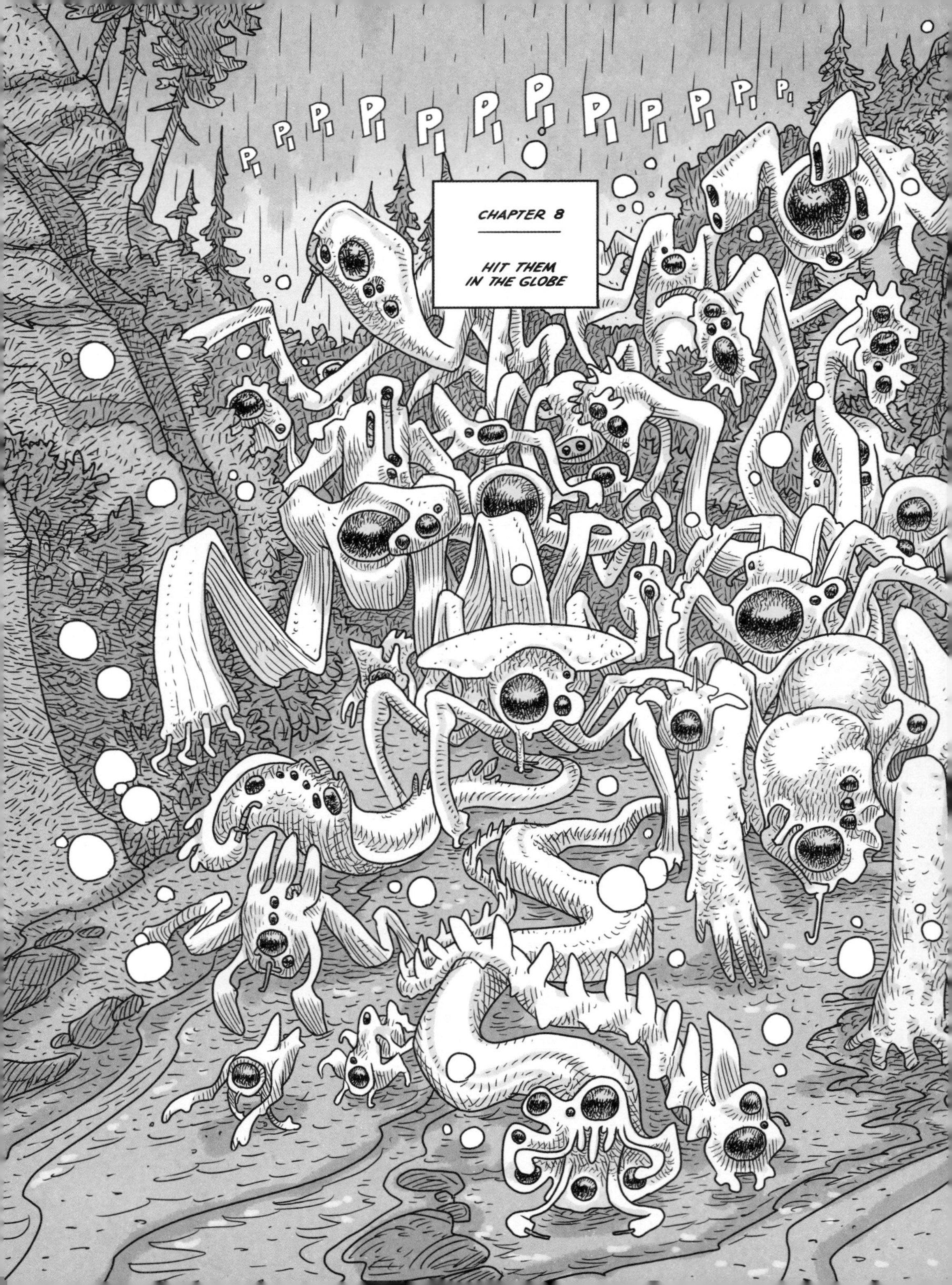

PI PI PI PI PI PI PI PI PI PI PI PI PI PI
CHAPTER 8
HIT THEM
IN THE GLOBE

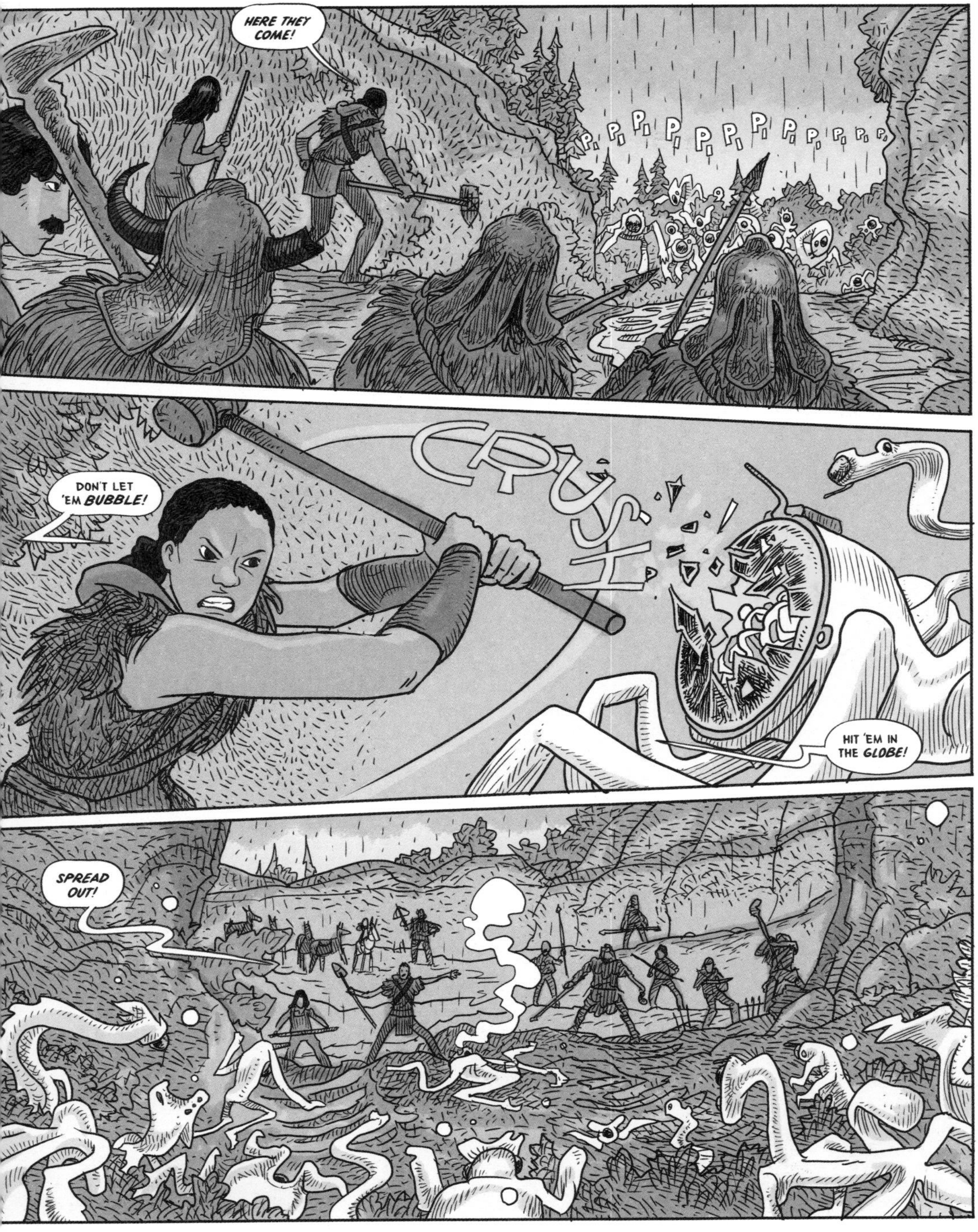
HERE THEY COME!
PPPPPPPPPPPPP
CRUSH
DON'T LET 'EM BUBBLE!
HIT 'EM IN THE GLOBE!
SPREAD OUT!

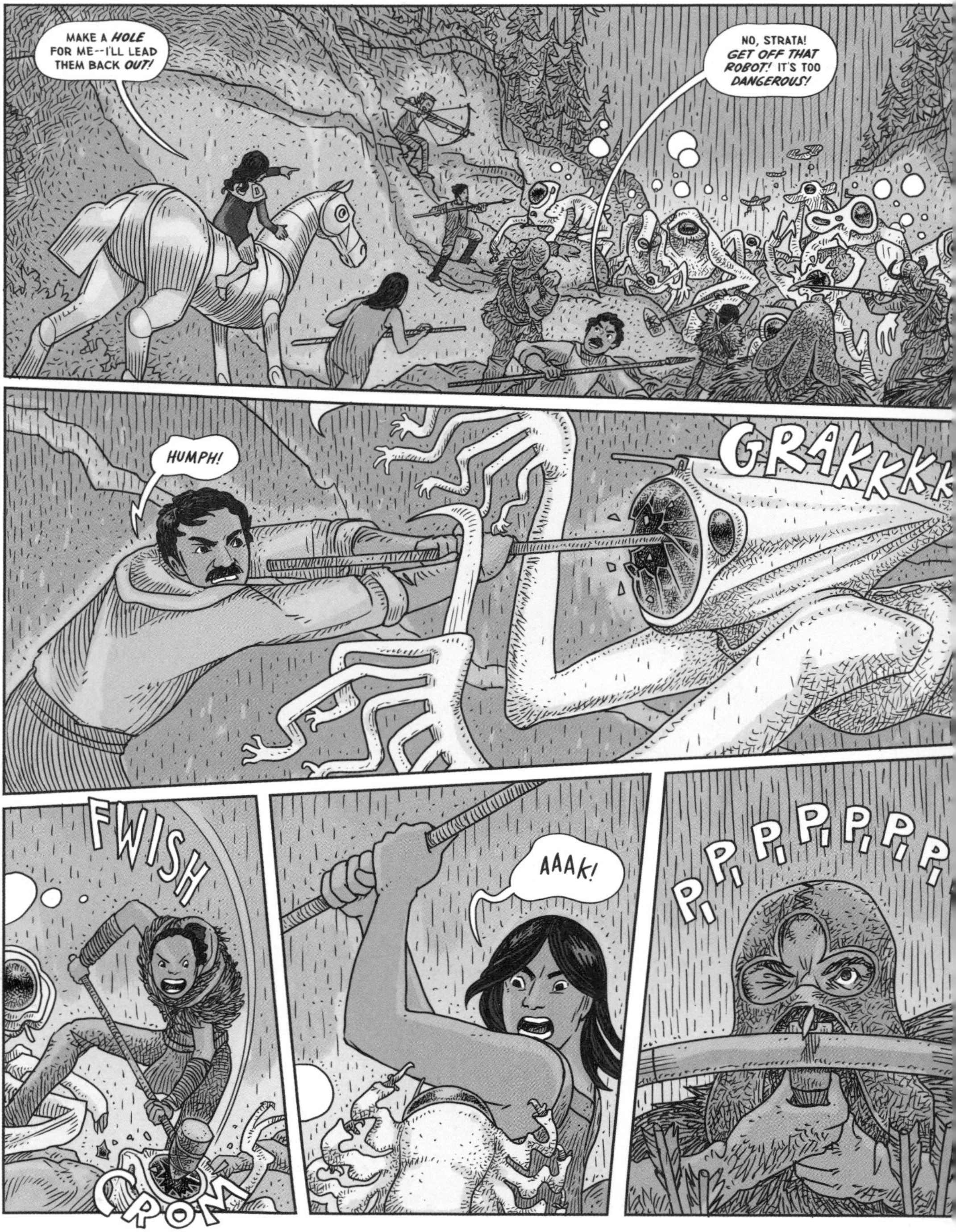

MAKE A *HOLE* FOR ME--I'LL LEAD THEM BACK *OUT!*
NO, STRATA! *GET OFF THAT ROBOT!* IT'S TOO *DANGEROUS!*
HUMPH!
GRAKKKK
FWISH
CROM
AAAK!
P P P P P P P P P

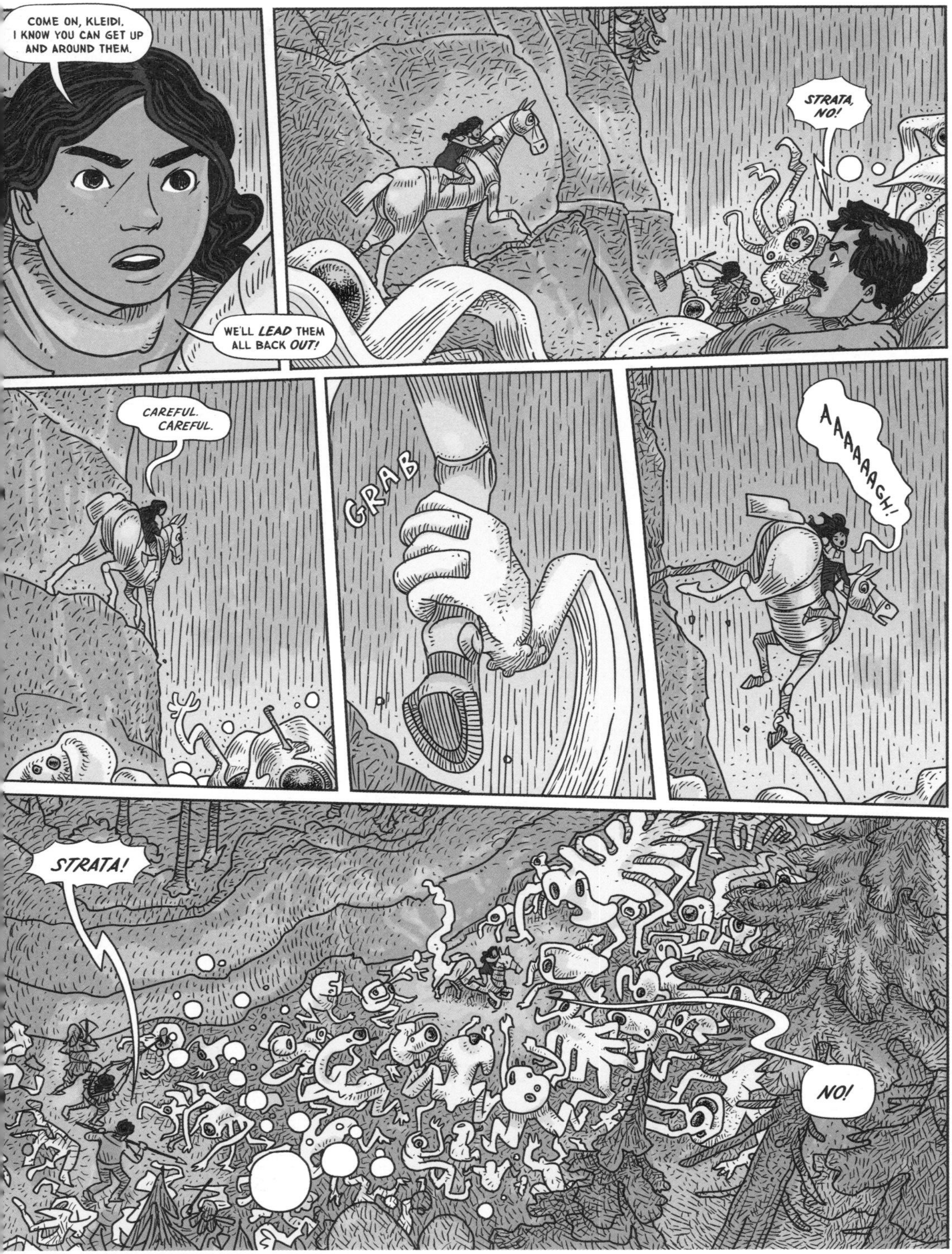
COME ON, KLEIDI. I KNOW YOU CAN GET UP AND AROUND THEM.
WE'LL LEAD THEM ALL BACK OUT!
STRATA, NO!
CAREFUL. CAREFUL.
GRAB
AAAAAAAGH!
STRATA!
NO!

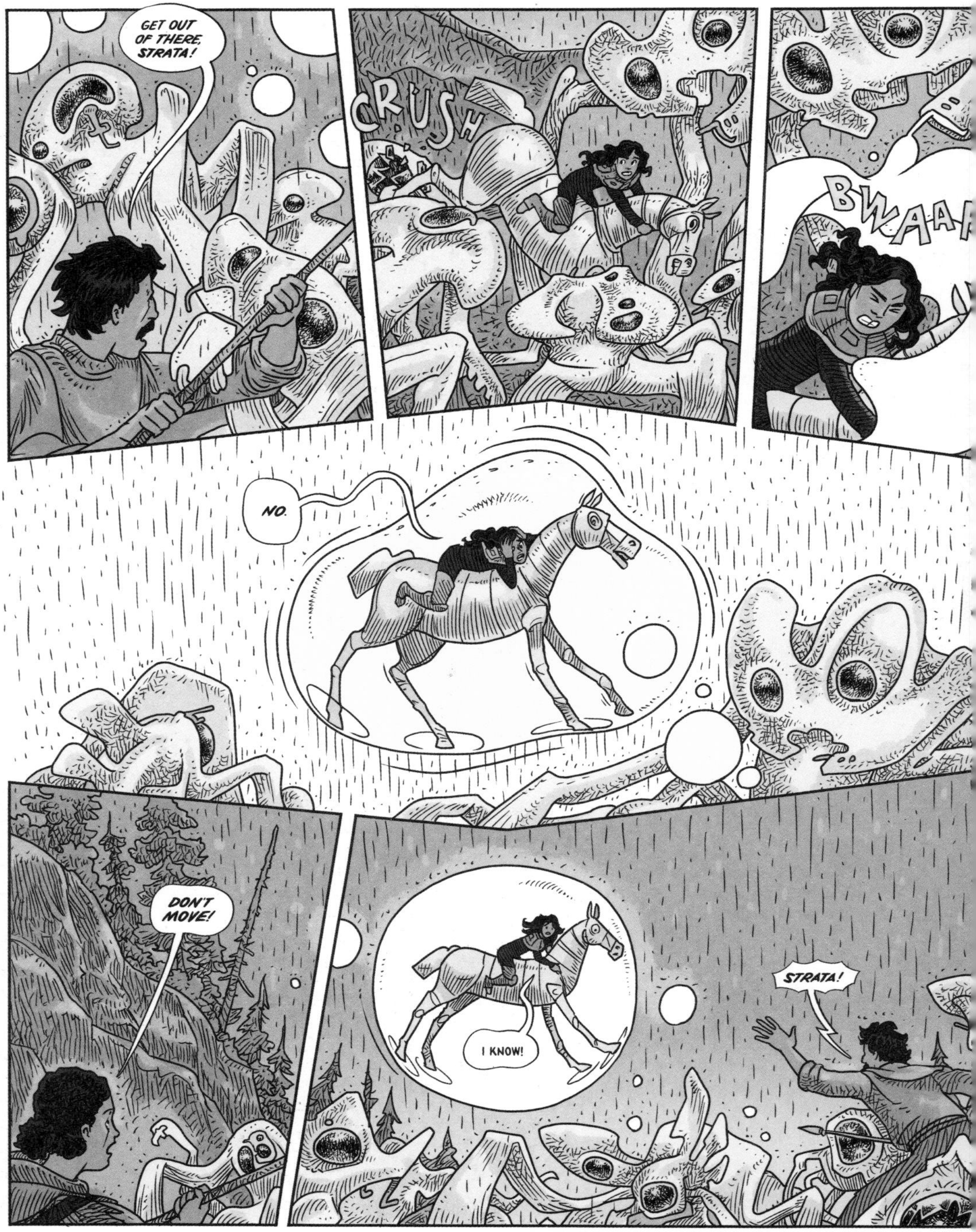
GET OUT OF THERE, STRATA!
CRUSH
BWAA!
NO.
DON'T MOVE!
I KNOW!
STRATA!

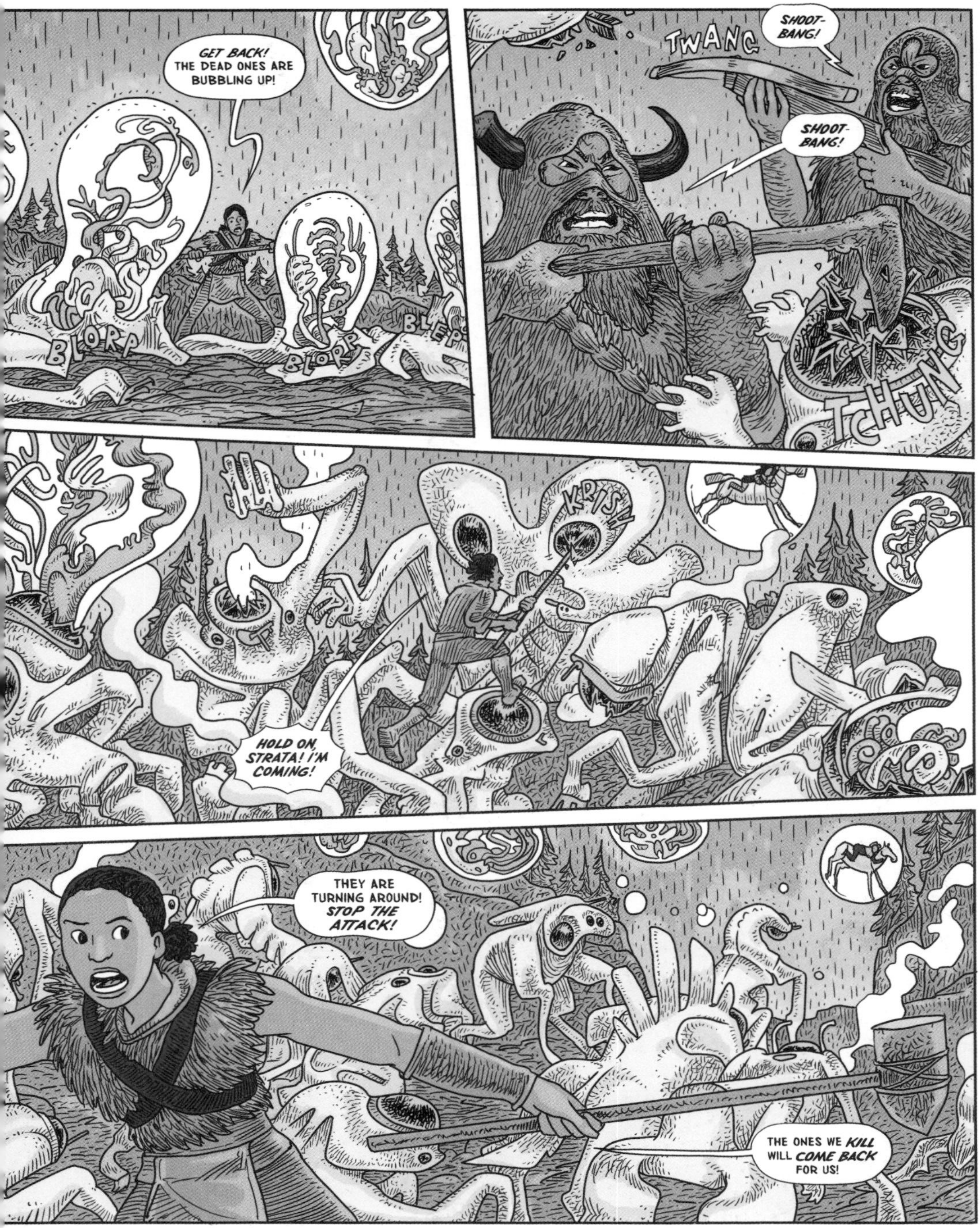
GET BACK! THE DEAD ONES ARE BUBBLING UP!
BLORP
BLORP
BLEP
TWANG
SHOOT-BANG!
SHOOT-BANG!
TCHUNG
KRISH
HOLD ON, STRATA! I'M COMING!
THEY ARE TURNING AROUND! STOP THE ATTACK!
THE ONES WE KILL WILL COME BACK FOR US!

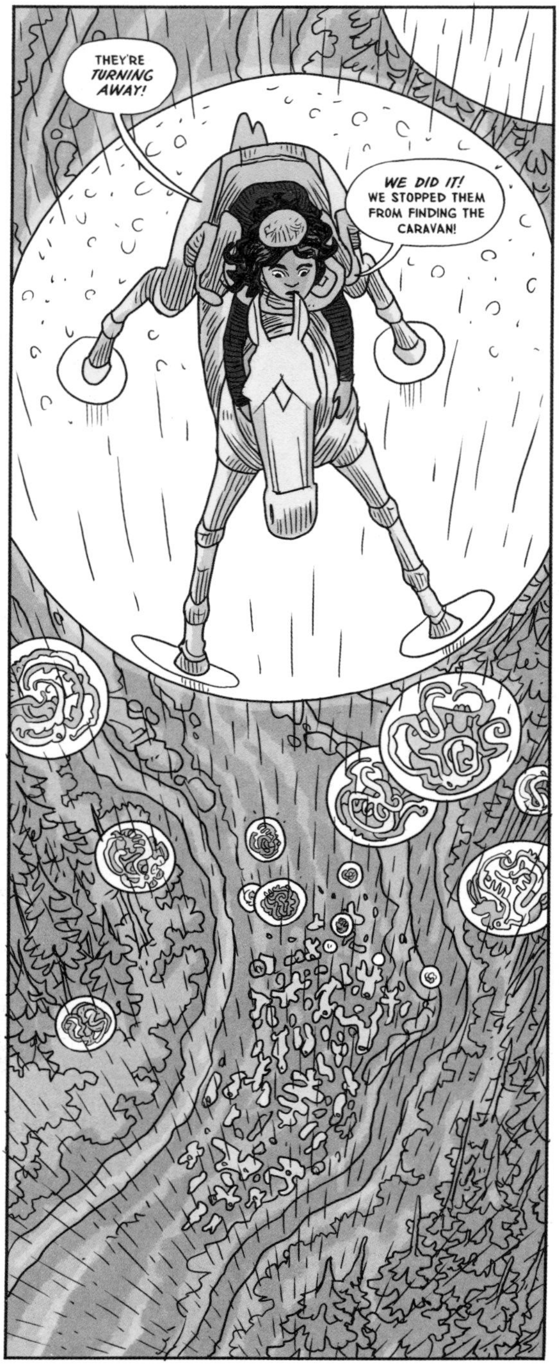
THEY'RE *TURNING AWAY!*
WE DID IT! WE STOPPED THEM FROM FINDING THE CARAVAN!

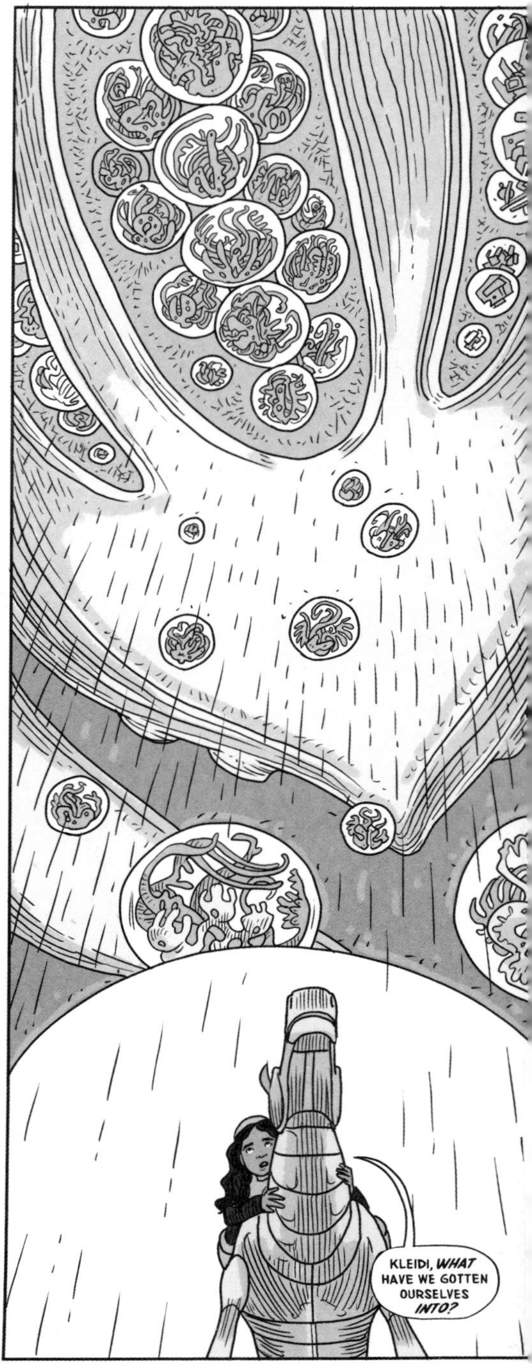
KLEIDI, *WHAT* HAVE WE GOTTEN OURSELVES *INTO?*

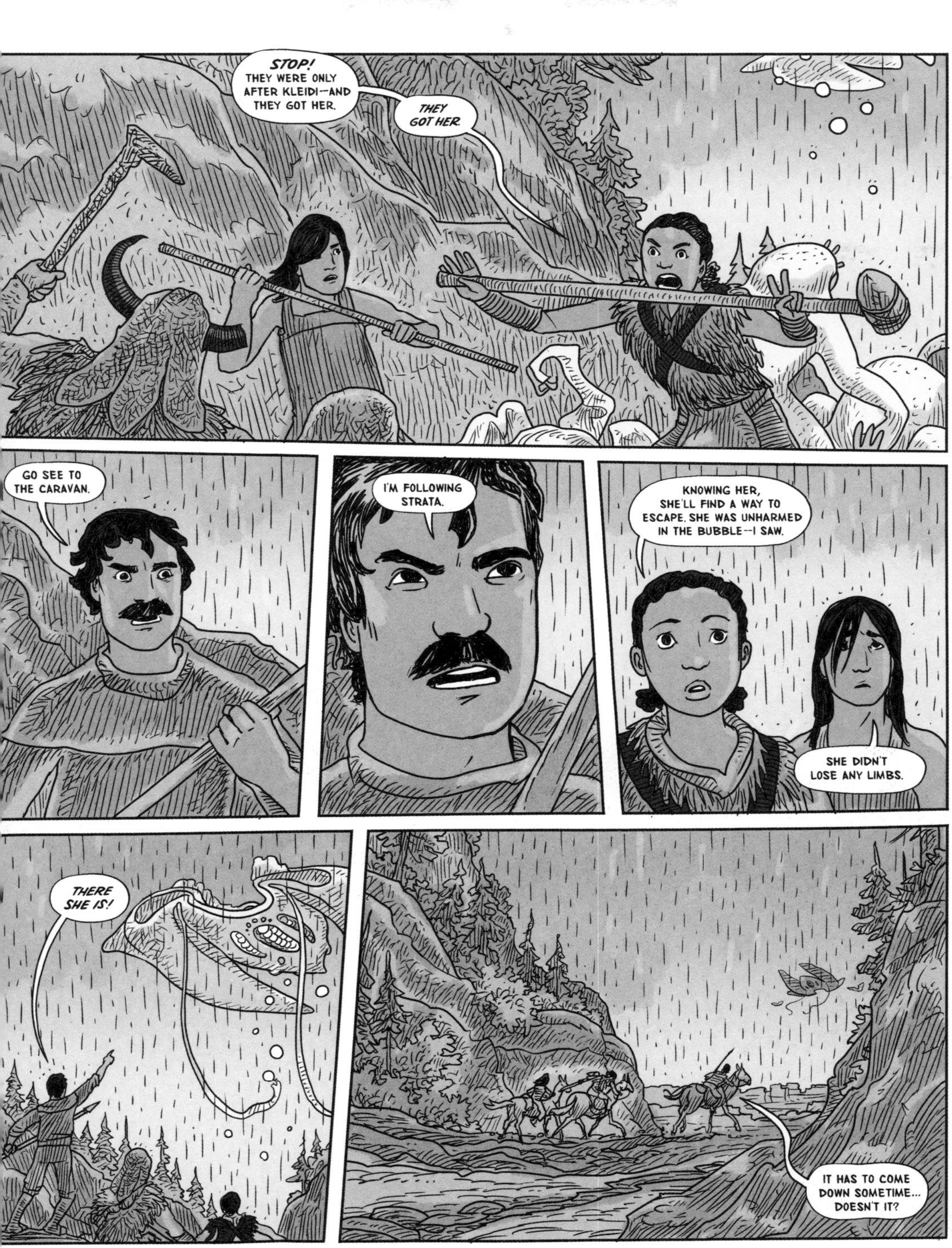
STOP! THEY WERE ONLY AFTER KLEIDI--AND THEY GOT HER.
THEY GOT HER.
GO SEE TO THE CARAVAN.
I'M FOLLOWING STRATA.
KNOWING HER, SHE'LL FIND A WAY TO ESCAPE. SHE WAS UNHARMED IN THE BUBBLE--I SAW.
SHE DIDN'T LOSE ANY LIMBS.
THERE SHE IS!
IT HAS TO COME DOWN SOMETIME... DOESN'T IT?

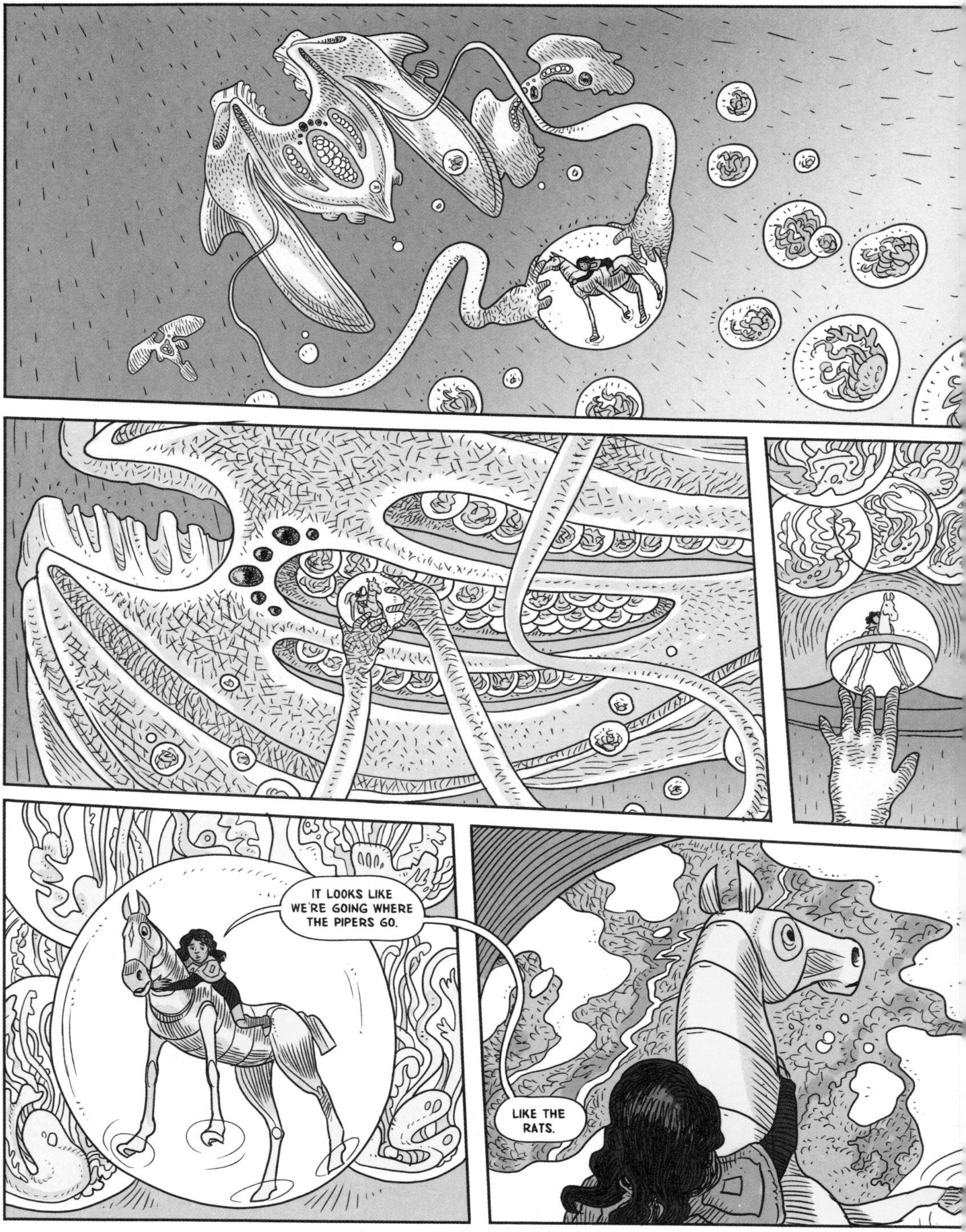
IT LOOKS LIKE WE'RE GOING WHERE THE PIPERS GO.
LIKE THE RATS.

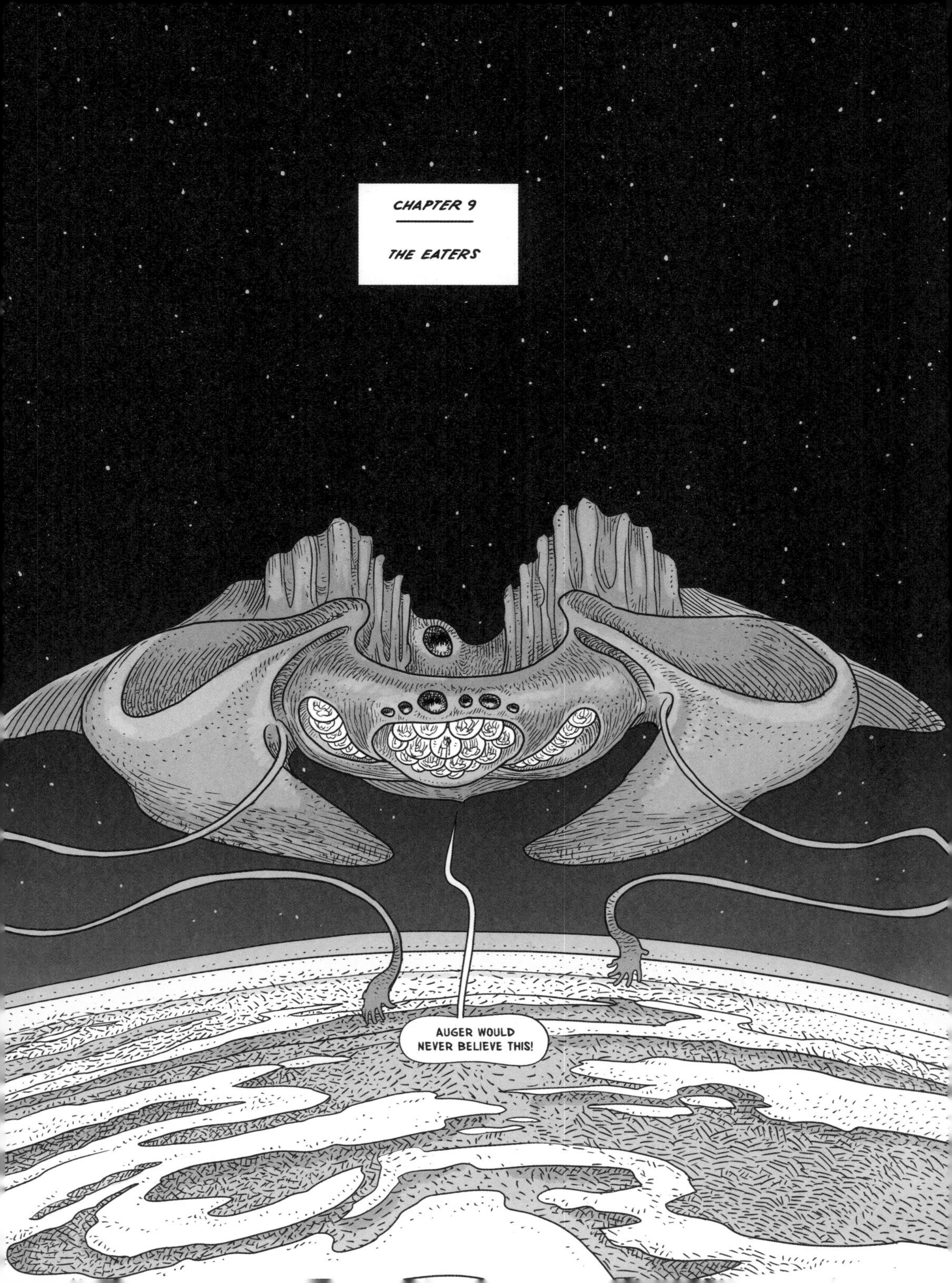
CHAPTER 9
THE EATERS
AUGER WOULD NEVER BELIEVE THIS!

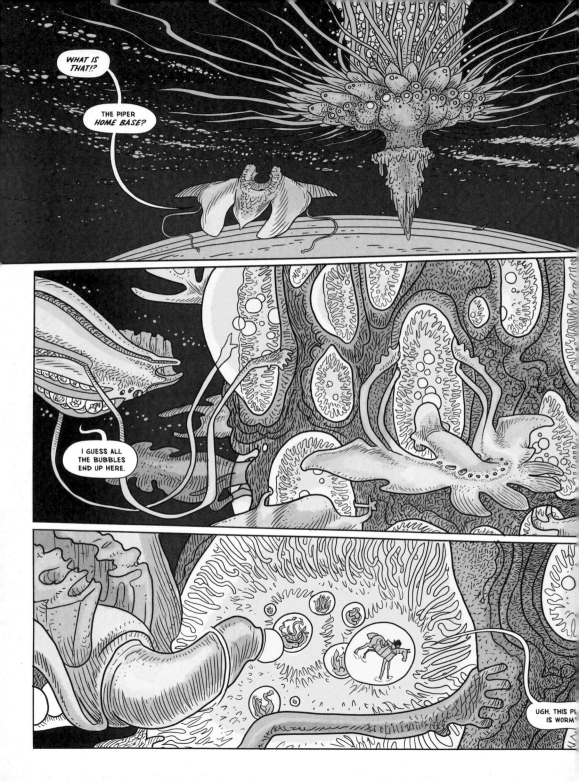

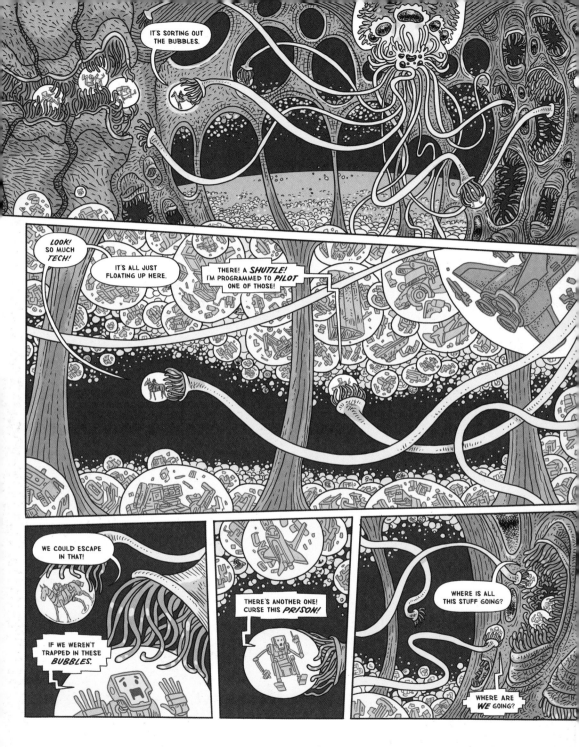

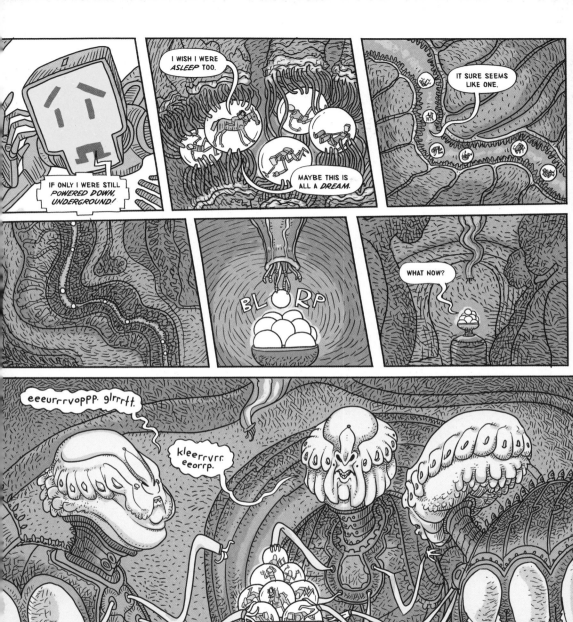

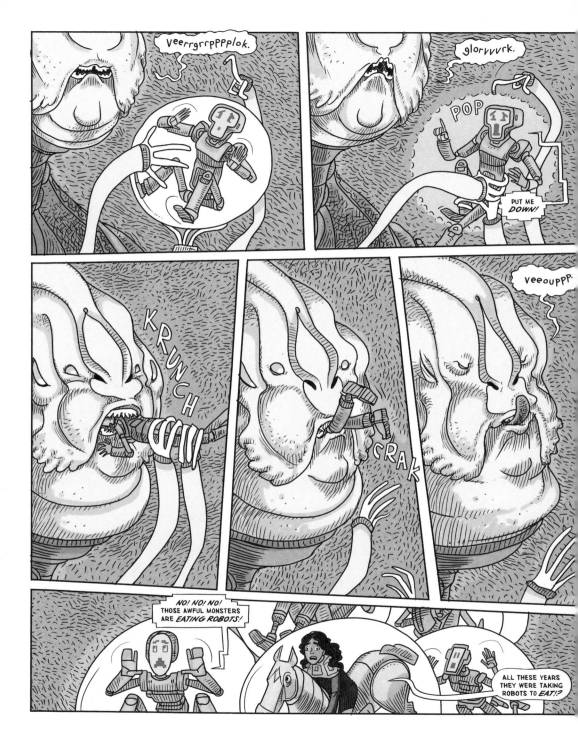

NO! NO!

GET IT OFF! KLEIDI, FIGHT!

QUIT STRUGGLING, EARTH CHILD.

HUH?

DO YOU UNDERSTAND MY SPEECH NOW?

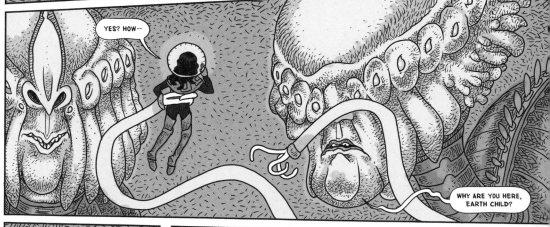

YES? HOW—

WHY ARE YOU HERE, EARTH CHILD?

YOU HAVE MY PONY.

YOU RODE IN THAT BUBBLE ALL THE WAY HERE TO SAVE THIS?

THAT IS, HMM, *BRAVE.*

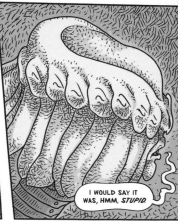

I WOULD SAY IT WAS, HMM, *STUPID.*

WHO *ARE* YOU? WHAT'S *GOING ON* HERE? WHY ARE YOU *STEALING* EVERYTHING?

HOW *TIRESOME.*

I ALWAYS ENJOY A CHANCE TO SPEAK WITH THE, ER, *LOCALS.*

I *DON'T.*

YOUR QUESTIONS ARE CONCISE.

TELL ME CHILD, DO YOUR PEOPLE STILL HAVE A WRITTEN LANGUAGE?

YES, WE—

COULD YOU *PLEASE* STOP DOING THAT!?

I'M *HUNGRY.* DO *YOU* STOP EATING WHEN *YOU* ARE HUNGRY?

YOU *EAT* ROBOTS?

I THINK WE'VE ESTABLISHED THAT.

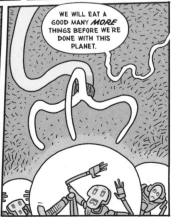

WE WILL EAT A GOOD MANY *MORE* THINGS BEFORE WE'RE DONE WITH THIS PLANET.

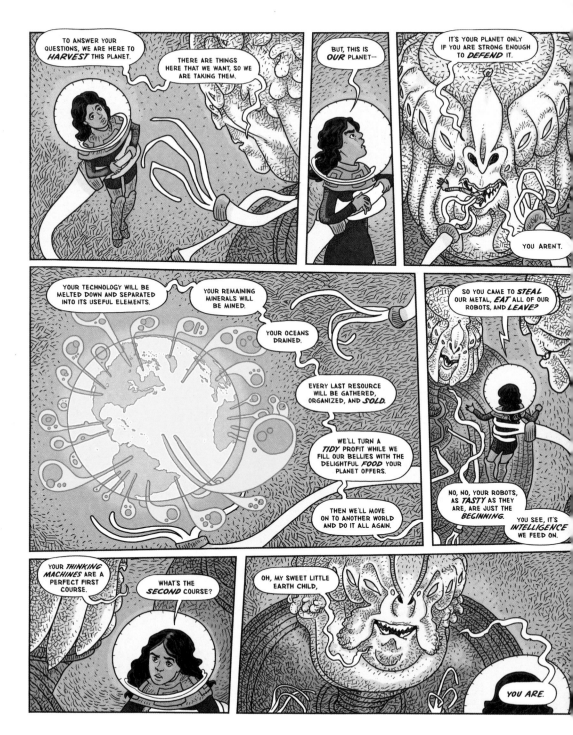

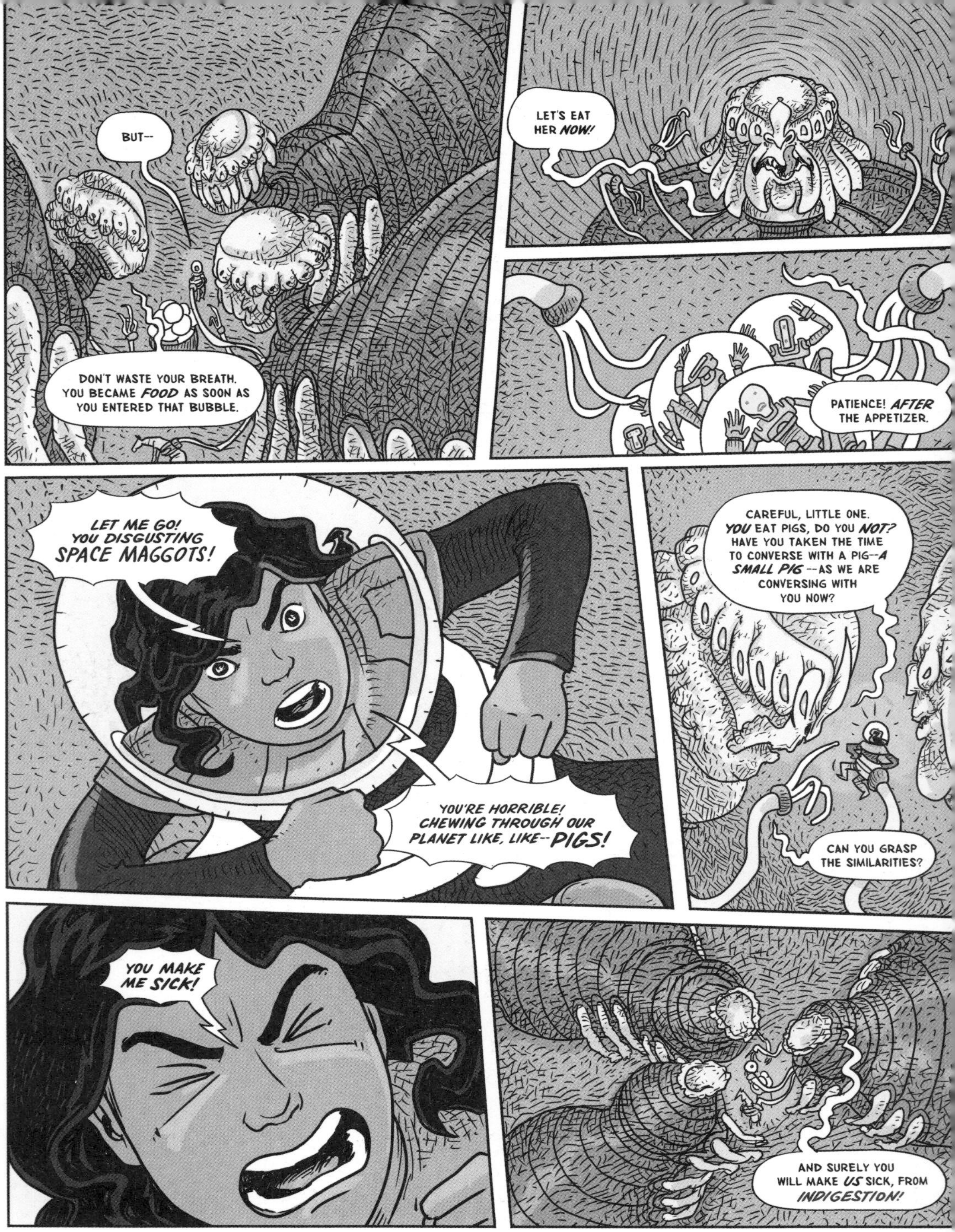
BUT--
DON'T WASTE YOUR BREATH. YOU BECAME FOOD AS SOON AS YOU ENTERED THAT BUBBLE.
LET'S EAT HER NOW!
PATIENCE! AFTER THE APPETIZER.
LET ME GO! YOU DISGUSTING SPACE MAGGOTS!
YOU'RE HORRIBLE! CHEWING THROUGH OUR PLANET LIKE, LIKE--PIGS!
CAREFUL, LITTLE ONE. YOU EAT PIGS, DO YOU NOT? HAVE YOU TAKEN THE TIME TO CONVERSE WITH A PIG--A SMALL PIG --AS WE ARE CONVERSING WITH YOU NOW?
CAN YOU GRASP THE SIMILARITIES?
YOU MAKE ME SICK!
AND SURELY YOU WILL MAKE US SICK, FROM INDIGESTION!

113

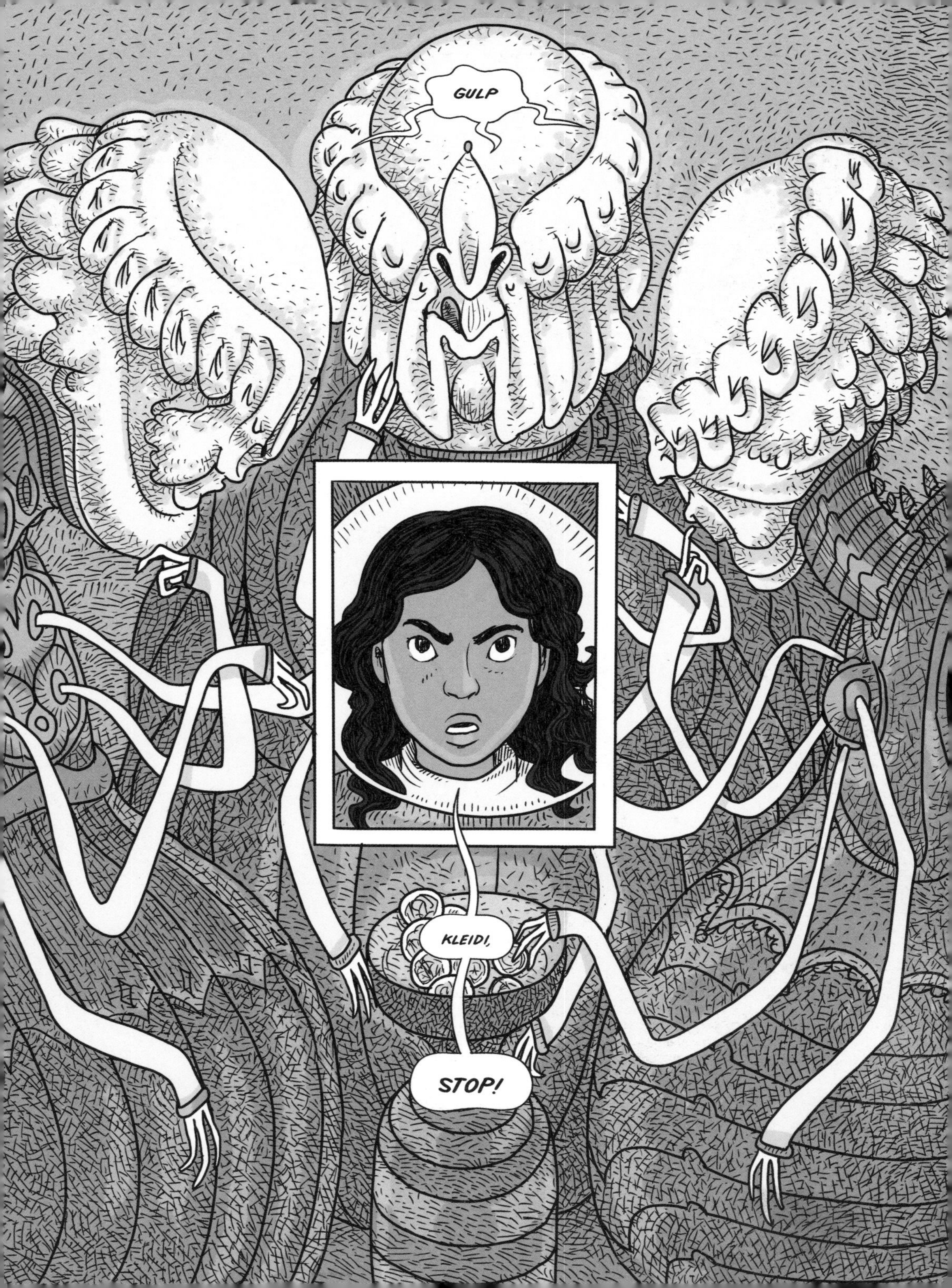
GULP
KLEIDI,
STOP!

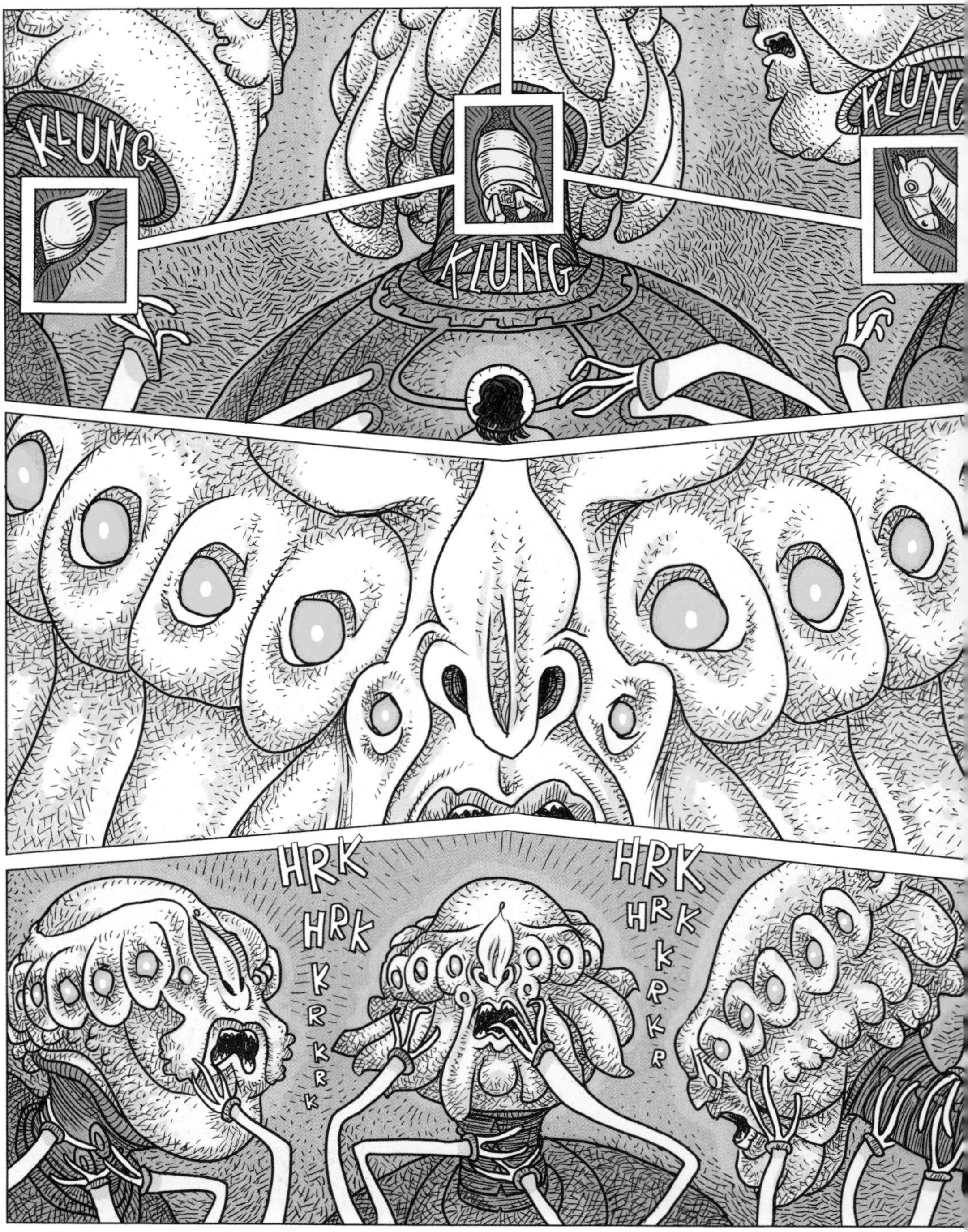
KLUNG
KLUNG
HRK
HRK
KRKRK
HRK
HRK
KRKR

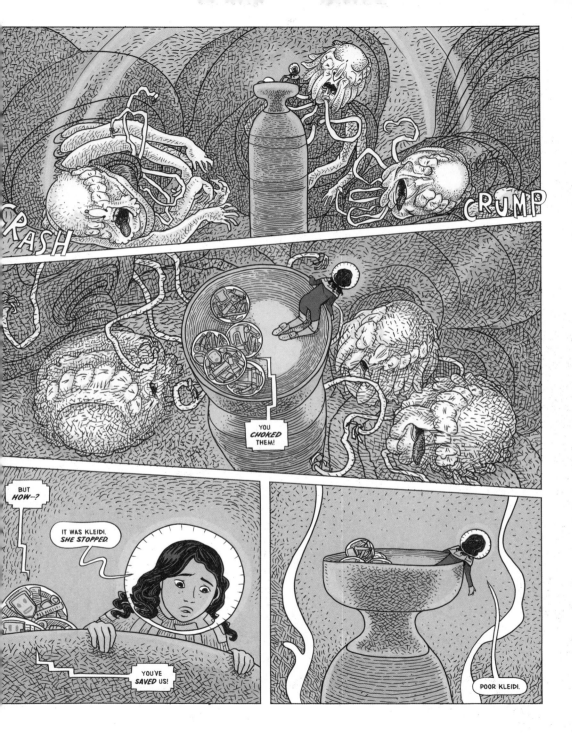

119

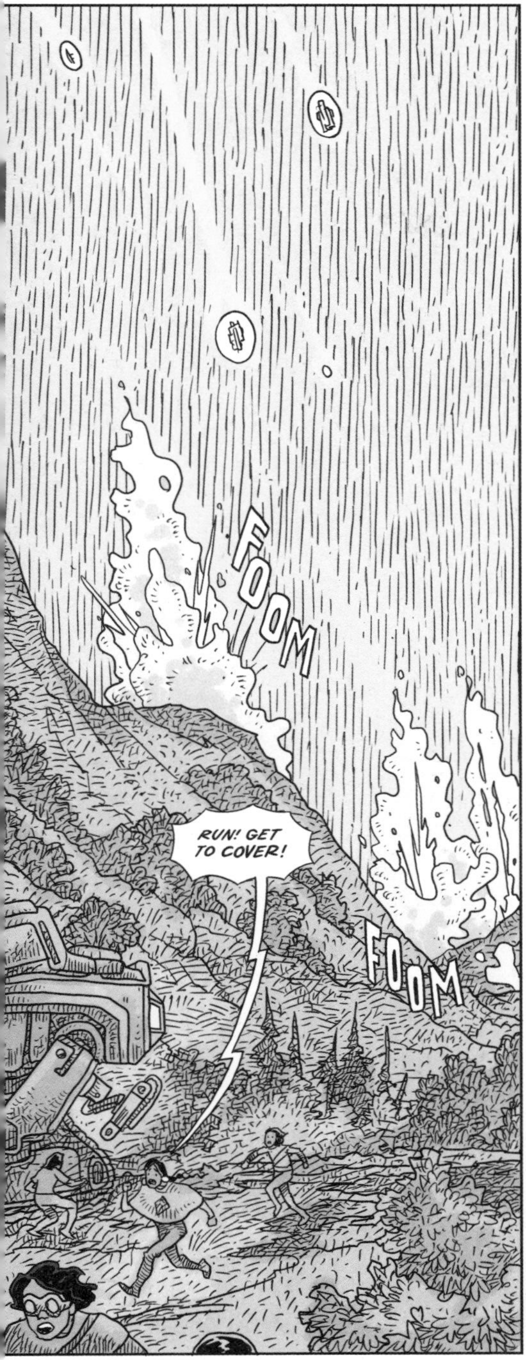
FOOM
RUN! GET TO COVER!
FOOM

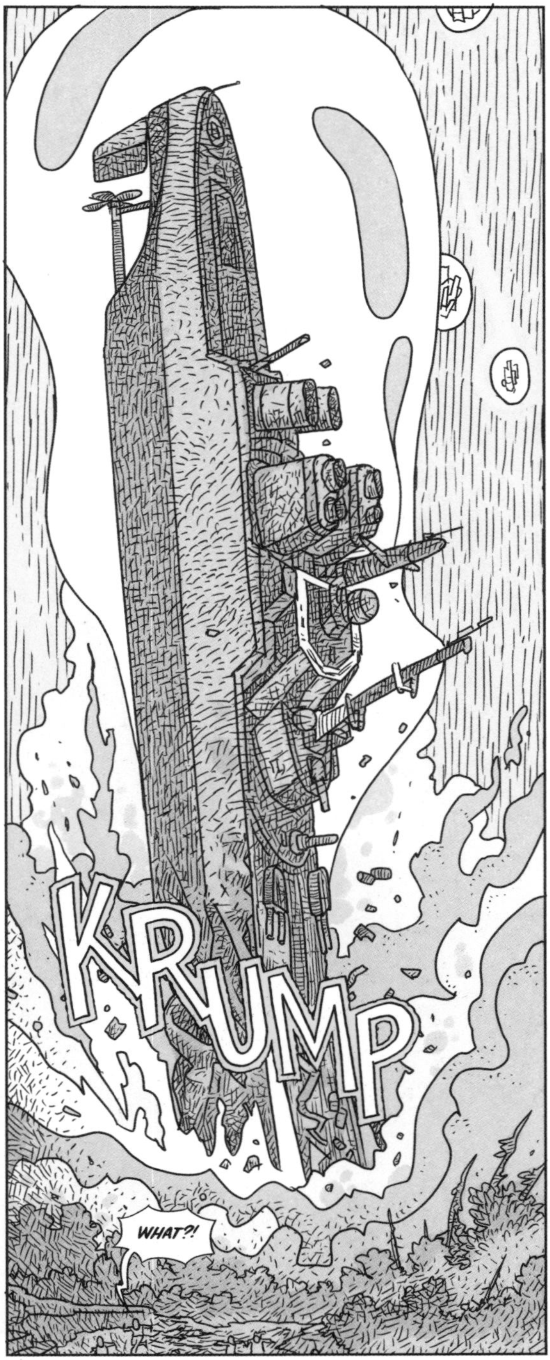
KRUMP
WHAT?!

123

WHAT IS IT?

STRATA?

IS THAT
REALLY *HER?*

IT IS!

HOW DID YOU—
WHERE DID YOU—
WHAT'S *GOING ON!?*

IT'S OVER.

THE PIPERS
ARE ALL DEAD—
REALLY *DEAD.*

SHE SAVED US ALL!
SHE STOPPED THE
PIPERS FOR GOOD!

IT WASN'T ME.
IT WAS *KLEID!*

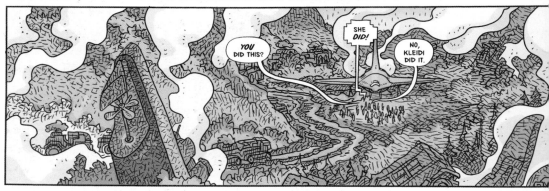

THE END

NATHAN HALE IS THE AUTHOR AND ILLUSTRATOR OF THE #1 *NEW YORK TIMES*
BESTSELLING SERIES HAZARDOUS TALES, NONFICTION COMICS ON AMERICAN HISTORY.

ONE TRICK PONY IS THE NINTH GRAPHIC NOVEL ILLUSTRATED BY NATHAN HALE.
HE CREATED THE ARTWORK FOR THE FAIRY TALE EPIC *RAPUNZEL'S REVENEGE* AND ITS
SEQUEL *CALAMITY JACK*, WRITTEN BY SHANNON AND DEAN HALE (NO RELATION).

HE LIVES IN UTAH.

EXCUSE ME, BUT THE HAZARDOUS
TALES SERIES ISN'T OVER, IS IT?

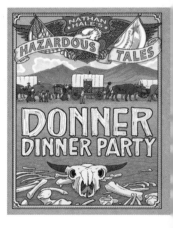

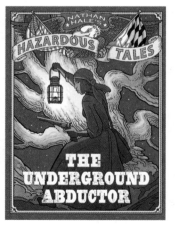

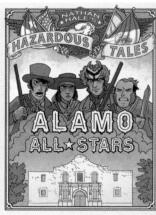

WATCH FOR MORE *NATHAN HALE'S HAZARDOUS TALES*, COMING SOON!

WOO HOD!